SAME PLACE, SAME STARS

A NOVEL BY

KATEY TAYLOR

SAME PLACE, SAME STARS

Copyright © 2025 by Katey Taylor

ISBN 978-1-7327504-4-9

E-Book 978-1-7327504-5-6

AUTHOR'S NOTE

Dear Reader,

This story addresses difficult topics, including mentions of suicide, sexual abuse, eating disorders, and mental illness, which may be triggering for some. Please read with caution.

My desire is to bring hope, not despair.
If you're struggling, please know you're not alone—reach out to someone you trust, or to a professional, for support.

With love and care,

Katey Taylor

CONTENTS

PROLOGUE

Tiny vessels surround her dilated eyes, but her mind remains unaware as she trades warmth and safety for the chilly night. An unknown force drags her feet through the dirt. Her fingers claw upward, pulling herself higher. Her legs scrape against the edges of rough wood, blood soaking into her silk gown.

Two voices scream at her: one calls from below, a distant plea, begging her to stop, but the other is raging inside her head, drowning out any sound.

She wavers in a forward motion while her extended arms sway, trying to balance the harsh wind. Plagued by a torrent of disarray and fear, she's lured to the edge—against her will. She doesn't want to do what she's told, but she has no choice but to obey.

All her physical movements have succumbed to mental compulsion. With a sharp gasp, she steps out into the abyss. Letting out a piercing cry that steals her breath, her body slams against the cold ground.

Her vision fades to the same shade of darkness as the pitch-black sky above.

CHAPTER 1

No sharp objects. Pack light.

My instinct is to run, but I don't know how far my sore limbs will carry me.

Apathy is my last line of defense.

I reach for a baggy sweatshirt and leggings. This has become my uniform when I go away, not for any fashion statement but its functionality—it can be easily taken off before my body is searched by a nurse's gloved hands. The pressure from the fabric causes me to hiss in pain. I carefully step each leg in to cover the tender scrapes and deep purple bruises along my pale white shins and thighs. The bruises are a reminder that I've messed up again.

I drag my worn leather suitcase that's on its last leg away from our cottage and into the trunk of Olga's station wagon. She doesn't say a word as we head out of our driveway and onto the tree-dense highway. The branches are grayer than normal, though it could be my mood filtering the world in a cloud of indifference.

Olga rolls every window down even though it's a brisk fifty-two degrees. Long drives make her sweat. I think she would never leave our small town if it were up to her, but I remain her forcing agent.

My eyes wander from the pastures filled with cows and horses to Olga and her wild blowing hair that is unusually more silver than black for someone in their thirties.

"So, what's this ward like?" I ask, trying to break the tense silence.

"Don't call it that. That's not what it's called. This is a treatment center."

She turns up her classical piano playlist, the one she plays to calm her nerves, then hands me a folded piece of stock paper filled with smiling faces of young adults—those who, like me, are not teenagers anymore but not quite what I would consider adults either. Much like our mental state, we're something in between.

The brochure states this center isn't government funded. By the looks of it, it seems far out of the budget of Olga's ballet studio salary and my unemployed status, but it claims as part of their philosophy that they take on special cases free of charge. Just my luck, they happened to have room for a last-minute drop-in.

After the stunt I pulled last night, I'm sure Olga would be willing to pay any price.

"Stop biting your fingernails," Olga snaps.

Because of her tone, I won't remind her that it's not the nail I'm biting but the skin around the nails. Although tearing my thumbs with my teeth probably isn't a better habit.

I glance at my shredded nail beds and notice the dirt under my fingernails. My eyes squeeze shut in the hope that any flash of memory will come through from last night. I went from falling asleep under my warm quilt to abruptly waking up on the cold ground, above jagged sticks and rocks yet under Olga's fear-filled eyes. But everything in between stays black, and my frustration turns into a heavy weight of guilt. I know I shouldn't feel ashamed of my illness, but being afraid of who you'll turn into after you shut your eyes at night brings more than shame—it fills you with terror.

I am often devoured by terror.

I wish I could remember what I did last night and how I ended up bruised and battered on the lawn, not only for my sake but for Olga's. But I can't. I have never been able to remember the moments between when the world goes dark and when I wake up being deemed a threat to myself or others. The forgetfulness isn't the most horrifying part. The real fear lies in not knowing who inflicts the wounds covering my body. Self-betrayal at its finest: my body unconsciously acting of its own accord, without me having a clue as to what possesses it.

I know how much it hurts Olga when I have to leave. Though she won't allow me to call her Mother, she deserves that title. Olga is my savior, but it's days like today that I wonder if she regrets saving me.

I open my eyes to a lush plot of land surrounded by tall redwoods. The bumpy dirt path leads to two ranch-style homes. We park in front of a tattered sign welcoming us to Awana's Treatment in the Trees. The abundance of nature is a lot homier than the wards in bland cement buildings or large sterile hospitals housing hundreds of patients.

We step out into brisk air as the sun is tucking behind the dark trees. The sound of rushing water distracts me. I catch a glimpse of a river flowing behind a row of redwoods. I walk away from my luggage for a closer look. The powerful white rapids smashing against rocks send a chill up my spine. There's something familiar about this river.

Olga's hand lands on my shoulder, startling me from my thoughts.

"Wrong way. The entrance is over here."

She guides my shoulders to follow her, but my feet won't let me leave the sight of the strong current.

"Come on, Natalia, let's go."

"I've been here before. I've seen that river! I just know it!" I blurt out.

The sounds of the water amplify in my head like a bad song you wish you could tune out. An uncomfortable heaviness seeps into my chest.

Have I been here before?

"You've never been here, dear. It's just a river," Olga says, reading the puzzled expression on my face. "You've probably seen one like it on TV or something." She rubs my back, trying to reassure me.

"But it's not the look of the river—it's the feeling I get when I look at it. Something strange—"

"Stop! You know what I say about bringing up these kinds of thoughts. You better keep them to yourself if you ever want to live a life outside confined walls and timed medication."

Ouch. And it never hurts any less each time she reminds me.

I stay silent. I wish I could tell her that the vast stream of murky water set off an alarm in me, one filled with amorphous dread.

I know she only means well. I gulp down my fear. You learn to when you don't have any other choice. She grabs my hand, and her tiny frame pulls me on the small trail to the white wooden house.

A bell rings as we walk through a stained-glass door. It leads to an open living room with a wood-burning fire and sofas that face each other on a bohemian-style carpet. To the right, a woman with tight curls sits behind a desk, clicking away at her computer. Olga clears her throat, and the thicker middle-aged woman notices us and grins.

"Oh, I'm sorry! Hi! You must be Olga and Natalia. I hope finding our facility didn't cause too much trouble. I know those roads get winding," she says, standing up to greet us.

Olga returns a friendly hello, but I choose to remain meek in my silence. The woman, in a crisp trench coat with colorful beads and crystals draped around her neck, steps toward us with an open hand to shake.

"Oh, your hands are so cold." Her voice rises after touching mine. Her warm hands and demeanor ease my reluctance. "We're all wondering when the sun is going to show up this spring. Anyways, welcome! We're so happy to have you. I'm Dr. Cassidy, one of the four doctors overseeing Awana. Dr. Beckham is running a few errands, so you'll have to meet him later. He's the other lead doctor here on the women's side."

"Women's side?" both Olga and I ask in synchrony as we take our seats.

Olga's eyes widen with concern as Dr. Cassidy slides into the chair behind her desk and continues on. "Yes. This is the women's building. Dr. Lee and Dr. Sanford are in charge of the men's building."

"Wait, the house *right* next door?" Olga interrupts, her voice slightly louder than it had been.

"Yes. Though we are a coed facility, we do keep patients strictly separated based on gender identity due to traumas certain guests who stay with us have."

I chew at my pinkie nervously until Olga tugs my hand.

"So, they're completely separated?" she reiterates.

Olga believes having boys around will only create problems for a young woman who has enough of her own, but she doesn't seem to realize that of all the worries I cause her, that should be the least of them. Guys hardly look in my direction.

"Yes. Meetings, meals, and recreational activities are all separate," Dr. Cassidy confirms.

The thought of having the opposite sex yards away creates an excitement in me I wasn't expecting. I don't have too much history with guys around my age. Growing up, she's always placed me in the all-girls' wards. This is a surprising added bonus to staying at Awana.

"I'll need to go over a few standard rules. The policies here are fairly relaxed. As you know already, the boys' house and recreational areas are off-limits. We strive to have open communication and a strong bond of trust here. We believe having independence is a crucial part to our treatment. No cameras in the rooms, no lockdowns at night, and most of your day is up to you."

These rules are a steep contrast from what I'm used to. A place that doesn't treat its patients like lab rats seems too good to be true.

"Sounds like a lot of freedom. Will she be supervised at all?" Olga asks with crossed arms. A fair question for someone who can turn into an escape artist at night.

"Yes, of course. Our staff lives on the property, so we're available for our patients twenty-four seven."

Olga relaxes her shoulders.

"Now, the next rule is the hardest one for our young adults to hear," she continues. "We do have a strict no-phones policy, as you probably saw on your packing list. Will this be a problem?"

"Nope," I answer quickly.

I think Dr. Cassidy was expecting a moan or a debate, but the truth is, I hardly used mine anyway. You need good reception and friends for a cell phone to mean much to you. I lacked both.

"Well, that's good to hear. We find them to be distracting and conflicting to our practices, but we do have a computer in the main room for research and games. We pride ourselves on giving our patients more of a retreat experience, and part of that is enjoying your time with us here at Awana. If you need anything, don't hesitate to let us know. Do you have any questions for me?"

I look at Olga, and she presses her lips together in a smile.

I can't return one. Not this time. I don't have the energy to help relieve her guilt about dumping me in the hands of total strangers.

"No, not that I can think of."

All these places are the same. I've been in enough to know the drill by now.

"Well, if any come up, I'm always here. Now, if you don't mind, Olga, please sign." She hands a pen and clipboard filled with papers toward us.

The state doesn't even trust me to make sound mental decisions on my own account. Olga was granted conservatorship the moment I turned eighteen. Though I'm twenty-one, sometimes I still feel like a child. The years of my life all blend together. The milestones that most have, like graduations or going to prom, or college, were events I only watched on television.

Olga reaches for the clipboard, signing my rights away faster than I was expecting.

Wow. She can't wait to get rid of me.

I guess she shouldn't have to put up with me any longer.

Dr. Cassidy takes the clipboard back from her, then turns to me. "Well, Natalia, shall we show you to your new sanctuary?"

Before I can reach for my bag, Dr. Cassidy grabs it first, placing it behind her desk. "We just need to do a quick search. You'll be reunited with your belongings soon."

"Is this the part where I strip down and get searched too?" I ask, pulling on my sweatshirt sleeve.

Dr. Cassidy cracks a smile as if I told her a joke, but it disappears when I reach for my pants.

"No, sweetheart, we do not enforce any kind of strip search here. It's a dated practice, so you may leave your clothes on, please."

She has no idea how much relief her words bring me.

Dr. Cassidy's leather sandals click with each step she takes on the hardwood floors. "We do have a daily schedule. Meals are the same time every day, as well as arts, yoga, and afternoon free time. We'd like you to stick to being on time, unless you're sick."

She leads us through the kitchen to a large mahogany dining table decorated with fresh flowers and candles, nestled under a beautiful black chandelier.

"Here is where you'll eat your three meals a day, and if you find yourself hungry between meals, our cabinets are always stocked with snacks."

We follow Dr. Cassidy down a long hallway with colorful art displayed on the walls. The abstract strokes all blend together in each painting, creating a harmonious story as you walk down the hall.

"This place is stunning," Olga whispers to me.

I have to admit, it's not bad so far. This place has a homey feel, almost like staying at a relative's house. I've never felt that way at any ward before.

The hallway is lined with closed oak doors, and we stop at the one with an iron number four. Dr. Cassidy swings it open to loud rock music blaring and a view of two parallel beds, one empty and one occupied by a girl with blue hair and a septum ring.

"Lindsay, music down, please! Your new roommate is here!" Dr. Cassidy shouts.

Lindsay's enormous amber eyes meet mine, and her pursed lips turn into full teeth. She turns down a speaker before hopping up to greet me with open arms.

"Hi, I'm Lindsay. Nice to meet you!" Her hug is tight and seems sincere, much different from my last roommate, who didn't like to be touched; she had a full-blown, hysterical panic attack if I accidentally rubbed shoulders with her.

"Natalia, wow, look at the size of that window. Perfect for viewing the birds outside." Olga points to the massive window above the tightly made bed adjacent to Lindsay's, covered in clothes and magazines. The lack of bars shocks me, allowing an unobstructed view of a grassy field and a jagged landscape of pine trees, standing tall beneath the stars.

Dr. Cassidy chimes in. "Yes, we truly believe natural sunlight does wonders for the mind and spirit." She smiles at me. "Well, Natalia, I know this is the hard part, but I think the time has come to say your goodbyes."

Olga turns to me. The whites around her eyes burn crimson, but she doesn't shed a tear. I've never seen her cry, but it's these moments when I know she's fighting the instinct more than ever. She grabs my hand and brings me in so that our foreheads touch, lowering her voice so only I can hear.

"I've hit my breaking point. I'm not sure what I'll do if these doctors can't fix you."

Fix me. As if I'm a damaged old doll who just needs to be glued back together before it can be loved again.

Her words plunge a sadness into my heart, leaving me speechless. I wish it was that simple. I know she's fed up with me. I can't say I blame her. I want to promise her that things will be different this time, but looming doubt holds me back.

What if I never get better?

She kisses my forehead, but before she leaves, she squeezes my hand. "Take care, Natalia. I'll be back for you. I'm hoping sooner than later this time."

"I'll miss you" is all I can muster.

She doesn't say any more, just squeezes my hand one last time before heading out. Dr. Cassidy follows her out the door.

Desolation consumes me. It never gets easier when Olga has to leave. She's been my crutch for so long, and without her, I'm stuck with this constant fear of falling. I worry most that this time she won't come back. The strain in her stare and voice confirms she's had enough. She legally could go to court and try to leave me, but if she left me for good, I don't think I'd be able to survive without her. The thought causes my stomach to ache.

"Your mom is hot!" Lindsay hollers.

"She's not my mom," I inform her while taking in the scenery outside my window. It's too dark now to see any birds. They're probably all sleeping, something I should be doing in a matter of moments.

"Oh, right. I thought she looked too young. Sisters? You guys have the exact same eye color." Lindsay's voice rises, so I bring my attention back to her.

"Probably because we're both from the same place in Russia. But no relation."

"Russia! So that's where her accent is from. Why don't you have one?" she asks, sitting on the edge of her bed, tapping her feet against the floor.

"I didn't live there for very long."

"Still cool either way. I couldn't put my finger on it, but I knew you looked different."

I raise a brow. "Uh, thanks?"

"No, like in a good way! You're kind of like Snow White, if she never had a haircut in her life."

I've also never had a roommate be so blunt.

I'm slightly shocked by her candor. I pick up my black ends off my waist to examine them.

"You know, I was at a high-end cosmetology school down in Santa Barbara before this. I was planning to move to LA and cut the hair of celebrities. So, if you ever want to do the chop, I'm your girl," she says, making a snipping motion with two fingers.

Her locks, the color of a Kool-Aid flavor, now make sense. Her hair isn't the only thing that stands out. Lindsay is in hot pink shorts and a matching flannel pajama top. It's refreshing to see that I'll be able to wear the clothes to bed that I packed and not some backless mint gown that's been covered in human shit at some point.

Lindsay's staring at me with widened eyes, and I think she wants to continue the conversation.

"Santa Barbara is far. What brought you all the way up here?" I ask politely to appease her.

"My parents kicked me out after my third rehab stay. My grandma in Sonoma was the only one willing to take me in, but poor Grams, it wasn't long till I was back to my old tricks. I'm basically wired to be addicted to everything: pills, alcohol, sex. Anything that provides a thrill, I want it."

She shares this without flinching and almost with pride. These are all things I've never indulged in. My life, spent mostly confined at our cottage, gave me little freedom to try anything rebellious outside Olga's watchful eye.

Lindsay lies on her bed below a wall covered in music posters of her favorite bands, many I've never heard of. Despite her addictive personality, she seems like your average twentysomething, bubbly with a zest for life. But from what I've learned about meeting people in places like this, your exterior is usually just a shell hiding what's broken inside.

"So, what about you? Do you live close by? Were you in college?" she asks.

"No and no" is all I want to say. I prefer to keep to myself. My home life only tends to puzzle people, but I force myself to elaborate. "I live about two hours away in Latent Valley with a population less than a thousand, and no, I've only ever been homeschooled," I admit, despite the overwhelming urge to keep that bit of information to myself.

Why did I tell her that? She's definitely going to think I'm a freak now.

Lindsay's blinks slow down.

"Wow. That sounds… interesting. So, wait, how did you make friends being homeschooled?"

Her question stings.

I didn't.

Ironically, wards have been the closest thing I've had to a normal social structure. I face my window to hide the warmth growing on my cheeks.

"Sorry, I ask too many questions sometimes. But hey, I'm going to go grab some lemonade from downstairs. You want some?" She jumps up and heads for the door.

"No, thanks." I look back at her.

"Suit yourself!" Lindsay slides her feet into furry slippers before she exits our room.

I plop down on my bed, glancing around the small but modernly decorated space, then let out a heavy sigh.

Home sweet home.

Shortly after, a knock on the door surprises me. Dr. Cassidy peeks her head in with my bag.

"All cleared for unpacking. I know you got in late, so be sure to take things easy tonight. Lights go off in an hour, alarms are set for seven, and breakfast starts at eight. Your nurse will be in with your nighttime medication."

Dr. Cassidy leaves, and an older woman with a neatly styled bun steps in with a name tag that reads *Grace*. She doesn't say anything to me, just hands me two paper cups: one with a yellow pill and one with water. There's nothing warm or fuzzy about this woman which tracks with the typical nighttime-nurse demeanor that I've encountered in the past. I grab the cup, assuming it's a sedative like the ones I've taken my whole life to prevent me from leaving my bed. I swallow the pill in front of her, and once she leaves, I empty my bag into my designated dresser. I take out a bra and stick my finger in the small slit I made in one of the cups, pulling out a baggie filled with birdseed. The people assigned to search my things always find it and throw it out, every time. I'm not sure why seeds seem to pose such a threat. I'm convinced that some facilities just want to strip you of anything that reminds you of home. I'm proud it made it through the search but equally perplexed that they didn't catch it.

What if this bag was filled with drugs? This place is proving to be more relaxed than most. I'm not sure if that's a good or bad thing.

I tuck the bag away and change into an oversized shirt. Lindsay isn't back yet, but this sedative is strong. My entire body feels as if it's wilting. My muscles relax and my eyelids grow heavier with each deep breath I take. I'm too exhausted to wait for her.

When I pull back my soft comforter, I reveal restraints buckled to the sides of the bed frame. Disturbing images flash bright in my mind of the times my arms and legs were bound against my will.

As lovely as this place may look, the leather straps remind me that I'm still stuck in a cage, and these doctors are the only ones who hold the keys to my release.

CHAPTER 2

The soothing song on the alarm wakes me, but it doesn't take away the blaring in my head. I press the top of the clock to end the elevator music and stick my palm to my forehead. My head is throbbing.

Ugh, what is this?

My eyes gain focus and find Lindsay staring at the yellow-and-brown bruises along my exposed legs. I hop up and head straight to the shower, avoiding any chance for conversation.

I think the private bathroom is the best part of Awana—no locks, which is a fair trade for being able to close a door. For a virgin, my body has been seen naked more than I'd like. Our shower stall has toiletries like the kind you see in a hotel, not the usual soap dispenser filled with pink goo. After my shower, I change into jeans and a black long-sleeve shirt, then brush the tangles from my hair. My headache has subsided, but I still hear a faint ringing in my ears.

I'm running a few minutes late for breakfast, and the nerves kick in as I realize that I'll be meeting the other girls who reside here. Lindsay is already gone, so I'll have to go on my own. Light on my feet, I try to make a quiet entrance until I make it to the kitchen. A buffet of eggs, fruit, and different pastries lies across the island counter, and it actually smells appetizing. I fill my plate and head for the dining room.

"Hey, girl, hey!" Lindsay chants with a muffin stuffed halfway in her mouth.

I wave with a smile and am surprised to see only Lindsay and one other girl at the table. The girl across from Lindsay looks a little older than me and has strawberry-blonde hair styled in two braids. Her thick-rimmed glasses make her green eyes stand out.

"Sit here, Natalia!" Lindsay pulls out the chair to the right of her.

Who? Me?

I do a double take to make sure I heard that right. Once we make eye contact again, she grins and signals for me to come over.

I wouldn't say I'm antisocial. I just tend to keep to myself. Trying to make friends in these types of settings has been nearly impossible for me. I think I shut people out because I'm terrified of their judgment, but then again, rarely have others acted as inviting as Lindsay. It does feel nice to have someone want to sit next to me for a change.

I do as she says, setting my plate on the table.

"This is Abby. Abby, this is Natalia, my roommate," Lindsay introduces us.

I say hello but get nothing in return. Abby keeps her head a few inches from her food.

Did I say something wrong?

"She's not a talker, like at all. She's a mute. She shares a wall with us, and it's great because she'll never on tell me when I play my music loud." Lindsay speaks as if Abby's not right in front of us, but the impolite comment doesn't seem to bother her.

"Where are the rest of the girls?" I ask.

17

"Oh, the EDs eat separately."

"The what?"

"Oh, eating disorder. Can you believe out of the six of us, only three of us are trusted to eat our food?"

"Yeah, I guess that's a substantial ratio."

"I mean, it makes sense. EDs will always be the trendiest of mental illnesses. That's why so many girls have them. It's basically glorified on social media. I don't know about you, but I would be pretty fucking miserable to be hungry all the time," Lindsay says, talking with her mouth full.

I don't reply because I know Lindsay has a diluted view on eating disorders. She doesn't realize how lucky we are that we *don't* have to share a meal with them. It's gut-wrenching to watch. I've seen girls rip their hair out at the sight of food. I've seen teenagers with tears streaming down their eyes being spoon-fed like babies. It's awful, and I don't think anyone chooses a disorder because it's trendy.

I hear sandals clapping on the floor, and Dr. Cassidy comes in with a smile.

"Hope you gals enjoyed your breakfast. Natalia, you have your first session with Dr. Beckham in about ten minutes, so if you could rinse your dish off and head to Room 9, that would be greatly appreciated."

I agree, and when Dr. Cassidy leaves, I stand up from the table, but Lindsay grabs my arm, pulling me close to her.

"Have a nice time with Dr. Big Bulge Beckham. If he's wearing his black trousers, you're in for a real treat," Lindsay cackles.

My cheeks feel warm, and I don't know how to respond, so I don't, leaving the dining room as quickly as I can.

I wash my plate and head to Room 9. Even with Lindsay's awkward introduction of Dr. Beckman, I'm not fazed by the idea of therapy. I've spoken to doctors on a regular basis for most of my life. Olga placed me in therapy as soon as they would take me.

I knock, and a deep voice invites me in. I crack the door, and when it opens all the way, I'm stopped dead in my tracks. Dr. Beckman is painstakingly gorgeous. I was not expecting this. Sitting at his desk, he rests a hand on his thigh, sporting a gold watch and a band that matches on his ring finger. My eyes slowly trail the rest of the way up. His white coat contrasts against a black V-neck that exposes about four inches of his chest. His sharp jawline is covered in dark brown stubble around his soft-looking lips. I now fully understand the meaning of "ocean eyes."

"It's okay, Natalia. Don't be nervous. Come on in," he says with a smile I've only seen on models in magazines. I hope the sound of my pounding heart didn't give away my nerves. I take a deep breath and step in closer to him. "You can sit down. Make yourself comfortable."

I take two awkwardly large steps to the leather sofa and plop myself down as if I were a bag of bricks. Dr. Beckham rolls his office chair closer in front of me, and I lower my gaze, taking notice of his black trousers.

Dammit, Lindsay.

"Natalia, did you hear me?" he asks, and I shake myself out of my hypnosis.

Pull it together, Natalia.

"Uh, sorry. I didn't catch that."

"How are you liking it here at Awana?"

"Oh, it's great," I say, admiring the way his mouth moves when he talks.

"Great?" He raises a brow.

I clear my throat. "Well, I mean, you guys have some nice amenities."

"Yes, we try to keep things as close to home as possible. Glad you're enjoying them."

While he moves away to jot something down on paper, the excruciating pain I felt when I opened my eyes reminds me to speak up.

"Well, actually there's one thing."

"What's that?" He looks back up at me.

"Whatever medicine I took last night gave me a terrible headache this morning. Can we consider switching?"

"That is a known side effect. I'm sorry, but it's what I want to keep you on until we can pinpoint the type of delusion you had."

Delusion?

The word feels like a slap across the face.

"I've never had any delusions." My voice rises.

He folds his hands together, and his tone softens. "Natalia, let's talk about what happened before you came here. What do you remember?"

The whole night is a void, only a burning vision of the terror on Olga's face above me when she found me outside, and she refused to tell me what happened.

"I'm sorry, I don't remember anything. But this isn't the first time I've woken up outside."

"How often do you sleepwalk?" he asks.

"At my best, once, maybe twice a month. Lately, though, it's been happening every few days. As the years go by, it seems my episodes are only becoming more frequent and less innocent... hence why I'm here."

"I don't want to scare you, but there's a reason Olga chose not to tell you what happened before you woke up. She thought it'd be best for us to discuss."

My chest tightens at what he might say.

"She found you standing on the limb of the oak tree in your front yard next to a steep hillside. You had gone out the front door and climbed up the branches in your nightgown. She said you were in a panicked state, furiously screaming, 'No,' as if someone were forcing you to jump, but there was no one there. Olga tried to talk you down, but you either couldn't hear her or you just weren't listening. She was terrified that you were going to accidentally fall and hurt yourself until you willingly leaped out of the tree, your arms spread out like you were on a cross, fifteen feet to the ground. Olga thought she was watching you jump to your death, but somehow you managed not to hit your head or break your back. A few feet farther out and you could have fallen hundreds more down a dangerous rocky slope. You're very lucky."

My chest now feels as if someone is squeezing it with their fists, making air hard to expel.

"Hold your breath in, Natalia. One, two, three. Now release it." Dr. Beckman repeats the instructions until I have control of my lungs again.

"This might be a hard question, but do you remember who you were yelling at?" he asks softly once I'm calmed down.

"I have no memory. My mind is blank," I confess.

He sighs as he writes more. He has no idea how desperately I want to be able to give him more information. I know potentially falling to my death seems like the scariest part of last night's event, but for me, it's the slipping away. The lack of control over my own body and mind and the inability for anyone to explain what drives me to do such horrid things to myself are the most frightening parts of these episodes. I'm left with the fear that one day I'll fall asleep and my worsening condition will take over, and I'll tumble down a flight a stairs or take a fatal walk off a cliff.

Every time I close my eyes, I take the risk that they'll never open again.

My shoe rapidly taps the ground until Dr. Beckham notices my foot. I cross my legs, trying to regain my composure.

"I mean, it was probably just a nightmare, right?" I ask, wishing it was just that.

"I don't have a definite answer for you yet. Maybe it was a nightmare. Many people deal with sleep disorders. But we get involved when these disorders put you at risk of harming yourself and so we can prevent this from happening again. You really are lucky you walked away with only minor injuries. Has this type of occurrence happened before?"

"Jumping out of a tree?" I raise a brow.

"No, self-harm in your sleep."

"It has."

"Can you tell me what happened?"

I glance around to avoid his eye contact. I think he catches on to my purposeful delay when he briefly places his hand on my knee.

"This is a safe place," he assures me.

"I created bad habits in my sleep," I admit with a heavy exhale.

"What kind of habits?" he asks, bringing his pen back to his notepad.

I hate replaying the moments in my head. I squeeze my eyes shut for a moment, and when I open them, I explain.

"Small ones at first, like chewing my lip or tearing out my eyebrow hairs, but then it got worse. I started scratching myself every time I'd fall asleep. I didn't realize it until one morning I woke up with bleeding collarbones. I thought I'd been attacked until I noticed dried blood under my fingernails. But I couldn't stop myself. Every night, I'd scratch at the same places, reopening the scabs. It got so bad it left scars."

Having to bring this up is like picking at emotional scars that release guilt and shame. Sometimes the mental wounds hurt more than the physical ones.

"Would you be comfortable showing me these scars?" He rolls his chair closer to me.

I hesitate, but there's something in his gaze that brings me to pull the collar of my shirt aside to show him the faint marks on my skin, the ones I keep covered to avoid being reminded of my insanity.

He brings his stubbled chin inches from me to examine them, and it causes my breath to stop. I fidget when his fingers lightly brush the delicate skin below my neck.

"Excoriation during a sleep cycle is very interesting," he says, moving back to his desk.

"Excoriation?"

"Picking or scratching at yourself in a compulsive manner. In some cases, it can act as a coping mechanism for severe stress, but since you do it in your sleep, it does pique questions of what the root behind it is."

What's the root of any of the crazy things I do?

I've been asking myself the same question for as long as I can remember. I want nothing more than to know what causes me to do such awful things, but I guess I'd rather hurt myself instead of hurting anyone else. Unfortunately, that's what earned me my first ward stay at six years old. It's when we realized my sleepwalking was more than just night terrors about monsters under the bed. I became the monster that night. I woke up to Olga gasping for air and my hands wrapped around her neck.

My body breaks out in chills remembering that night. Though Olga doesn't hold it against me, I still hate myself for doing it, even if it was during some sort of sleep trance.

"Natalia," Dr. Beckham says, trying to recapture my attention from the horrible memories replaying in my head. "Does this make sense to you? Do you understand why I need you to stay on the medication? We're dealing with a whole different issue now. You put yourself in grave danger this time, and your regular medication wasn't enough."

"Yes, I understand."

I'm fully aware of the liability I've become. I must be some sort of monster if they need to severely sedate me so my mistakes won't fatally affect myself or others.

"Great. I know you're as eager as we are to have this all sorted out."

"Do you have a timeframe of when you think I'll be able to go home?"

"Every patient and situation is different here at Awana. For some, it's several weeks; for others, months. We do even take in a few long-term patients on a case-by-case basis."

My nerves are starting to seep moisture into my palms.

I can't stay locked up forever.

"You don't think I'll be long term, do you?"

"Don't worry about it too much. Take this one day at a time, and before you know it, it'll be your time to leave."

His optimistic quote that belongs on a coffee mug doesn't reassure me. It's unsettling to have your fate depend on your own faulty mind.

"Well, I think that's enough for today. Just wanted a quick meet and to check in. You have arts and crafts in the living room until lunch, and after that you have free time. Maybe go enjoy some fresh air outside. The sun should be making an appearance this afternoon."

He stands to shake my hand.

When our hands cup, I find my fingers not wanting to leave his warm skin, but I pry them away and hurry out.

***

Arts and crafts is a typical ward activity and happens to be my favorite. Creative expression has been treating mental illness for centuries. Vincent van Gogh once said, "Art is to console those who are broken by life." Inspiring words from the man who cut his own ear off in the name of love, though scholars will argue his intent.

Learning about van Gogh was the first time in my life I didn't feel alone in my illness. He suffered sporadic breakdowns and had attacks where he couldn't remember what he was doing or saying. He would momentarily lose his mind, but then he would bounce back and regain awareness. Although these episodes were debilitating, once he was in his right mind again, he did his best to sew the threads of his life back together. I know exactly how it feels to have your life be a quilt with no idea how some of the patches were woven in.

The living room has been transformed into an art room. A long table is set up with plenty of items to choose from: brushes, paint, fabrics, old magazines. There's another round one nearby where other patients are working quietly.

Out of all the scraps, an empty soda bottle, yarn, and a metal bell stick out to me. I know exactly what to do with them.

Lindsay isn't here, but I see Abby's braids and take a seat next to her. My hello goes unanswered again, but knowing what I do now, I don't take it personally. I peer over at the painting she's working on and am shocked at her skills. She's created an exact replica of Awana from an outside view. Most illustrative artists need their subject in front of them, but she's just going off what she sees in her head.

"Abby, your painting is incredible. You have some serious talent," I tell her. I wonder if anyone has checked her hearing, because she doesn't acknowledge me at all.

I focus on my project, cutting the plastic bottle in half and using the bottom as a bowl. I poke holes on each side of the bowl, then attach the bell to the yarn. Finally, I string yawn through each hole, creating a handle so the cylinder dangles in the air. Every time the bowl moves, the bell rings. Eager to try my new contraption, I scoot out to head back to my room.

Lindsay isn't in the room when I get there, and I'm excited to have some time to myself. I reach into my top drawer, grab the bag of birdseed I have tucked away, and pour it into the bottom of my plastic contraption. I crank open my window enough to slip the seed carrier through, hook the long yarn over the window handle, and admire it hanging outside below.

The door creaks, and I'm startled by Lindsay singing a song as she enters.

"Whatcha doing, Nat? Spying on the boys outside?" she teases and skips over to sit next to me on my bed. "What in the world is that?" she asks, looking out the window.

"A bird feeder."

"A bird feeder? Why? So you can sing to the birds? You really are Snow White, aren't you?"

Her joke makes me smile.

"I guess I must be. I love birds more than anything else."

"Okay, well, since you have no bites from the birds yet, look over there. That's a sight to see." Lindsay points to the far left, where two shirtless guys are throwing a football back and forth.

I catch myself admiring the way their muscles flex with each throw.

"You got a boyfriend, Nat?" Lindsay interrupts my male anatomy study.

"Oh, um, no. I've never had one."

"What?" she shouts so loud that the boys all turn their heads in our direction. She grins back with a flirty wave. They laugh and give us a nod, and it makes my stomach flutter. "Wait, so you've *never* had a boyfriend? That seems insane. You're freaking gorgeous."

Mental note: Lindsay needs to get her eyes checked.

My cheeks feel warm, probably because it's not an adjective I usually hear to describe me.

"I guess being homeschooled in a small town has its disadvantages. What about you? Do you have one?" I ask.

Lindsay's smile is ear to ear. "Yes, I do. He's so great. Super hot. Makes good money, great bod. He's a little older and very straitlaced, but you know what they say: opposites attract."

"He sounds nice. So, are you guys sort of long distance now that you're here?"

"Um… something like that." Lindsay abruptly ends our conversation to continue singing and dancing her way to the door. "See you at lunch!"

CHAPTER 3

Lunch had a similar routine as breakfast, and afterward, Dr. Cassidy led a yoga class for all the girls outside. I stood in the back, embarrassed of my inability to even touch my toes. You can tell the girls are divided. The ED girls stick together. Abby seems like a loner by nature, and if it wasn't for me, I think Lindsay would be one too.

After yoga, I want to head back to my room to check on the feeder, but Lindsay calls out for me before I can step away. I wish she would ignore me the way she does Abby, but for some reason, she has her eyes set on me.

"Hey! Come with me."

I don't want to be rude to the girl I'll be living with for who knows how long, so I do as she says. On our way through the grass, we pass a rainbow of lilacs and carnations. I can smell the fresh tomato vines planted along the picket fence that surrounds the quaint garden.

We are now closer to the boys' house than the girls. We stop in front of a weeping willow tree with cascading leaves that hang like teardrops from their branches. Lindsay leans against the thick trunk.

"Come on. Sit back and relax," she says.

I cross my arms and peer up at the sun shining through the leaves.

"This spot is my favorite. This tree gets great sun, and we even get a little privacy from the house. Trust me, you'll want it. It gets tiresome being a spectacle for doctors all day." She tears off her shirt, revealing her sports bra. "Plus, the boys enjoy the view." She points to their sliding glass door a short distance away.

When she pats the ground, her exaggerated grin convinces me to sit next to her, but I inform her that I'll be leaving my long-sleeve shirt on. My pale skin has never agreed much with UV rays, but I'll hand it to her, the warmth is relaxing.

Lindsay plucks the dandelions in the grass, showing me how to pierce the stems to weave the flowers together, creating nature-made necklaces for us all while talking my ear off about reality TV shows I've never seen. She reminds me of a hummingbird, the way her mouth moves a mile a minute.

I'm finding myself enjoying the company.

Dinner approaches, and we head back inside to the same table I've eaten all my meals at so far. Hot dogs are the main course tonight. Lindsay makes inappropriate gestures with her phallic food, but it's when she goes in for her first real bite and the hot dog slips from the bun into her lap that both of us crack up.

"Five-second rule!" she yells before picking it back up and chomping it like a carrot stick.

After dinner, I head back to check if my feeder has had any success and am disappointed that the seeds look untouched. To pass time, Lindsay plays me upbeat electronic music.

"I've never heard any of these songs." I tell her and find myself bobbing my head to the catchy beat.

"Please don't tell me you like country." She fakes a gag.

"Definitely not. My musical knowledge is just a little behind."

"Why is that?" She tilts her head.

"I really only listened to what Olga likes."

"And what kind of music is that?"

"Classical, opera, occasionally some jazz when she's in a good mood."

Lately, classical has been the go-to. Her moods haven't been the best recently, and I'm afraid it's because of having to deal with me.

Lindsay cringes. "Well, time to expand your horizons, Nat. The first thing you need to know is that anything you hear on the top charts is trash. Second—"

The nurse enters our room and interrupts her rant with my nightly medication. She hands me one of the paper cups with a lone pill, which I pop into my mouth and wash it down with a swish of water. I expect her to hand something to Lindsay as well, but she turns around and leaves after only giving me mine.

"You don't take medication?" I ask.

"Nope. None for this addict. I'm not opposed, though, if you ever want to share." She wiggles her brows with an evil smile, but I glare back. "Sheesh. I'm only kidding. Night, Nat. I'll see you in the morning."

She sticks in her earbuds, then rolls over.

It's interesting that she doesn't take anything, and I almost find myself jealous of her and the fact that she doesn't require pills. I'd give anything to not need medication to be normal, and ironically, Lindsay abuses pills for the chance to escape normalcy.

***

My throbbing head wakes me again, and it's the worst way to be woken up. I'm in so much pain it's hard to move. It's been this way for a week now with no improvement.

Within minutes, Lindsay hits our nagging alarm and heads to the bathroom first. I close my eyes again, pressing hard on my temples, trying to find relief. I hear a bell jingle, and excitement distracts me from the pain. When I open my eyes and look out my window, I find two beautiful cardinals enjoying a morning snack.

Lindsay steps back out, and I place my finger over my lips and signal for her to come over. She tiptoes to my side, and I point to our first little visitors.

"Oh my God, they're so cute," she whispers, but her slipper catches on the carpet runner between our beds. "Oh shit!" she yells, and the delicate birds vanish. She winces. "My bad. I'm so sorry. I know those were your first ones to show. This stupid rug insists on tripping me at least once a day," she says, trying to even out the kink with her foot.

"Don't worry about it. They'll be back. Once cardinals find a source of food, they tend to stick around."

"Why do you love birds so much?" Lindsay asks.

I take a minute to answer a question not even Olga has asked.

"Hmm. I mean, I've always thought they were stunning and fascinating as long as I can remember, but I think I fell in love with them the moment I realized they're a symbol of love."

Lindsay raises a brow.

"Ninety-five percent of birds are monogamous. That's way more than our species. Some birds do courtship dances or wait several years in hopes to find their one perfect mate, and when they do, they remain together until death. They're actually the most romantic creatures on earth, in my opinion."

"Wow, that's pretty deep." She pauses for a moment before saying, "Hey, Nat."

"What?"

"Maybe you haven't found a boyfriend 'cause you're like the birds. You just have to wait for the perfect one to come along," she says with a genuine smile.

Aw, what a nice way to think about it.

I just hope she's right and that my bird is out there waiting for me, because at this point, boys are an endangered species in my life.

"Maybe." I smile back, thankful Lindsay didn't judge me for my nerdy obsession.

"Well, if you're a bird, I'm definitely more like a lion. I look at men like they're my prey." She lets out a roar and scratches the air.

We both giggle until Lindsay heads out.

***

Breakfast goes per usual, Lindsay dominating the conversation while Abby and I stay quiet. After Lindsay ends our meal in a tirade about why it's unfair that we aren't allowed to check social media, I sneak back to our room to freshen up. I comb my hair out of the messy bun I wore to breakfast and slip on my favorite black chiffon turtleneck blouse that cinches at my waist, giving evidence to my womanly curves that normally look nonexistent.

Wait, why am I getting ready for therapy?

I've never cared at all before.

I quit analyzing myself in the mirror to check my feeder one last time before heading out to my session with Dr. Beckham. To my disappointment, there's no sign of a bird anywhere.

On the dot, I'm at Dr. Beckham's door with a knock. He allows me in, and his appearance doesn't disappoint. His dark hair is meticulously styled without a strand out of place. He's wearing thick-rimmed glasses and takes them off after he sees me.

"Good morning, Natalia. Please have a seat. How are you feeling? Still dealing with the headaches?" he asks, grabbing a pen.

"I'm fine. The headaches aren't, though." I say, crossing my arms as I plop down.

"I'm sorry to hear that. Once we finish this trial of medication, we can look into switching you to something new."

I should have known that my treatment plan wouldn't be easy, even in a progressive place like Awana.

"How long will that be?"

"At least three weeks."

Ugh.

"Can I take something for the pain?"

"I'm sorry, but no. We don't want any adverse reactions. So, can you hang in there for me?"

His Disney prince smile appears, making it impossible to argue with him. I nod, and he continues. "So, today I want to discuss your last facility visit about a year ago. Your charts indicate you were suffering from an extreme form of insomnia. Can you tell me a bit about what you were experiencing during that time and the moments leading to it?"

"Um, yeah. It's pretty simple. I just couldn't sleep. It would happen every once in a while, and I would go a few days without sleep. But one night turned into three, then a week. I didn't want to worry Olga, so I passed the time with night walks, hoping it would tire me out. But on the eighth night, she found me out of bed and forced me to explain. The next morning, we went to the hospital."

"Well, good thing you did. That's an unusually long time for the body to not demand sleep. In another few days, your organs would have shut down. Sleep deprivation will eventually kill you."

Scarily, he's right. When I arrived at the hospital, the doctors were astonished that I was still standing. Physically, I could feel myself shutting down. It's the strangest sensation to have every inch of you ache and beg for sleep, but your brain just won't allow it.

"Apparently so," I say, wondering why my body likes to betray me.

"I see this particular hospital kept you for a four-week sleep study."

If he wants to call drugging me to the point of barely functioning and strapping me to a bed at night a sleep study, then yes.

"I find it rather fascinating that you experience different types of sleep disturbance," he continues. "With your consent, I'd like to try a sleep study here."

I'm reminded of the leather straps on my bed. I'd rather die of sleep deprivation than wake up with those attached to my limbs. My lip quivers as I clench my eyes to rid myself of the thought.

"Natalia, what's wrong?" he asks, and I try to calm myself down, but all I can do is vehemently shake my head. "Open your eyes. Tell me what you're feeling."

My eyes open, and his curled lips allow my crunched shoulders to move away from my ears.

I huff. "I just hate sleep studies. I saw what's attached to my bed, and I won't allow you to strap me down. It obviously did nothing before to help me or else I wouldn't need to be here," I say, tensing again.

"I see the method they used in the notes, and that's not at all what I had planned for you. I don't think those restraints have ever needed to be used here. The only straps involved in this sleep study would be the ones I would place around your head to monitor brain activity, and we would only do it once a week. It's only a small part of figuring out this puzzle."

I'm still reluctant, but I know if my illness was some sort of puzzle, it would be the impossible kind with thousands of pieces that no one ever finishes.

"What exactly would you be monitoring?" I ask.

"Sleep is vital to every human being. We spend at least one-third of our lives doing it. It affects almost every major tissue and organ in us. It's the foundation to keep our body and mind healthy. Poor sleep patterns can create a multitude of issues. I need to make sure you're reaching a REM stage without any disturbances while you're here with us. This will ensure the medication and treatment here is working for you."

"What's REM again?" I know I've heard the word before, but I can't place it at the moment.

"REM—rapid eye movement—is the most crucial of the sleep patterns, especially with someone who has your types of sleep disturbances. It's the stage that causes all your muscles to become temporarily paralyzed to prevent you from acting out your dreams. There are a lot of mysteries revolving around sleep, some scientists have yet to solve, but I think as long as we focus on achieving REM sleep, it could help you lead a normal life."

What if he's wrong? What if no one will ever be able to solve my issues?

I hate to be a cynic, but it's hard not to be when nothing in the past has seemed to work.

My leg won't stop shaking, and he stops for a moment to take my hand, giving it a gentle squeeze. My gaze goes from down at my feet up to his eyes.

"I promise we'll get you through this, and I'll do everything in my power to help you."

The shaking stops, but the beating in my chest picks up speed. I can only focus on his soothing voice. I've never had anyone be able to change my emotions so quickly from full-blown panic to a peaceful bliss.

In an infatuated trance, I agree to his sleep study, and he lets go of my hand to conclude our session. We say goodbye, and when I leave, I worry about the mess my heart made when it melted on his floor.

It's official. I have my first crush, and it's on the one person who is completely out of reach: my married psychologist.

***

After another half-assed attempt at yoga class, I grab a glass of water inside and then head back out to find Lindsay to see if she's up for some afternoon sun. Our trips to the clearing by the willow tree have become a daily ritual. Happy to see her lying in our spot, I walk over, but the ED girls reach her before me.

"Put some clothes on," one sneers.

Still staring up at the sky in her bra and sunglasses, Lindsay replies with a waving middle finger in the air.

"Fucking slut," a taller girl with pretty features and hair down to her hip bones hisses. I'm shocked when she spits on Lindsay's exposed stomach.

Lindsay's jaw drops, and for the first time, I think she's speechless. For once, I can't hold my tongue. My boiling blood brings out my defenses for her.

"Hey! Back off!" I yell and rush over.

"Oh, you got the schizo fighting your battles now. Guess she's too delusional to see the whore you are."

"You don't have to be cruel," I say, standing firm, mere inches from the spitter.

She rolls her thickly mascara-coated eyes, and the group marches away.

"Are you okay?" I ask Lindsay, helping her sit up. She uses her sock to wipe her stomach.

"Yeah, I'm fine," she mumbles, but her lowered voice worries me that they've gotten to her. "Hey, thanks for that. Those girls hate me. I don't know what I did to them."

I wonder if it has to do with her insensitive theories on their disorder.

"Yeah, they definitely aren't warm and friendly by any means. What's up with calling me a schizo? I don't have schizophrenia."

"Don't let them get to you. The tall one with the hairy upper lip is the biggest rumor starter. I'm telling you, being that hungry will turn anyone into a bitch."

I crack a smile but try to hide it, knowing it's not something we should joke about. I'm just glad she's back to her comedic self.

We forget the EDs by lying back to enjoy the warm afternoon. After an hour of baking in the sun, my porcelain shoulders are officially pink. Lindsay leaves for her therapy session, and I decide to spend the short rest of my free time indoors.

I open my room door and am greeted with the sweetest sound: the ringing of a bell. I creep over and find a striking blue jay chomping away. I wish Lindsay was here to see. Blue jays are often disliked because of their bold personalities, but to me, they're one of the most enchanting birds. Their temperament mirrors Lindsay's, and their feathers perfectly match her hair color. I don't know if it could be more fitting.

Excited to tell Lindsay about the blue jay, I rush down the stairs to find that she isn't at dinner. I didn't know we were allowed to skip meals. I scoop some pasta and take a seat near Abby. We both sit in awkward silence until I finally have to break it.

"I love spaghetti! What about you?" I realize that saying it out loud was even more awkward.

Abby twirls her noodles with a fork, not acknowledging a word I said and making the rest of our dinner painfully silent.

The quiet brings reflection as I finish my last few bites. I don't want to get my hopes up or jinx myself, but Awana isn't so bad. These dinners sure beat Olga's leftover goulash we often eat for weeks at a time. Is it wrong for me to enjoy myself here? Sometimes when you feel like you've been a burden to others your whole life, you start believing that being uncomfortable or miserable is all you deserve.

"Well, I'm full. I guess I'll get going," I tell an unresponsive Abby, then clear my plate into the trash.

I come back to an empty room, so I lie down and watch the orange setting sun through my window.

Moments later, Lindsay comes in with a smile full of teeth and her hands behind her back.

"Hey, why weren't you at dinner?" I ask.

"My session with Dr. Beckham ran late. But never mind that. I brought you a gift."

"What for?"

"For having my back with the EDs." She pulls out a paper bag from behind her. "Look inside!"

I grab the bag and open it to reveal a bunch of crushed nuts and sunflower seeds.

"I made you some more birdseed! I raided the snack cabinet and got inspired when I saw the trail mix. Don't worry, I ate all the M&M's first before crushing it all up. I assumed chocolate wasn't good for birds. I mean, I hope it's even usable."

Oh my God, this is so thoughtful. Only a true friend would do something like this.

"It's absolutely perfect." I wrap my arms around her.

Nurse Grace comes in, breaking our embrace. I toss back my pill while Lindsay blasts her music so loud, I can hear it playing from her earbuds.

Later, as the lights go out and I'm lying in bed, I realize today was filled with so many firsts. I discovered what a crush is, and even if it will never be more than that, the new sensation is thrilling. But what I'm excited for most is finding my first friend.

I look at Lindsay's shut eyes, but the familiar dread of falling asleep prevents me from closing mine. What if I ruin everything good right now with one of my freakish night accidents? I try to sit up to stay awake, but the medication flowing through my bloodstream weighs down every part of me. Fright and anxiety fill my motionless body until my eyes can no longer fight to stay open.

CHAPTER 4

My splitting headache shoots down to my gut, and I think I'm going to hurl. My feet pick up as much speed to the closed bathroom door as I can muster. Lindsay yells out from the shower, but I ignore her to grip the toilet seat and spew out last night's spaghetti.

She peeks her head out from behind the shower curtain. "You good, girl? That smells awful."

If throwing up my insides counts as good, then I'm great.

"Yeah, I'm fine. Just a migraine from my medication, I think," I reply, toning down my dramatics.

"Must be some serious shit they got you on."

I shrug and cradle my stomach, walking back out to go lie in bed.

Lindsay comes out in a towel and says I should just rest, that she'll tell Dr. Cassidy I don't feel well. I agree, and once she's dressed, she rubs my back.

"Feel better," she says before slipping out.

I pull the blanket over my head to block out any light and try to rest. As awful as I feel, it's a relief that I didn't wake up outside or with any physical harm.

Almost asleep again, I hear a ringing, but not from the migraine; it's coming from the window. I peek outside, and the sight of the two cardinals makes the sunlight worth the pain.

The door opens, startling the cardinals and causing them to fly away. Dr. Cassidy comes in with a glass and a plate of crackers.

"I'm sorry you're not feeling well. Here's some Alka-Seltzer to ease your stomach."

I thank her and take a sip of the bubbly drink.

"Take it easy today. Do you want to skip your session?" she offers.

"No, I'll be fine," I answer quickly.

Seeing Dr. Beckham is the only thing that will make leaving this bed worthwhile.

"Okay, I'll let him know you'll still be attending. I'd sit yoga out this afternoon, though."

I assure her I will.

After she leaves, I push myself up. In the bathroom, I splash some water on my face and brush the bitter taste out of my mouth. A shiny black lipstick tube Lindsay left out catches my eye. I pop off the lid and swivel the stick up, then dab a bit on my finger and smear it on my lips. After pressing my lips together, I admire the rouge stain. I open our vanity drawer to grab my hairbrush, and a pack of cigarettes stands out. I carefully slide one out with my finger and place it in front of my lips, careful to not leave any red residue.

"I'm more like a lion. I look at men like they're my prey," I copy Lindsay's words, pretending to blow out smoke.

Who am I kidding?

I place the white stick back in its pack and let out a lengthy exhale.

Time for therapy.

When I arrive at Dr. Beckham's office, his door is open, and he signals for me to come in. After closing the door behind me, I notice he's distracted by his computer. It takes a few minutes for him to acknowledge me, and when he does, he jumps right into psychiatry talk.

"Today, I want to talk about your relationship with Olga. She's been your guardian since you were three, right?"

"Yes. She's really all I know. I don't know any life without her."

Imagining her delicate features creates a homesick pit in my stomach.

"You two had a rather unique meeting. Can you dive into it for me?"

"Um, it's kind of a long story," I say, hoping he'll move on to something else.

"All we have is time, Natalia." Dr. Beckham lifts his lips in a small smile.

I've heard that phrase before. In other words, I better divulge if I ever want to leave this leather couch, even if it's a question I hate answering. Sometimes I wish Olga was simply my mother. That story would be more normal and easier to tell. Unfortunately, the beginning of our relationship is far from that.

I glance away from his persistent eyes, searching the room until my gaze lands on a lone succulent plant on his cluttered desk. I find it easier to talk to nature than humans. I focus on the mint-green spiky leaves and force myself to begin.

"Olga found me eighteen years ago before she fled a small town near Moscow. There I was, wandering alone at the train station. She told me my nightgown was ripped, and I had tangled hair and a dirty diaper. She asked around, praying someone would claim me, but by the looks of it, it was apparent I had been abandoned. In a rash moment, she had to make a gut decision: hop on the train with or without me."

Bringing up the fact that I was neglected by whoever birthed me makes me want to curl up and hide. It never feels good to be reminded that nobody wanted me.

"That's a real brave choice to make." He stops and writes something on his notepad.

He's right.

My life may be far from perfect, but I know without Olga, it could have been cut short, or worse, I could have ended up in an orphanage or fallen into the hands of someone sinister.

"Does Olga suffer from any mental disorders? Depression? Anxiety?"

No one has ever asked me about Olga's mental history, only mine.

"I would say she has a bit of anxiety. Her life before me and America wasn't easy by any means."

A loud beeping causes me to flinch. Dr. Beckham grabs his ringing cell phone and silences it before sliding it into his jacket pocket.

"Sorry about that. Would you be able to go into more—"

The blaring ringtone cuts him off again until he presses the side repeatedly to stop it.

He clears his throat. "All right, back to Olga and her life in Russia."

He leans toward me, and I think I finally have his undivided attention.

"I don't know too much detail. Olga doesn't like to talk about her past. I've only gotten a few glimpses over the years. I know she was born into a poor family and was raised by her single mom. It was her mom who taught her the basics of ballet, and that's how she fell in love with dance. Her mom tragically passed when she was a teenager, and she was left in the care of her uncle. He was an evil man, as Olga described him, but she never went into too much depth. She hates when I ask too many questions."

This has always bothered me about Olga. I've been dissected by doctors my whole childhood, yet she shuts down any time I ask about hers.

I look at Dr. Beckham for his reaction, but his eyes are back on his vibrating pocket. He leaves it and shift his focus back to me.

"Has Olga been to therapy?"

"Nope, I think I've been given the starring role in that department."

He cracks a smile at that.

"Well, I know you haven't been feeling well, so let's end today early. I'll be beginning the first sleep study at the end of the week." He ends our conversation, then digs out his phone and taps away.

"Can't wait!" I cheer, hoping to catch another smile, but the only grin he gives is to the screen in his hands.

"Someone sure is eager to talk to you," I remark.

He retracts his smile and pushes his fingers through his hair.

"Just a personal matter. I'll see you a few days." he says shortly.

I take the hint that he wants me to leave and shut his door hard before heading to my room.

Dr. Beckham was off today. He seemed distracted by whatever was happening on his phone.

I hate to admit it, but I'm kind of disappointed.

As I reach the door to my room, my headache pounds it way back to the forefront of my mind. I jump into bed and hide under my covers, hoping it will be over soon.

***

My eyes slowly blink open, and a blurry body is standing over me.

"Oh, good! You're awake." Lindsay grins.

My eyes adjust to the light and find Lindsay with a pair of scissors in her hand.

"Whoa! You can't wake people up by hovering over them with sharp objects!" I yell, scooting back away from her.

"Oh shit. My bad… Especially not in a psych house."

I laugh. "What's with the scissors?"

"Well, I grabbed a pair from arts and craft this morning, and I was thinking we could give you a new look."

"Have you lost it?" I glare at her.

"Not fully, yet. Oh, come on! I'm having hair-cutting withdrawals, and you'd be the perfect model to work on with that head of hair."

I grab a chunk of my thick black strands. I can barely count on one hand the number of haircuts I've had. The locks that hang down my waist represent security to me. When your life is filled with tumultuous ups and down, it's comforting to have one thing that consistently stays the same.

I look up at Lindsay, who has her bottom lip poked out.

"Pretty please? I promise you'll love it."

I glance back and forth between my hair and her pouting face.

"Ugh. Fine. But nothing too short."

I give in, knowing that if Olga sees I chopped it, she might kill me. I'm not allowed to do much without her consent. I think it's because of the chaotic nature of my illness; she can't discipline my disorder. It's the one thing in life she can't control, so maybe dictating everything else in my life brings her a sense of stability.

Lindsay jumps up and down, cheering and waving her arms wildly.

"Hey, watch the scissors!" I shout.

After soaking my hair in the bathroom sink and getting water everywhere, Lindsay sits me at our desk.

"We'll just trim those dead ends, then give your hair some life with some layers," she says, removing the damp towel from my head. Her makeshift salon only has a tiny mirror that she turned me away from, so all my faith is in her hands.

My stomach churns imagining what she might do, but I try and keep my cool.

After an hour of hair falling to the floor and a few accidental blow-dry burns, Lindsay forces me to cover my eyes. She leads me to the bathroom, then pulls my hands from my face.

Oh my gosh. Is this really me?

My reflection brings out an emotional response I wasn't expecting. Not disappointment but total awe. It definitely isn't too short. It's perfect. In fact, I don't think I've ever loved the way my hair has looked this much. The volume bounces delicately, luminous and full, as I wave my head back and forth. Lindsay transformed me from an ordinary girl to a breathtaking vision. It's the complete opposite of the straight-across trims I received at the cheap "in-and-out" salon back in Latent Valley.

Admiring myself has never come easy, but with this new look, it's difficult not to.

"Hello, cheekbones!" she shouts, shaking the layers that now have definition and shine. "So, do you like it?"

"I love it. I absolutely do," I assure her and run my fingers through my smooth hair, adoring how soft it feels.

A haircut might not mean much to some, and for me it usually doesn't, but this is one of the first times I've felt like an actual young woman. Growing up reclusively in a home where my illness took the forefront stole those moments from me. I didn't have friends or a mother who taught me how to do makeup or use fashion to express my femininity. All I've ever wanted is to experience the simple joys that come with a girl growing up. Today, Lindsay has gifted me with one, and she'll never know how thankful I am.

She shrieks and gives me a side hug as I take in the new me. I can't take my eyes off the image in the mirror. The wide-eyed girl staring back at me is stunning, and I don't want to look away. My newfound confidence is towering over any previous worries I had or my ever-present fear of change.

I hop up and squeeze her tight. "Thank you so much. You're really talented. I mean, the fact that you can bring someone so much happiness with a pair of dull paper scissors says something."

"Thanks, girl." She rests her hands on my shoulders. "It brings me joy too. I was feeling a little down today, so thank you for trusting me."

My posture is straighter as I wear my new hair to dinner, and Lindsay shows me off as her masterpiece. Afterward, we head back to our room together, and Dr. Beckham brushes past us.

"Nice hair, Natalia," he says, and my feet stop dead in their tracks.

Did Dr. Beckham just compliment me?

"Thanks to me!" Lindsay boasts, pulling my arm away from him, as I hide my blushing.

As we get ready for bed and I wait for my pill that caused my day-long headache, Lindsay whispers something to me, but I can't make out what she's trying to say.

"I can't hear you," I tell her, moving closer to her.

"You don't always have to take them. I mean, if they make you so sick. I don't think skipping one once in a while will hurt."

Is she actually being serious?

The mantra that ward rules are in place for a reason and medication needs to be taken have been drilled into me since I was a little girl. There's no way I'd ever do such a thing.

I tilt my head sideways and squint at her. "Yeah, right."

"I'm serious. I knew a girl at my last rehab who did it."

"And how would I get away with that? Grace checks."

"She only checks under the tongue. I watch her. Close your mouth and slip it under your top lip. It's simple," she whispers, then slides her tongue along her gum.

"I don't know. I've never done anything like that before."

"Well, if I was being forced to take something that made me sick, I'd do it. I just hated seeing you in so much pain in the bathroom this morning."

I'm not the rebellious type—though I guess in a way, my body rebels every time I have a nighttime incident. It's the consciously choosing to do something wrong that's so foreign.

Grace walks in, and Lindsay hurries under her covers. The nurse drops the pill into my palm, and I hesitate for a few seconds. Maybe Lindsay is right. I could really use a break from feeling like I'm dying.

Could one time really hurt?

In one swift movement, I place the pill on my tongue, using the tip to slide it under my lip, pressing it tight against my upper gum as water slides down my throat. She does an under-the-tongue check, and I clench my fist, trying to calm my racing nerves.

I'm gonna get caught. This was so stupid. Maybe I should just swallow it now?

Grace doesn't think a thing, walking back out with no suspicion. The door shuts behind her, and I spit the yellow pill into my hand. My nerves are now on an adrenaline high.

"Holy shit, you actually did it! I didn't think you had it in ya!"

"Me either, to be honest."

"Maybe it's the new hair? I made sure in between the layers to cut in some badass bitch. You should probably go flush it now, though," Lindsay says, putting in her earbuds.

Me and "badass bitch" have never been in the same sentence, but they do sound pretty good together right now.

Something in me doesn't want to swirl it down the drain, though. This pill is a trophy of the first time I've ever broken a rule. My life has always been controlled with medication by doctors, and it's strangely liberating to take a small bit of that control back. Instead of flushing it, I grab my bra that first was used to hide birdseed and slip the soggy pill into the cup.

Lindsay is rolled over, and I lie in bed enjoying these moments of falling asleep without an induced drowsiness. I imagine a different version of my life, one more like Lindsay's, where boys lust after me and girls all want to be my friend. I wonder what I'd be like if I was a normal girl my age, going to college parties or spending the summer traveling.

I soak in all these sweet visions and allow them to tuck me away into the night.

***

The rising sun creates a glow over my bed, and the warmth radiating from it is the most wonderful way to wake up. Lindsay is still asleep, and I have a triumphant feeling waking before the alarm. I crank open my window to let in the fresh springtime air. The gentle wind brings in the scent of jasmine from the bushes outside. Everything is clear; everything is calm. And best of all, I feel no pain.

I take my time in the shower, enjoying the different sensations: the icy cold water warming and then turning into steam, sliding my fingers through my hair, and running the fingertips along the softness of my skin. All my senses feel intensified, perfectly complementing my heightened emotions.

An overwhelming sadness hits me when I realize there will always be heavy chains locked to my wrists because of my life sentence to medication. A lump forms in my throat as moisture gathers in my eyes. Tears pour down my face, and I can't stop them. I place my hands on my aching chest as I crouch to the shower floor and mourn the life I'm not allowed to live. It's like my body is purging something that has been stuck deep down inside me. I weep until there isn't anything left in me to give. And I actually feel a little better.

The sorrow dissipates, turning into a sudden burst of euphoric energy throughout my body, creating a therapeutic release.

Letting out that dumpster fire of emotions was much needed.

Maybe this is what happens when you're constantly numbed, and everything that has been bottled up forces its way out of you.

I shut the water off and use the walls to push me up.

"Everything okay? You've been in there for a while. How are you feeling?" Lindsay shouts through the door.

"Everything is great! I feel great," I shout back and stand tall, staring at the crystal-blue eyes of my reflection.

I could just be trying to convince myself, but if I can choose one emotion to dominate my drug-free holiday, I will do everything in my power to keep it a positive one.

***

My session with Dr. Beckham was canceled today, due to some personal time he had to take. The day goes by slowly, and I don't mind because I'm taking in every scent and sound.

Lindsay isn't her sprightly self today. It's like we traded personalities. We lie in the grass, and she doesn't say a word, staring off behind her sunglasses.

"You okay?" I check in.

She lets out a heavy breath, "I'm just missing my life outside here."

"Your boyfriend?"

"No," she says sharply, then changes her tone. "I mean, boyfriends are nice. Most of the time, at least. I miss the old things I used to do—and no, not drugs. I miss being able to go to concerts. I miss shaking my hair and screaming the lyrics to my favorite songs. This place is the same routine, over and over, and I feel like I might lose it." She pulls out the grass at her sides, letting out a frustrated grunt.

Oh, I understand that more than she'll ever know.

I may not know what a concert is like, but feeling like I might lose it is all too familiar.

"I've never been to a concert," I admit.

Lindsay sits up, removing her shades to look at me. "You've never been to a concert? Oh, honey, I'm pitying the wrong person here. Come on. Let's go inside," she demands, helping me up.

We walk back inside the house, where the ED girls are on the sofa, sending Lindsay dirty looks. As we take the hallway corner, one coughs out the word "Whore."

It doesn't faze Lindsay, who keeps on walking, so I keep following her until we're in our room.

"How do you deal with them?" I ask.

"Who, the EDs? Oh, I'm used to it, I guess. Something with cliques of girls. It's like I have a bright red target on my back."

She turns on her speaker and plays a song. It's a blend of rock mixed with a fast-paced electric beat.

I like it.

She sighs. "He was the hottest singer with the most amazing voice. It's really too bad he died last fall."

"What happened?"

"Heroin overdose."

"Oh, wow. That's scary."

"Yeah, overdoses suck. One minute, you're enjoying the best high of your life, and in a flash, your body is fighting to stay alive."

Why does she know so much about them?

"Have you ever…?" My voice trails off. I'm afraid to ask.

"Overdosed? Not on heroin and not fatally, obviously. But yeah, why else do you think I'd be stuck in a place like this?"

Lindsay never has a problem sharing her past, and it's not something I'm used to.

Turning up the speaker, she thrashes her head to the beat and yells out to me, "Come on! Dance with me!"

Oh no, here we go.

She grabs my hands, and I follow her lead, throwing my body into the rhythm. Our bodies sway until Lindsay drops her butt down provocatively to the floor, but she can't lift herself back up. We both burst out laughing.

"You're better than I was expecting," Lindsay cheers as I help her to her feet.

"I grew up in a ballet studio. I may have picked up a few things."

We continue to prance around, jumping on and off our beds. The music radiates around us, and we grip each other's hands, spinning until everything blurs. All I see is Lindsay's gleaming expression. We both collapse to the floor, cracking up. This is a moment I could stay in forever—an unfamiliar cloud nine, brought on by simply dancing with a friend.

Our door opens, and Dr. Cassidy sticks her head in. "Can you girls turn off the music, please? It's disrupting some of the girls in the living room."

Of course it is.

Lindsay rolls her eyes, then turns off the speaker. I fall back onto my bed, but what's out the window steals away my dancing bliss. A black starling is staring back at me. The hauntingly beautiful black bird is sitting on my feeder, its flecks of iridescent indigo and violet shimmering in the sun.

This is the last bird I was hoping I'd see.

"No, no, no!" I yell. "Shoo! Go away," I say, frantically fanning at the window.

"What is it?" Lindsay asks.

"A starling found my feeder. This isn't good."

"What's wrong with that? I thought you loved all birds."

"Starlings are one of the most stunning of the species, but they're dominant and aggressive to other birds. Once they find your feeder, there's a good chance no other birds will go near it now. Here, take a look."

I turn, waving for her to come over, but by the time she does, the bird is gone.

I sigh. "You just missed it. But unfortunately, I'm sure it'll be back."

"Well, if it's feeling like me at all, then it probably just wants to eat. Come on, let's go grab some dinner."

After we eat, we return to our room, and I dread Grace coming in. These are my last moments of mental freedom. Today was a shock to my emotional state, but in the best way possible. It's like I've spent my life staring at a dark sky, and then suddenly neon fireworks exploded and lit up everything around me. Sadly, I know it can't always be like this, but I don't have any choice in the matter. I never have. It's time to go back to living in a dimly lit dungeon.

Like clockwork, Grace comes in and hands over my pill. I place it in my mouth, swallowing it down this time. I retire to my bed, waiting for the heaviness to take control of my eyelids and the numbness to fill my mind.

***

I'm awakened by a high-pitched screeching sound. When I'm finally able to open my heavy lids, I'm mortified when I find myself standing over Lindsay. Her eyes are struck with fear as she peers out from under the covers like a child who's just seen a ghost. Could skipping my pill just once be what caused this?

"Holy shit! You scared me! What the hell are you doing?" she gasps, pulling off her blanket.

I'm asking myself the same question.

Panic sets in. I have no idea what's happening or how I got here.

Our door swings wide open, and there stand Nurse Grace and Dr. Beckham. Neither of them look pleased. I step away from Lindsay's bed to sit on my own.

"Is everyone okay?" Dr. Beckham questions while inspecting the room with crossed arms.

Lindsay makes eye contact with me as I anxiously chew on my thumb.

"I'm fine. Just a little startled," she assures him with lifted lips.

Dr. Beckham turns toward me. "Natalia, did you wake up out of bed?"

"I guess so." I speak at a low volume while staring at my feet. I'm too ashamed to look at him. I messed up. Everything was going absolutely perfectly, and now I've ruined it all. The self-loathing begins absorbing into me like a sponge.

"We will discuss this more tomorrow. But right now, we're going to need to give you an extra dose of your usual medication," he explains.

"Won't that be too much?" I protest.

"Please don't make a fuss." He raises his voice, dismissing me.

I look past him at Lindsay, and her brows furrow as she mouths the word "Sorry."

This isn't her fault at all. It's mine.

I give in to Dr. Beckham's orders because it doesn't seem like I'm left with a choice.

Nurse Grace hands me the pill, and they both watch me swallow it down.

Dr. Beckham helps me back into bed, and after he lays the covers over me, they head back out.

Right as the door shuts, Lindsay rolls over to face me.

"Oh my God. Were you sleepwalking?" she asks.

"Uh, yeah, I'm afraid so," I say, feeling shame sink in further. My cheeks flush red from embarrassment.

"Whoa. That's so cool."

"Cool" isn't how I would describe it whatsoever.

I'm just thankful she didn't call me a freak.

"I didn't do anything, uh, weird?" I ask nervously.

"Nope. You just were staring at me, kind of emotionless. I thought you were awake at first since your eyes were wide open. I hope you don't take offense to the scream. It's always a little terrifying to wake up to a pale figure with long black hair lurking over your sleeping body."

Her smirk allows me to smile.

"No offense taken. I'm sorry about that," I reply as a wave of drowsiness hits me. I think this double dosage is going to take me out any minute.

"Don't be sorry at all. It happens to the best of us."

"Does it, though?" I doubtfully squint my eyes.

Does the rest of the world worry about wandering around in the middle of the night, completely unaware of what they're doing? Do other people happen to find themselves jumping out of trees when they're in a dead sleep? I appreciate her trying to make me feel less self-conscious, but there's nothing common about my disorder.

"Well, maybe not. But trust me, it really didn't bother me."

After saying good night, she turns over and nestles against her pillow. I'm so grateful Lindsay didn't make fun of me, or worse, want to switch rooms because she's afraid of me.

Though her reaction was a pleasant one, I'm anxious about what Dr. Beckham will have to say about this tomorrow.

CHAPTER 5

Nothing ever goes unpunished. My headache is back and showing me no mercy. I grasp my head, trying to think of anything else but the drilling in my skull. The window bell and the alarm are both going off, but I can't tend to either. My stomach expels last night's dinner onto the floor in the middle of our beds.

Lindsay throws her blanket off and hops out of bed. She grabs the back of my hair as I gag with drool dripping from my mouth.

"Someone help! We need help!" Lindsay screams toward the door.

Dr. Cassidy comes in fast. "Oh, boy, this doesn't look good. Come on, Lindsay. Make your way to breakfast, and I'll take over."

Dr. Cassidy pulls out her walkie-talkie and calls for a nurse to assist her. She reaches down and wraps my arm over her shoulder, then grabs onto my waist, lifting me to my feet. My legs tremble as she helps me back into my bed.

A younger male nurse I've never met shows up with a mug and two pills.

"Here. Sip this ginger tea, and then I have some anti-nausea pills for you," Dr. Cassidy says, handing me the warm cup.

"Will these mix badly with my medication?"

"Nope, they're gentle but effective. These were my saving grace during my first pregnancy."

I thank her and let the chalky pills dissolve under my tongue.

"There's no chance you're pregnant, right?" she checks.

I almost spit out my tea, but I just shake my head sternly instead. If she only knew how impossible that would be. I've never even kissed anyone.

"I didn't think so, but always safe to be sure. Nausea is a listed side effect on your medication, so I'll have a nurse stock your bedside with a supply of these."

The pills and warm ginger begin to calm the rumbling pain in my gut.

"That would be amazing. Thank you."

She pats my hand. "Of course. We want to make sure you're as comfortable as possible under our care. Now, you should be feeling better in a matter of minutes. Go ahead and clean up, then grab something light at breakfast. I'll have someone deal with the mess."

Although I don't love that someone has to clean my projectile vomit, Dr. Cassidy's kindness does help ease the embarrassment.

The smell alone could cause me to hurl again. I hold my breath and dodge the chunks on the floor to go wash off the leftover residue on my face and gargle some mouthwash. I spit the minty liquid into the sink. My reflection shows something ghoulish. These side effects are now affecting my appearance. I pinch my cheeks to give my pasty complexion some color and force a smile on the face in the mirror. The medication is doing its job, altering my state of mind, making all my emotions feel bland in comparison to the incredible way I felt when I skipped them. Back to my reality, the watered-down version of who I wish I could be.

I get down the hall and realize Lindsay and Abby must have already eaten, because the dining room table is empty. My stomach feels better, but I have absolutely no appetite, so I ditch the kitchen and hang out in the empty living room, hoping time will slow down before my session with Dr. Beckham. It's never fun to have to explain and go over my mess-ups. When I was younger, I did everything in my power to hide them from Olga. If I woke up outside my bed, I'd quietly sneak back in, or if I had a nightmare, no matter how terrifying it was, I would force myself back to sleep, pretending it didn't happen. When possible, I'd keep the erratic episodes and dark dreams to myself. I knew they stressed her out too much.

But my incidents eventually got to a point where I couldn't just shake them off or hide them. As they increasingly became more dangerous, Olga's tactics to protect me from myself became more severe. She started off with smaller solutions, like locking me in my room after I fell asleep or duct-taping my windows shut, but then things escalated. A psychiatrist recommended a restraint jacket for me to wear during the night—the kind you see in movies for the criminally insane. That's exactly how I felt, like some sort of criminal receiving a punishment. I'd cry myself to sleep every time Olga had to help strap me in it. She tried to assure me that it was for my own good, but it felt like cruel and unusual punishment. Finally, after a month of having to sleep in the scratchy, suffocating nighttime uniform, it disappeared. Olga never made me wear anything like it again. I didn't question her decision, and she never brought up it. I think she realized the damaging consequences that awful thing was having on me were worse than any of my sleep disturbances.

I wonder what Dr. Beckham's reaction will be like in therapy today. I know I'm not happy with myself. Lindsay claims nothing happened, but what if I was just moments away from doing something terrible—something that would make her want to stay away from me indefinitely? I can't handle the thought of my crazy behavior threatening my first real friendship because God knows what I'll do after I fall asleep. Who wants to be around someone who can't control themselves?

I try my best to not let my broken record of thoughts get the best of me, so I pick a spot on a sofa to zone out and pass the time. My eyes gloss over until I hear a voice.

"You alive?"

I refocus my vision on the tall ED girl who was picking on Lindsay. She's waving her hand manically in front of me.

"Yeah. I'm fine," I mumble, shaking out of my trance.

"Can I sit?" she asks. Before I can answer, she settles onto the cushion next to me. "I'm Cookie with a K," she introduces herself.

Could that really be her given name? It sounds like a Muppet.

"I'm Natalia."

"I know. You're Lindsay's friend." Kookie smacks her gum. I'm not too keen on the behavior that I've witnessed from her so far, but I guess I could give her a chance to redeem herself.

"Uh, yeah. I am."

"Well, you seem cool, but there's something you should know about Lindsay. I mean, I think it's something you would want to know. Especially since you're with her all the time."

"What's that?" I perk up, curious about what she could possibly say.

"Well, I'm sure you know she's an addict, because she loves to announce it any chance she gets. But that's not why she's really here." I raise my brow at her. "She's a psycho."

61

I squint, irked by the harsh label. "That's pretty fucking rude. Have you even taken the time to get to know her?" So far, this girl is doing an awful job at gaining any sort of redemption in my eyes.

"I don't want to after what I heard." And even though I don't ask, she continues to tell me. "I heard at her last rehab center, she fucked every guy, but one guy wouldn't touch her. When he told her he didn't like her like that, she freaked out. So, in some sort of twisted revenge, she hid all her withdrawal medication until she had enough to sneak into his drink at a mealtime. Thankfully, he ended up being fine, and when they traced what was in his system, it matched up with her medication. So yeah, the psycho tried to poison someone, so they sent her here."

This is beginning to smell like bullshit. How could she find out this kind of information about Lindsay?

Before I get the chance to ask, another ED girl calls out for Kookie, and she hops up to leave.

"I would be careful if I were you, that's all," she warns, then links arms with the other girl and leaves the room.

What a bizarre story. Lindsay did say Kookie loves to start rumors, so I should probably add it up to her just being the bully she is quickly proving herself to be. Then the memory of two nights ago pops into my head, when Lindsay gave me instructions on how to avoid my medications, and it does match up in a weird way. I'm sure it means nothing, but why would Kookie have such a far-fetched story?

I have to push all my questions aside, because the hands on the clock across the room tell me that I'm now running late to my session.

I jump to my feet and speed out of the living room toward Room 9, and when I knock on the door, I'm winded. I twist the doorknob to a pleasant view of Dr. Beckham standing tall. One thing my medicine doesn't surpass is the way my heart leaps at the sight of him. I step in, but my racing heart turns into a spinning dizziness, and not a good kind. I try to take my next step, but my legs lose all feeling, releasing the weight of my body.

Dr. Beckham catches me before I hit the ground, and I dangle my arms around his neck. I feel my eyes roll back, and I lose view of him.

Air being fanned in my face brings me back to consciousness, and the first thing I see is Dr. Beckham's smile.

God, he's a sight to open your eyes to.

"There she is," he praises.

"Did you eat anything at breakfast, Natalia?" I hear Dr. Cassidy, but I don't want to break my gaze into Dr. Beckham's eyes inches over me.

"Here, let's sit you up," he says and places a hand behind my head to help lift me. "Did you eat anything today, Natalia?" he repeats Dr. Cassidy's question.

"No, I'm sorry. I wasn't feeling very hungry,"

Dr. Cassidy chimes in. "You don't need to be sorry. But this is why we encourage you to eat at every meal. You must have been lightheaded. Your medication is strong, so without food in your system, fainting or vertigo is not uncommon. Here, eat this."

She hands me a banana, and I happily peel it back and chew off a few bites.

"Do you feel well enough to finish your session?" she asks.

I no longer feel like my head has been stuck in a blender, so I sit up taller and try to forget that I just awkwardly wilted in Dr. Beckham's arms.

"Yes. I'm fine," I answer her.

"Okay, I'll let you get to it, then." Dr. Cassidy steps out.

Dr. Beckham returns to his chair, and I slouch back down into his couch.

"I'm sorry you're not feeling well. It must be the extra dose of medication," he states.

I almost forgot I had taken the extra pill, but the extreme nausea now makes sense.

"I hate to tell you this, but we're going to need to keep you on the higher dose, as it was proven last night that the lower amount isn't enough."

It feels like the floor beneath me has dropped. I cradle my inflamed stomach.

No! No more medication!

The thought clings to me with an unbearable weight.

"I don't know if I can live with such horrible side effects. Please, there has to be another option."

"Sorry, Natalia. Actions have consequences, and last night showed me that I need to take more aggressive measures to contain you." he scolds callously.

Contain me?

His words strike me as strange. They feel like a punch in the gut, nothing like his normally comforting ones. I feel judged for something I don't even have control over.

"Are you upset with me?" I ask timidly.

He trades his serious scowl for a softened smile. "Of course not. Slipups happen, and we're looking for progress here, not perfection. I wouldn't be doing my job if I allowed you to wander freely in the night. My best interest is always in your safety and well-being."

This is something closer to what I was hoping he'd tell me, but I can't let go of what he just said before. I'm constantly chastising myself already. He's the last person I need to try and reprimand me. It triggers uncertainty and fear, feeling like a doctor is not on my side. It takes me back to the deeply traumatic times that I was incapacitated against my will—strapped down or tied up in a straitjacket. Those barbaric solutions always seemed like lazy, careless options. The best therapists are supposed to be supportive and helpful, not make you feel worse, or like a monster deserving of discipline because of your illness.

"Well, I won't keep you long. You've had a rough morning and can use some rest, but tonight is your first sleep study, so I want to make sure you're prepared." He starts going through a list of things to avoid today and any day we have a sleep study scheduled. "No caffeine, no napping, no hair gel—"

"Why no hair gel?"

"It can get in the way of our recordings."

"Recordings of what?"

"We'll be using a device that will record your brain waves and measure your eye and muscle activity. You had a similar study when you were six and had an incident with Olga, if you remember."

I hate that the only thing I can remember is what I did to Olga.

I was so young that I don't have much memory of my life back then, except that one terrible night. The only time someone else was physically hurt because of my disorder. I'm thankful nothing like it has ever happened since, but there's always that shadowing fear that it could.

"Oh, right. Yeah, I don't exactly remember how the study works," I tell him, trying my best to block out the intrusive images of my fingers locked around Olga's neck.

"That's okay. The activity we'll be monitoring is basically our map to the sleep stages going on in your head. Normal activity equals normal sleep, which is all we want for you."

Ha! Good luck. Normal sleep is a foreign concept in my world.
"What is abnormal?"

"Abnormal activity shows up similarly as it would when you're awake. Simply put, the less active you are, the better.

"That seems easy enough," I lie, knowing all my body wants to do is be active after I pass out.

"Easy as pie. So, I'll be seeing you tonight, then," he says, taking one of my hands to help me up.

"I guess you will be," I reply dryly, wondering why I don't feel my usual bliss after this session.

***

After art and lunch, I meet Lindsay for yoga. Her appearance is off. She's not in her normal skintight athletic wear but rather in a loose shirt and sweats, and she doesn't have her usual enthusiasm where she basically leads the class herself.

"You feeling all right?" I pry.

"Eh, I think I'm coming down with something."

I think she might be right. Her skin is almost as white as mine, even with her SoCal tan. She barely gets through yoga and then drags herself to our afternoon meeting spot to lie down.

"I guess we've both seen better days," I joke, sitting next to her.

She lets out a light laugh. "Yeah, I guess so. Are you feeling better?"

"Yeah, but I'm sort of nervous for my sleep study tonight."

"Sleep study? Is it because you sleepwalked?"

She moves her hands from her eyes to look at me. I realize I've never shared with Lindsay about my sleep disorders—or anyone other than doctors, for that matter—but I guess no one has ever really asked.

"I have a bit of parasomnia," I admit, anxious for her reaction.

"What is that? Sounds like something you'd hear on a ghost-hunting show." She grins so I know she's kidding.

"Ha! No ghosts here. Parasomnia is basically an intense sleeping disorder."

"Do you care to share more?" She stares at me, I think wanting a more in-depth answer, which I normally hate to give, but I feel comfortable enough with her to elaborate.

"I do sort of weird things when I'm asleep that I have no control over and can't ever remember doing. Like you saw, sometimes I sleepwalk. Sometimes I have vivid night terrors that aren't fun. I also suffer from bouts of insomnia, which involves no sleep whatsoever, which is the exact opposite of parasomnia. I'm all over the place when it comes to sleep issues. Which is why doctors love to use the term 'interesting case' when trying to figure me out."

"Damn, you might be the *most* interesting case here. I mean, I'm not exactly sure what's up with Abby, but I think you take the cake with that," she teases sarcastically.

I shrug. "Not sure if it's the kind of cake I want to win."

Lindsay's nonchalant, slightly offensive reaction is actually a breath of fresh air. The idea of making friends has always been intimidating because of my worry about being outed as "the girl with a strange sleep disease." I assumed sharing my disorder would scare people off, but I'm realizing I've never actually given anyone the chance to learn more about it.

"Well, I think it's kind of badass. And you might as well take the cake, 'cause the ED girls aren't going to eat it." She laughs at herself. Her joke reminds me of my talk with Kookie this morning.

"Can I ask you something, Lindsay?"

I figure since I just shared something personal with her, she wouldn't mind doing the same.

"Sure. Shoot," she says, picking at a dandelion she plucked from the grass.

"So, why this place and not another rehab option instead?"

She tosses the mauled flower. "Well, other than the proximity to my grandma's house, I'm here to find out if there's something deeper influencing my addictions since traditional rehab hasn't worked. Also, they think it's great for a sex addict like me to be separated from male patients. They're afraid I might screw every boy in sight, which is probably a good call."

I can't tell if she's being serious about the boys. Our sexual histories are like night and day.

"What's being a sex addict like?" I ask, genuinely curious about a disorder that involves something I know nothing about. I mean, I've seen sex happen on TV and read about it in books, but it's always wrapped in the Hollywood illusion. Usually, there are two people who are in love, and it's filled with lots of cheesy passion. It's hard for me to imagine it in a way where it would be considered an illness, or something dangerous to yourself.

Just when I think she's going to make another joke, she sits up and blows out a breath.

"It's complicated. Drugs are addictive because of all the chemicals and shit inside them. But with sex addiction, all I have to blame is myself, and it's not because I really like to fuck. It's a mental turmoil I've created. Every time I have sex with someone, I feel on top of the world for a moment, this indescribable high.

But when it's over, I'm slammed right back down and left feeling more broken than I did before." Lindsay pauses, pulling out her hair tie to release her ponytail. "You sort of start to feel like each boy, each time, takes a part of you. I finally hit a place where I didn't think I had anything left to give, but I keep on giving myself away anyway. The rush I felt before was gone, and the only similar one I've found has been drugs. So yeah, I guess I'm more of a fucked-up case rather than an interesting one."

She wraps her arms around her legs, and for once, she's not bragging about why she's here. I can see now how destructive this could be to one's mental state. Sex is a vicious cycle for Lindsay. Nothing seems enjoyable about her addiction at all. I know what it's like to be your own worst critic, so I try to give her some consoling words.

"You're not fucked up. It sounds like this rush you're talking about is affection or love, but you've only found it in the wrong places. Sometimes we find comfort in routines, even shitty ones."

I speak from experience.

Sometimes you're forced to seek any glimmer of light in the darkest situations. It's a form of survival.

She ponders for a moment, then nods her head.

"Damn, you really hit me hard with the deep topics sometimes. I feel like my parents should be paying you instead of these doctors." She wraps an arm around my shoulders and squeezes me. "Whenever we're both out of here, we better stay friends."

"I'd really like that," I tell her, and it warms my heart knowing there's nothing I'd want more.

Lindsay falls back onto the grass, and I do the same. As we watch the clouds move across the sky filled with blue, I take in a new understanding. Lindsay and I do have one thing in common. We both have parts of us that we wish didn't exist. I know what it's like to feel like mental illness is your greatest flaw, and it's a heavy burden to have to carry.

I'm going to chalk up Kookie's elaborate story as a cruel fib. She has no right to judge Lindsay and spread lies without any clue of what Lindsay's been though or endures on the daily.

***

I did a decent job at distracting myself from thinking of my sleep study today, but now it's happening in a matter of minutes. My heart is racing, maybe because I'm not sure what this test might prove. I hate to be a pessimist, but my mind loves to go to the worst places.

What if it just confirms that I'm incurable?

Lindsay and I changed into our pajamas, and we're settled in bed. Nurse Grace comes in, and when I see my new higher dosage in the cup, I fill with dread. The two pills cut my throat on their way down. It's as if two bombs dropped into my stomach, waiting to set off the horrible side effects in the morning,

After she leaves, we hear a knock.

"Come in," I call out.

Dr. Beckham enters, rolling a monitor with different wires and straps attached to it. As I stare at the dated-looking machine, my neck hairs stand up.

"*He's* doing the sleep study?" Lindsay looks puzzled, and I nod. I'm not sure who else she was expecting would do it.

"Good evening, ladies," Dr. Beckham greets us with a wide grin as he comes over to my bedside.

"Good evening," I reply, but Lindsay only returns a cutting scowl in his direction. She's apparently not in the best mood.

"Okay, Natalia. I'm going to get you wired in, and you should be good to sleep as you normally do."

Although I'm not exactly thrilled with our session earlier, his perfect teeth situated above his strong jawline are never disappointing. He kneels close enough that I can smell his aftershave, and it's heavenly. He attaches two wires to each side of my head and pulls down my blanket to expose my chest and arms. He moves in closer and gently tugs my top down to stick a wire over my heart, and it causes my toes to curl.

"Um, excuse me, Dr. Beckham, but aren't you not supposed to be undressing patients?" Lindsay blurts out, clearly irritated.

I can't tell if she's being protective of me or sexualizing this, but either way, my cheeks radiate heat. I hope Dr. Beckham doesn't see me blushing.

"Yes, that's true. However, medical tests and procedures are the exception. This test requires electrodes be placed in specific places in order to be effective, but, Lindsay, if you're uncomfortable, you don't have to watch," he explains in a slightly condescending tone.

Annoyed, Lindsay rolls her eyes, then faces the far wall.

"Now relax and sleep as you would normally, Natalia. There's nothing to be afraid of. This is just a way for me to find out more of what's going on in that head of yours," he says reassuringly, then pulls my blanket back over me.

"Good night, Natalia. Good night, Lindsay."

He glances at me, then at her, but Lindsay stays faced against the wall. He turns off our lights before shutting the door.

As the machine hums, I observe all the various wires that make me feel like I'm a science experiment. My racing heart is slowing. It's probably the extra sedative, or could it be the sleep study isn't as bad as I imagined it to be?

A few minutes pass, and an overpowering drowsy sensation is pulsating throughout my body, but I want to make sure Lindsay's okay.

"Lindsay, are you awake?" I whisper, but she must be sleeping because she doesn't answer.

I take a deep breath and let the sedation sweep me away into a black void.

CHAPTER 6

My unbalanced equilibrium feels like I spent the night violently shaking my head. I know it's the higher medication, so I reach for my nausea pills before I spew all over the floor. The wires running down onto my chest reminds me that I'm hooked up to a monitor. Behind the machine is Lindsay, still wrapped under her covers.

A knock on the door makes the pounding in my head worse. When it opens, Nurse Grace comes through. She peels off the wires and rolls the screen out. It takes all my strength to get out of bed and plaster on an expression that doesn't show misery as I head to the dining room.

After I force down water and toast, my pain finally eases. I'm hoping it's because my body is adjusting to the new dosage.

Lindsay was quieter than usual at breakfast. I wonder if she's still upset. She didn't seem excited to have Dr. Beckham in our room. Maybe he's a threat to her addiction. If he can make me think dirty thoughts, I can only imagine what he does to her.

I don't have a session today, so I try to kill time by spending extra hours in arts and crafts. Lunch tasted bland, and everyone is moving at a lazy pace in yoga. The gray skies seem to have an influence on all of us.

I head to our spot, but Lindsay isn't there. Maybe the weather is too cold for her today. I lie in the grass alone, stretching out. The boys' house is in the corner of my eye, and I turn my head for a better view. If I squint hard enough, I can see figures of them and what looks like a TV playing.

"Spying on the opposite sex, I see!" Lindsay shouts from behind, startling me.

I turn around, happy she's back to her normal self. She's sporting a baby pink minidress and a full face of makeup.

"I still think it's crazy you've never had a boyfriend," she says, sitting cross-legged next to me.

If she knew my life, she wouldn't be saying that, but I can imagine how peculiar it sounds to her.

"Yeah. I mean, it's not like I don't want one. I've just never had an opportunity."

Boys my age were far and few between back in Latent Valley. Strangely, mostly women reside there. A lot of widows, divorcées, and empty nesters. I almost wonder if Olga chose to live there because of that reason. She never showed interest in dating anyone. I think in her eyes, men have always equaled trouble. Olga was completely fine avoiding them, I assume because of the way she spoke of her uncle or that her father left her and her mother to fend for themselves. Men haven't proven themselves to be anything else but distress in her life.

"So, you never even had a date? Didn't you go to prom?"

"Homeschooled, remember?" I remind her.

"Oh shit. Yeah, I guess you don't have proms at home." She chuckles. "Well, you didn't miss anything. Just a bunch of testosterone and insecurity crammed into a dancing hall."

"You went to prom?"

"Oh boy, did I. This blue hair was once blonde and huge, and my sequined dress barely covered my goods. I was prom queen my senior year." She fluffs up her straight hair and pokes out her chest.

She was prom queen, and I've never even been to a dance.

Prom is just another event that makes me mourn a normal teen life.

"What? That's so cool. You must have been pretty popular, then," I say, realizing Lindsay would make a perfect prom queen.

"Eh, yeah, I guess you could say I was popular—mostly with the boys. But it wasn't all it's cracked up to be. The more eyes on you, the more people talk and feel like they have some sort of right to hold a magnifying glass over you. Honestly, your life sounds refreshing. Nobody knows you. You can go anywhere and be someone new."

"Refreshing" isn't exactly how I'd describe being a nobody, but I get what she was trying to say. It sounds like Lindsay has always had people cast judgments on her. The same way Kookie did.

"Well, can't you too? Maybe you just need to find different places to go," I state.

She peers upward as she thinks. "Yeah, I guess you're right. Can't I just stay here and have a session with you instead of Dr. Beckham?"

"I don't think I'm qualified." I crack a smile.

"Sure you are. More so than I think you know." Lindsay gets up to dust off her dress. "Well, it's session time for me. I'll catch you at dinner."

"See you then," I say, then watch as she heads inside.

Lindsay and I have had polar-opposite lives outside Awana. I spent my teens chasing birds and reading books while she wore sparkling dresses to proms and parties. But the more I talk to her, the more I wonder if I was the one who lucked out.

I head back to my room before dinner to check on my feeder and am disappointed that nothing is there. That stupid starling must be coming back and scaring away my other feathered visitors.

I spy Lindsay's speaker and turn it on. The song we were dancing and having fun to days before comes on. This kind of dancing was different from what Olga always taught me. There was freedom in my newfound movements. It was nothing like the disciplined repetition in ballet.

Ballet was Olga's thing. She wanted me to love that style of dance the way she did, but I never could, no matter how much I wish I did. She dances every night and looks so beautiful when she does. Even with bloody calluses and sore feet, she would tuck them away into a pretty pink slipper, and you'd never know the pain she was in. She throws all of herself into her ballet studio, leaving me feeling isolated most of my life.

Behind the music, I hear a faint screech. Pulling out the earbud, I realize a screaming cry is coming from the other side of my door, in the hallway. I open it to find out what's going on and freeze at what I see down the hall.

Dr. Beckham is behind Lindsay with his arms gripped around her waist as she kicks her legs frantically. His eyes tense and his mouth snarls as he uses visible strength to restrain her.

"Get off me, you stupid fucking asshole!" she yells so hard tears fall from her eyes.

"Stop resisting!" he shouts in her ear.

She's sobbing and wailing for him to let her go, but he doesn't. One of his hands tightly grasps the back of her head. Then, in a vigorous motion, he slams the side of her face against the ground, hard enough that it makes a sound. Like a cop bringing down a gunman, his knees pin her, holding her arms crossed behind her back. The other male nurse runs in with a syringe. Lindsay screams so loud that I have to cover my ears.

"No, please, no," she begs between tearful gasps.

"Help keep her still," Dr. Beckham commands. The nurse hesitates. "Hold her down!" he orders the young man.

The nurse does as he's told and presses his palms against her shoulders to keep her flat.

For a moment, Lindsay stops moving with her cheek pushed against the wood. The helplessness and sorrow in her eyes make me want to cry with her. Dr. Beckham stabs the needle into her thigh, and Lindsay's last agonizing scream slowly fades as they drag her out of my view.

I slam my door behind me and sink to the floor.

What the hell did I just see?

***

My stomach is in knots, and it's not from my medication. I can't touch my dinner. Thinking of what happened to Lindsay makes me physically sick. I hate how aggressive Dr. Beckham was toward her, and it makes me think of him in a very different light. I've seen staff use force against patients in the past, but only toward the severely violent ones who were endangering themselves or someone else. A prom queen with a pill problem doesn't seem to fit that bill to me. Lindsay has never acted aggressively around me, even after I saw Kookie spit on her. She's completely harmless, and Dr. Beckham's actions were far out of line. This is the exact behavior from doctors that makes me anxious—a total misuse of power. If there's a side like this to Dr. Beckham, then what the hell would he do to me if history repeats itself, and I inadvertently walk, talk, jump, or—God forbid—choke someone in my sleep.

The Dr. Beckham manhandling situation has me uneasy all day. I just wish Lindsay was here, so I could at least make sure she's all right. After dinner, I pace, waiting for her to show up, but her side of the bedroom remains vacant.

Finally, the door opens, and I pray it's Lindsay, but I'm let down when Dr. Cassidy walks in.

"Natalia, I want to inform you that Lindsay won't be returning to bed for a few nights. I'm sure you heard the altercation earlier, but Dr. Beckham thinks it's best for Lindsay's care if she's separated for a while."

Separated? What? Where? Why?

I have so many questions flooding my mind, but I start off with the most important one.

"Is she okay?"

"She's fine. She just needs to rest."

I hate when doctors throw out generic phrases, but I won't give up on Lindsay yet.

"When can I see her?" I demand to know.

"I don't have an exact answer for that yet. She will return when she's ready," Dr. Cassidy explains in a calm manner.

The simmering anger that I've been trying to contain boils over.

"Where is she? I don't fucking get it. Is she in solitary confinement like some sort of prisoner?" I catch myself lashing out at Dr. Cassidy, so I sit on my bed to calm my flustered state.

She releases a deep breath and walks over, resting a hand on my back and softly rubbing. "I'm sorry, Natalia. As a respect to confidentiality, I can't discuss any more details about Lindsay's current treatment. But please believe me when I tell you that she is doing okay, and we're taking good care of her."

Dr. Cassidy's gentle nature is always appreciated, so I accept her response and stop interrogating her.

"Please get some rest, dear. Lindsay will be back soon." She stands up and turns off the lights before slipping out the door.

I guess I have no other choice but to hope what Dr. Cassidy said is true. I pray Lindsay's not scared or lonely, because God knows how much I am right now. Right when I find the one person who I can confide in, she's ripped from me by a doctor who I'm beginning to distrust. What if Awana truly isn't different than all the wards I've stayed at before, the ones where they treat their patients as if they're second-class citizens, undeserving of human decency? This dark, silent bedroom brings me back to every time I've been forcefully isolated, whether locked up back home or placed in an empty, cold room in an asylum. Suddenly, the four walls around me feel like a cement cell closing in. I ration my breaths and squeeze my eyes shut.

I'm not alone. I'm not alone. I'm not alone.

The self-soothing chant in my head halts when Grace comes in, breaking the darkness with the light from the hallway. My panic finally eases. She hands me a cup with my pills, and when I look down at them, I think of Dr. Beckham slamming Lindsay to the floor. I pop them in my mouth, and after Grace leaves, I spit them back into my hand using the trick my new friend taught me.

If Dr. Beckham wants to play by his own rules, then I'm going to play by mine.

***

The next morning when I open my eyes, Lindsay isn't next to me, but I don't wake up alone. A full-body chill breaks out at the sight of the piercing yellow eyes of a black starling staring at me through my window.

"Get out of here!" I yell, banging at the window until it flies away.

Why does this bird seem like it's stalking me?

I won't allow it to ruin my morning. Nothing can beat waking up to being side-effect free. My stomach is rumbling, so I get ready fast so that I can take care of these hunger pangs.

Abby is at the table, but there's still no sign of Lindsay. I can't stop fidgeting, and I have a feeling it's my nerves about going into my session in a few minutes with Dr. Beckham. For one, I'm not on my medication, and I hope he can't tell. Second, I'm still uncomfortable about what happened with Lindsay. I'm not sure where she is, but she has to eat, right? I thought skipping meals was frowned upon, so why isn't anyone bringing her food? What if they're starving her as some sort of twisted punishment or have her chained up somewhere?

I restrain my vibrating leg with my hands and realize I'm letting my mind get the best of me right now. I need to quit it before I'm late to my session. I push myself up from the table to head to Dr. Beckham's office.

His door is open, and I walk in to find his leg shaking more than mine was. His usually coiffed hair has fallen down in his eyes. He pushes it back when he sees me.

"Good morning, Natalia. Have a seat, will you?"

I sit down without returning his greeting.

"Before we begin, I wanted to talk about what you saw with Lindsay yesterday."

"Where is she? What happened?" I immediately ask.

"I know you're concerned, and I'm sure it's because you two have gotten close. Lindsay needs to go through private treatment right now. We find it's in her and everyone's best interest that she's separated for the time being."

It's not just that we've gotten close. It's the fact that I saw you violently force her down while she was crying out in pain.

This is what I want to scream at him, but I know better. Psychiatrists, especially ones who don't take well to patients who cause a commotion, are more likely to respond better if you keep things far from volatile.

"I don't get it. She seemed to be doing fine," I pry, trying to get more answers.

"It's our job to make these types of decisions, and it's your job to trust us," he says dismissively, placing his hand on my thigh. His touchiness that once gave me butterflies now causes me to jerk my knee away. He retracts his hand to his lap. "On a different note, your sleep study went well. Only normal activity was detected. Have you had any difficulties falling asleep or any dreams I should be aware of?"

He seems to be refusing to mention anything else about Lindsay and wants to change the subject, but I have to admit, it's a huge relief to hear about my results.

"No. Falling asleep has been okay, actually. No crazy dreams either."

Strangely, I haven't had a single dream since I've been here. I'm sure it's thanks to the horse-tranquilizer amount of medication I'm given every night.

"I'm glad to hear that. I still want to do the sleep study weekly until we have enough conclusive results, though."

"How many is conclusive?" I ask.

Maybe this will give me an idea of when I can be released.

"You don't worry about that. All I need you to do is let me know if you experience anything unusual or any changes in your sleep patterns."

"I can do that," I agree. "Dr. Beckham…" I say his name softly with lifted lips. I'm hoping a little sweetness could coax him into spilling something about Lindsay.

"Yes?" He tilts his head.

"When will I see her again?" I shoot my last shot on trying to find out any more information.

"That's another worry that shouldn't belong to you," he says, avoiding eye contact as he writes something down.

How can I not worry about her?

She may not be the perfect patient, but she certainly isn't the worst, and now she's separated from everyone and everything. My heart hurts just thinking about it.

I'm imagining the suffering she must be experiencing. I'm not exactly sure what "private treatment" entails here, but I sure know what it's like to be banished to a room all by yourself, unable to leave at your free will. It's demoralizing.

Dr. Beckham clears his throat to recapture my attention. "Now, let's focus back on you. Everyone has a conscious timeline of their lives. Events that gave us a strong emotional reaction are the things we remember most—fear, sadness, times of immense joy or accomplishment. Does this make sense?"

"Yes, I think so."

Where is he going with this?

"Other times, our mind can do the opposite. It can repress memories, especially ones that bring us great stress. You were found alone as a toddler. I wonder what your life may have looked like before then."

The early years of my life have always been an interest to doctors, but I can never give them the vivid memories they're looking for.

"Olga told me I was found in a very poor town in Russia. Sadly, it wasn't uncommon for someone to abandon a child who they couldn't take care of financially."

"Most adults don't remember much before the age of three, but I wish we had more of an insight into those years for you."

I shrug as he jots down more.

I may not ever know, but it's not like I haven't thought about it. I try to avoid the more realistic scenarios, like my parents being too poor to take care of me or that a knocked-up young woman simply didn't want a daughter, preferring to come up with my own narrative. Maybe my parents were spies, and I was tragically misplaced on a mission. Anything is better than considering that I was unloved and abandoned.

"Natalia?" Dr. Beckham cuts in, interrupting my daydreams.

"Sorry, I wish I could remember. I mean, how does a baby end up wandering around alone anyways?"

"I wish I had that answer for you." He cracks a pitiful smile. "Okay, now I know these are going to be some tough questions to ask, but it's my job. I have a couple, if that's okay?" I nod and allow him to proceed. "Has Olga ever shown signs of abusive behavior toward you physically or mentally? I can walk you through some examples."

Like when you shoved a girl half your size to the floor? I don't need him to list any examples of abuse. Dr. Beckham displayed a shining one yesterday right in front of me.

"No, I know what abuse is, and the answer is never. She's only ever shown me unconditional love." I scoff at the assumption. Yes, Olga has done things in the past that I may not have liked, but her intentions have always been to keep me safe. She's never purposely hurt me or inflicted pain.

"Okay, then, we'll jump right into the next one. Have you ever been sexually assaulted or molested?"

Wow! Dr. Beckham is really diving right into the gritty stuff today.

"No." I squirm inside at the directness of his question but answer with confidence that nothing like that has ever happened.

"Is there any event where you felt in danger or unsafe that you think I should know?" he reads off his clipboard.

Does every time I fall asleep count?

I take a moment to reflect on the scrapbook of my life, but there really isn't anything that stands out. Other than self-inflicted danger, my life has been spent at our cottage or in a ward, and nothing in between seems unusual.

"I don't think so. I've really lived a normal life—well, besides my sleeping habits."

He sets his pen down. "Okay, well, if at any time you feel something is worth mentioning, please do."

"Okay, I can do that," I assure him, even though I'm quite sure what he's looking for.

I could tell him that some of my most traumatizing moments have been at the hands of doctors, but I think I'm too afraid to share that now after seeing what *he's* capable of.

Dr. Beckham continues to ask me some lighter questions, like if I've ever broken a bone or if I know how to ride a bike. The more he asks, the more I think he realizes there's nothing notably special that has happened to me. Then one question catches me off guard.

"Are you sexually active?"

I sternly shake my head.

"Are you sure?" he asks, almost incredulously.

Wow! Okay, I've had enough now.

It's not only the question but the smirk he lets slip that causes my shoulders to curl and my arms to cross in an attempt to cover my now-uncomfortable body.

"Yes, I'm sure, and why is this question relevant?"

"I need to know your history in all aspects."

"Well, I think I've told you everything," I confirm, hearing the irritation in my own voice.

"Okay, that's fine. I think we're finished here, then," he says gruffly, straightening out some papers.

He stands to conclude our session, and I've never been more thankful because it was beginning to feel like it was taking an outlandish left turn. I can understand that in some cases knowing a patient's sexual history can be necessary, but there was an off feeling in his delivery.

Maybe I'm just still aggravated with the way he treated Lindsay and am reading too far into this.

***

The day has dragged. After dinner, I walk into my room to find Dr. Cassidy taking some of Lindsay's things, and it makes my heart sink. Life at Awana is stale without her vibrancy around.

Shortly afterward, Grace comes in with my medication. As she hands me the cup, an idea sparks. Dr. Beckham said it himself that I've been improving, and I really love waking up without the crippling side effects. Would one last night without it really hurt? With Lindsay gone, who is here to be disrupted if I were to sleepwalk? Which is worse, waking up in complete agony or fearing if I've left my bed?

Rashly, I place the paper cup to my mouth and slide the pills underneath my lip. Grace doesn't suspect a thing as she leaves. After I sneak the damp pills into my bra with the others, a victorious feeling tickles me inside. It's not just the thrill of breaking the rules. What feels good is making a choice for myself. But as empowering as it is, I have to promise myself that this will be the last time I do it. I've always been on medication. I'm not sure what would happen if I just suddenly quit.

I shut off my lights, but as I lie in the dark, I can't shut off my mind. I look at Lindsay's empty bed and wonder what it's like to be a prom queen, to have people like you enough to want you to win that title. I wonder if I went to a regular high school, if people would like me. Would Lindsay have liked me if we met outside here? She's so cool—her style, her magnetic energy, it's effortless. It's an artform to be able to attract the attention of everyone around you. I've never caught the eye of any guy. Psych wards and a hometown filled with mostly women prevented that. I've envisioned the kind of boyfriend I'd want based off celebrities and book characters, but sadly, that always stayed a fantasy.

Bringing up the timeline of my life in therapy has me thinking. I've always been painfully shy. Birds have been the closest things to friends I've had. Olga always bought all my clothes. When I put it all together, it actually sounds a little pathetic. I've been on such a short leash that I can't even have my own fashion sense or go places other people my age hang out for fun.

Coming to terms with my mild life saddens me. Have I completely missed out on being a teenage girl? I know my unusual disorder has a lot to do with it, but maybe if I grew up like everyone else, I wouldn't be the way I am. I don't want to resent Olga for anything, but what if distancing me from the world has only made it impossible for me to live normally in one?

The clock reads 2:00 a.m. already. My racing heart matches the two blinking dots on my clock. Every minute comes quicker than the last. I attempt to lie down and shut my eyes, but my legs won't stop twitching. My blanket is heavy and hot, so I throw it toward my feet. I toss and turn, trying to find a comfortable position, but nothing feels right. Could I be coming down with something? I count sheep, a trick that never worked with my insomnia, but for some reason, I give it a go anyway.

Fifteen, fourteen, thirteen—

A ringing bell causes me to jump. I perch on the window next to my bed, and I'm stunned by what I see outside.

A tall boy, around my age, is blowing smoke from a cigarette.

I keep quiet so he doesn't see me as I watch him. He's in gray sweats and an open flannel, exposing a white T-shirt. A black beanie covers his hair, and I can't get a good look at his face. He takes another exhale and moves his cigarette over to my feeder. He flicks the end, and the ash falls into the pile of seeds.

"Hey!" I pound the window with my fist.

He jumps, and I can tell I startled him. He looks like he just saw something supernatural.

He mouths, "What the fuck?" and turns around to walk away.

I crank open my window.

"That's not an ashtray," I say loud enough so he can hear me.

He turns around and looks up, and then I see him fully under an exterior light. My jaw drops.

He's beautiful.

His golden skin and eyes beam under the warm glow above him, and I now see a trace of black ink peeking out from the top of his T-shirt. His lips are rosy from the cold, and his cheekbones look like they would cut your skin if you touched them.

"Are you just going to stare?" he asks.

I snap out of it and close my mouth. "No, uh, sorry. I would just like it if you wouldn't use my feeder as an ashtray." I focus on articulating every word so my voice doesn't shake from the nerves of talking to this cute boy in front of me.

"This thing?" He rocks it with his fingers.

"Yes. It's a bird feeder, and as you can see, you're knocking the seed out, so please stop." Good-looking or not, I don't need him messing with the device that brings me my favorite feathery friends.

"Oh shit, my bad." he says, then pulls a cigarette from his pocket. "You want a smoke?"

"No, thanks. I'm good," I politely decline.

"So, what's your name?" he asks, lighting the end with a match.

"Natalia."

I quickly survey the area to see if anyone is watching. I don't need our little chat to get me into any trouble.

"It's just you and me out here, babe." He nods with a perfect grin.

Oh God, he's a charmer too.

I'm definitely in deep trouble now, because I don't want him to leave.

"Do you have a last name?" he continues.

"Sokolov."

"Natalia Sokolov. What a pretty name. I'm Gabriel King. Nice to meet you." He extends a hand up to my window, and I hesitate. "Just a handshake, Natalia. I promise my fucked-up head isn't contagious."

I smile nervously and reach out my fingers to his. His hands are cold but soft.

"Aren't you going to get in trouble for being out here?" I ask, pulling my hand back in the window.

"Nah, my doctors know I get restless at night. The night sky is the only thing that can help quiet my thoughts sometimes." I know exactly what he means. "May I ask why you're awake this late?"

"Couldn't sleep either."

"So, I take it you know exactly what I mean," he says, reading my mind and putting out the cigarette embers with his foot.

Gabriel won't let his eyes leave mine, and it causes my heartbeat to echo in my ears.

"Are *you* staring?" I ask him.

"Yes, I am. Your eyes are incredible," he says.

I have to look away from his gaze to hide the warmth on my cheeks that could light a fire.

"What do you think of this place, Natalia?" he asks, capturing my attention once more.

"It's not bad. I've been in worse."

"So, this isn't your first sentence?" He folds his arms across his chest.

"Nope," I reply.

"Mine either." Gabriel's eyes linger on mine. He looks like he could be a cutout on Lindsay's wall with his perfectly smooth complexion. "Sorry, I'm staring again, aren't I?" he asks, and I realize he's not the only one. "This may be a bit forward, but would you want to see me again?"

I press my lips together so I don't accidentally let out an excited shriek. I try to play it cool.

"We're not allowed," I remind him.

He places his hands in his pockets. "Well, what if I happen to be here again around the same time tomorrow night? Do you think you might want some fresh air?"

He bites his lip to hide a smile, and I can't take my eyes away from his lips.

He has an edge to him. I'm not sure if it scares me or allures me, but one thing I know for sure is that I want to see more of it.

"I mean, yeah, I could probably use more fresh air tomorrow night," I answer, trying not to sound too eager.

"I was hoping you would. Rest easy, Natalia," he says, releasing the corners of his mouth. He turns around and heads back in the direction of the boys' house.

I lie back in my bed, squeezing my pillow in my arms as the hopelessness I'd been feeling earlier dissolves into a humming excitement. Just when I was faced with my loneliest day at Awana, the night decided to gift me some company.

CHAPTER 7

Soft waves rock me back and forth in a relaxing trance until I realize my back is submerged in a murky pond with a thick haze floating above me. The serenity switches to terror when a dozen arms break through the still water, pulling me under. I try to fight the veiny limbs ripping at me, but every one of my bones stiffens.

A clouded light appears in the distance, echoing my name. I desperately scream out to the voice, but my vocal cords are silenced by the gorging water. The sound soon fades as I'm dragged into the darkness, sinking further into helplessness.

My eyes shoot open, and I struggle for air. More panic rises when my own hands are cinched around my neck. I'm not actually drowning. I'm in my bed, and I'd been choking myself. Releasing my clutched fingers, I dig them into my blanket, then blow out slow breaths and convince myself that I'm safe and sound in my room and the menacing water is gone.

I pray that this won't be like the scratches or climbing up the tree limb, because it would only indicate that things aren't getting any better.

Once my pounding heart rate lowers, I wipe the sweat off my forehead. This was just a horrifying nightmare. I try to shake it off by remembering the dreamy guy I met last night.

Gabriel King.

The thought of him soothes me, and prying myself out of bed becomes a little easier.

***

Breakfast was lonely without Lindsay, but a certain boy kept me company in my head. As I replayed our brief exchange, a tickling sensation filled my stomach. I need to know more about him. I wonder why he's here, or if he has a girlfriend. He has to— I mean, you don't look like that and stay single. But why would he ask me to see him again if he did have one?

Ugh, I can tell this day is going to last an eternity.

I have no session today, which is relieving. Funny how when I first arrived at Awana, I was starting to enjoy my time spent with Dr. Beckham. Now I'm more than grateful to avoid it.

Eager to waste the day, I try to spend extra time in arts and crafts. Abby is a seat away, and I peer over to see what masterpiece she's creating today. She's painting the river outside Awana, and in an instant, last night's nightmare of violent water rushing all around me replays in my mind. I jump in my chair.

Dr. Beckham did say to let him know if I had any unusual dreams, but something in me is afraid to tell him. What if he wants to prolong my treatment? What if he wants to give me more medication?

Fear continues to circle, but I break the cycle. I know I can't think like that. I need to be honest with him, even if it's the last thing I want to do. At the end of the day, I'm here to get better.

After yoga, I lie alone in our usual spot on the grass. I wish Lindsay was next to me tanning or telling me joke. For someone who is used to spending a ton of time in solitude, whether at home or in a ward, I'm beginning to despise it. A few silhouettes of boys stand out to me through the sliding glass doors of their house, and I try to see if any resemble the striking one who appeared at my window last night.

"You miss your crazy friend yet?"

I shield the sun to see who's talking to me and find Kookie.

"She's not crazy," I snap, combatting her insult.

"Whatever you say. They got her back in one of the doctor's cabins. I heard she's detoxing."

Oh no, here we go again.

"Detoxing? From what?"

"She must have gotten her hands on something. I overheard Dr. Beckham telling Dr. Cassidy that he thinks she had a friend bring her something during free time. He confronted her about it, and I guess that's when she had her mental freak-out."

I quicky come to her defense. "I'm with her all the time pretty much, and I've never seen her do drugs. Also, she doesn't have friends up here. Only her grandma, and I doubt she's helping Lindsay smuggle any in," I add with sarcasm, hoping it'll make Kookie feel as dumb as the lie she's conjuring.

"Aw, it's cute that you're defending her, but I think she's capable of a lot more than you know. Like a serpent in the grass, just waiting to strike," Kookie says before hissing at me.

I roll my eyes and turn over onto my stomach so she's out of my view. I hear her cackle off and rejoin the rest of the EDs.

I hope Kookie is just making up another tall tale to spice up the dramatics in her boring life here at Awana. Lindsay is usually with me or in a session with a doctor. There's no way she could have been using drugs.

Right?

Bedtime could not come faster, but now I'm conflicted. In order to see Gabriel tonight, I can't take my medication or else I'll be knocked out until morning. I know the circumstances are a bit unordinary, but this is the closest I've ever come to being asked out on a date. Plus, girls my age are supposed to be dating and flirting. It's human nature, and it's something I've missed out on. I've always been hidden from boys until this one finally found me.

I need this.

Grace comes in, and my desperation for some sort of companionship decides for me. After she leaves, so do the pills in my mouth. I stash them away and catch a glimpse of myself in my dresser mirror. My hair is a mess, and my lips are colorless and dry. I can't go to my window looking so drab. I brush out my knots and blot on some of Lindsay's lipstick before lying back in bed.

The anticipation could kill me. This whirling sensation in my chest increases with every minute passed.

What if he doesn't come? What if he was joking?

I push away the doubt in my head by holding on to the memory of his eyes. I've never had anyone look at me the way he did.

My arms and legs are twitching again like last night. It must be from the jitters of counting down the clock. Finally, it's almost 2:00 a.m. I don't want to be looking out the window when he comes, so I lie against my pillow and place my hands over my rapid heartbeat.

Ten minutes later, a tune plays outside, and I jump up. The sight on the other side of the glass makes me lightheaded. There Gabriel stands in his beanie and the same flannel, but this time there's no shirt underneath, exposing intricately woven tattoos stretched along his chest. His toned, tan skin brings goose bumps to mine. He pulls the small instrument away from his lips, revealing his bright smile.

I crank open my window, and he walks closer to me.

"Is that a harmonica?" I point at what he's holding. He blows into it once more, creating a short melody. I shush him. "You're going to wake someone up."

"A little late-night lullaby never hurt anyone," he teases, slipping it into his pocket.

I study the yard around him.

"Where did you get that?" I ask, feeling more relaxed about our rebellious meet and greet since it's clearly only us out during this breezy night.

"The harmonica? It's mine. Making music helps distract an unsettled mind. You should try it some time." He pauses a moment. "Can I just say something?" he says as I admire his warm eyes.

"Sure, what?"

"I'm not sure if it's the way the moonlight is shining tonight, but, Natalia, you look absolutely radiant."

I cover my mouth to hide my uncontrollable grin, and Gabriel keeps his eyes locked on me. This is the first time that I've been admired by the opposite sex, and the flattery feels like pure dopamine has been shot into my heart.

"So, will you let your hair down for me, Rapunzel, or will you keep me waiting in the cold?" He huffs into his hands, rubbing them together.

Though I'm sure he's been in plenty of girl's beds, he won't be in mine. Not tonight.

I lose my train of thought as I gaze at his lips blowing more warm air onto his fingers.

Gabriel whistles a tune, snapping me out of my infatuated stupor.

"I don't think so," I finally reply.

"Playing hard to get, I see. No problem. What do I have to do to get you out here with me, then?"

The five-foot drop from my window doesn't look too intimidating, but the guy standing outside it does. I think I'm okay with this safe distance between us. I mean, I'm just getting used to talking to a good-looking boy without stumbling over my words.

I shake my head coyly.

"All right, all right. Maybe another time?" he says, then bites his lip, and it causes my pulse to pound like a drumbeat.

He grabs a cigarette, then turns toward the river to blow smoke.

"How long have you been here?" he asks, turning back around.

"Two weeks on Friday. You?"

"Six months on Friday."

Ugh.

I don't envy him. But I've spent months in grimmer places than this. Awana is a world away from dated eerie hospitals with creaking hard beds and no windows in the rooms. I can still hear the cries filling the nighttime hallways as patients were locked away and forced to deal with their own torment.

"That's a decent amount of time," I tell him, trying to drown out the sounds in the flashbacks that still cause my skin to crawl.

"Well, either they like me a lot or they can't fix this," he jokes, tapping his head. "I'll let you choose." He turns toward my bird feeder. "So, what's with the ashtray—"

"Don't you dare come near it with that," I warn.

He chuckles and uncrosses his arms to flick the cigarette out of his mouth.

"It's a bird feeder. I like bird-watching. It helps distract an unsettled mind," I share, stealing his line.

He laughs again and inspects the feeder dangling in front of him.

"Homemade, I take it?" He spins the cut plastic bottle.

"Yes. Well, not home, but the arts and craft room."

I lean out my window a little farther to examine my contraption.

"Great work. And you actually get birds to eat off this thing?"

"Yes, actually. It's been successful. Well, up until a starling found it." I shudder thinking of the creature's malevolent eyes.

"A what?" he asks, raising a brow.

"A starling, a type of bird. And I hate it because it's scaring all the other birds from my window!"

"Sounds like my kind of bird." He grins, and I roll my eyes at him. "So, Natalia, you like birds, and arts and crafts, and you don't seem too fond of harmonicas."

"All are true but the last one. I'd say I'm impartial to the harmonica."

"You're kind of a nerd, aren't you?"

My jaw lowers.

He's a ballsy one!

"Hey! And you're kind of a jerk, aren't you?" I tease, dishing it right back.

"My apologies. I'm a bit of a nerd myself."

"So, Gabriel, you like music, I take it, and cigarettes. And let me guess, the nighttime sky?"

"You got me in a nutshell, babe."

He shows his pearly whites, and my heart hums a song louder than his harmonica.

"You don't sound like a nerd. You sound like the kind of guy who breaks hearts," I admit, and he grimaces.

"You got me all wrong. I guess we have some more learning to do about each other."

"I guess so," I respond quietly, even though all I hear are joyous horns setting off in my head because he actually wants to get to know me! I've never had a guy, let alone one this attractive, take an interest in me. The only ones who do wear a doctor's badge and are paid to.

He shivers and tugs on his beanie. "Well, unless you're willing to share some body heat, I think I better head back inside."

I don't want him to leave, but I'm not ready to share my body heat with anyone.

"Not tonight." I say softly, declining his third attempt to be closer to me.

"That's okay. I'll take you one night at a time if I have to. See you tomorrow? Same place, same stars?" he asks, glancing at the sky above us.

God, he's smooth.

I slant my head and peer up at the tiny specks in the distance that look like radiant glitter shining against the night.

"Sure," I reply, doing my best to tone down my smirk. "Wait, no, actually." The corners of my mouth release.

"Do you have plans already?" He tilts his head.

"No. Well, kind of. I have a sleep study—"

I catch myself admitting more than I intended. I want Gabriel to know me as the fun girl at the window, not the one with a troubling sleep disorder. But I also don't want him to think I don't want to see him again.

"A sleep study?" He pulls his head back.

I pause before I answer, and I think he notices my hesitation. Before I can speak, he continues, "You don't have to explain. How about the next night? Are you free then?"

"Yes, I'll be able to make it," I agree without a care about anything or anyone, only focusing on the fact that he wants to see me yet again.

"Perfect. Rest easy, Sleeping Beauty." He nods before turning around and walking in the direction of the other house.

I let out a deep breath and fall against my soft sheets. I'm afraid it will be impossible to sleep with all these butterflies dancing inside me. But I replay Gabriel's instrumental lullaby in my mind, and the sweet sound lulls me into a deep relaxation.

***

Gabriel King is lying next to me, staring at me with fiery eyes like a wolf. I close mine, and his fingertips brush my lips and move down my chest. His hand trails down to my thighs, but then it stops. His touch disappears, and when my eyes open, so has he. A thick, bloody wave takes his place, crashing into me, throwing my body around as I flail to keep my head above the vicious crimson tide.

My alarm lets out a jarring ring, and I wake up gasping. My fingernails are at my throat, tearing at my skin. My shaky hands feel around, checking to make sure I didn't draw blood, but I haven't broken through. I'm free from any more self-harm, for today at least.

I clutch my knees and rock to nurse my skittish state. Distorted pieces from my other nightmare appear. Strange waters always seem to dwell in my unconscious state. I hate these dreams, and I hate even more that I should tell Dr. Beckham about them.

I avoid people as much as I can today. I'm feeling worn out as my body alternates between sweats and chills. I can't seem to regulate my body temperature, and it's frustrating. Luckily, breakfast only involves Abby and me. I pour myself a bowl of cereal and sit at the opposite end of the table as her. She doesn't look up to acknowledge me, but I'm used to it.

My thoughts shift to Gabriel. He's incredibly handsome and a sweet talker, but he has this danger inside his eyes that I don't want to look away from. Part of me wonders if he could even really be into me or if I'm making this into something it isn't.

"I heard you last night," a lowered voice says, almost in a whisper.

What the hell?

The only person sitting at my table is Abby, but she's never spoken. I spin around and swiftly scan the room to see who else could have said that, but there's no one else within earshot. My eyes dart to Abby.

"Are you talking to me?" I check, but I go unanswered. Abby doesn't even look in my direction. "Abby, did you say you heard me last night? What exactly did you hear?"

Is it possible that Abby just spoke to me, and her first words were some kind of threat? If so, then why is she suddenly being so coy?

Abby scoots back from the table, tugging on one of her braids, and leaves without a word.

God, she can be creepy sometimes.

Did she really hear me? Did she hear Gabriel? I thought the girl doesn't talk. What if she tells on us? It would ruin the only thing I have to look forward to in here.

I find myself replaying the evening in my head all morning, worrying what exactly Abby could have heard or seen. The clouds are dense in the sky. We did our yoga class inside today because Dr. Cassidy feared it might rain.

My dry eyelids can barely stay open. My two late-night visits with Gabriel have left me with little sleep. I head to my room before dinner to lie down. I'm not supposed to nap on sleep study nights, so it takes physical effort to keep myself from dozing off. The wind rattles my window. Lindsay's absent bed still causes me pain. I wonder if she's able to look out wherever she is and see the storm outside. Rain pours down hard, and I watch the drops slide down the glass to pass the time.

My bird bell rings, and I stretch up to see past the dripping water. Through the glass, I see a figure of a dark bird and hear the cry of another. I crank open my window, and black wings fly away. My breath stops when I look to the ground. There lies a hurt blue jay. The rain pours over its panicking wings, but its struggle soon comes to an end. My eyes water, and I have to look away from the death that's happened right in front of me.

I won't allow the starling to stalk and hunt on my behalf. After pulling up my feeder, I rip it in two, and all the seeds drop into the grass and mud below.

The rain blew into my room and soaked my sheets, but I stay curled up in the dampness, trying to rid my mind of the awfulness I've just seen until it's time to go to the dining room.

Abby doesn't say a word at dinner, and I can't touch my food. My eyes are tearing from the stinging in chest. I can't help but think of how miserable my day has been: There was the poor, injured blue jay that I couldn't save. Lindsay is still missing, and I've been besieged with dread all day, knowing I have to bring up my taunting nightmares to a doctor whose temperament is unpredictable. This might be the first time I'm looking forward to taking my pills. At least when I'm on medication, the nights turn into pure nothingness, a place to escape disturbing dreams and the painful emotions from reality.

After dinner, I change into my pajamas and lie in bed waiting for Grace. I actually swallow the pills she gives me, and Dr. Beckham walks in shortly after with the monitor and wires.

"You must enjoy having the room to yourself," he presumes.

He's not in his usual doctor's coat and is dressed down in jeans and a V-neck T-shirt.

"It's okay," I lie.

"Lindsay should be joining you soon. She's doing much better."

I'm sure he's trying to be comforting, but I won't believe it until I see it.

Dr. Beckham's aftershave is extra strong tonight, and I notice his usually hidden arms flex as he reaches over to place the wires on my head.

I exhale. It's now or never.

"Dr. Beckham, I need to tell you something."

"Yes?" he says, stopping to look down at me.

"I had two weird dreams recently. In both, I think I was drowning."

I feel an internal flinch as I wait for his reaction.

He stands up straight, crossing his arms in concern. "Did you wake up out of bed, or did you hurt yourself?"

Tell the truth, Natalia. He's only here to help you.

"No. I just woke up out of breath both times," I explain, swirling my thumbs around each other.

The mentioning of physically choking myself must have gotten stuck on my tongue. It's like I've built up this new defense mechanism from all the previous dire consequences and berating I've experienced when doctors have found out how I've acted out during a dream.

He examines my fidgeting fingers, so I slip them under my comforter.

"These sound like typical nightmares, usually brought on by stress or a new sleep environment. Drowning in your dreams can symbolize something as simple as feeling overwhelmed. I don't think they pose a threat to your current treatment, but I'll make note of them, and I want you to tell me if these dreams escalate any further," he replies, then reaches for a clipboard behind the machine and begins to write.

"What happens if they do?"

He sets down the board. "Well, our sleep studies will need to become a nightly thing, or we might need to increase your medication until we can figure out what's happening."

Two things I feared he'd say. Both those options don't bring me any satisfaction, confirming that I made the right choice by not telling the full truth.

Gabriel comes to mind. This can't become a regular thing, or I'll never get the chance to see him.

Dr. Beckham slides down each strap on my tank top and presses a stickered wire a little lower than before, causing my body to quiver.

"Are you okay?" he asks.

I nod, but something feels uncomfortable about his meandering touch near my breast.

He moves his hands to turn on the machine and then stands up. "Sweet dreams, Natalia."

After I see him leave my room, in between slow blinks, I allow the powerful dose to take ahold of my senses and block out everything around me.

CHAPTER 8

I rip the wires off, praying I make it to the bathroom. My stomach hurls my insides into the toilet in the nick of time. After wiping saliva off my cheek, I push myself up from the ground, crouching as I walk back toward my anti-nausea pills. A loud leaf blower nearby is making my aching head hurt tenfold. I crawl back into bed with my hands cupped over my ears.

Once my stomach settles enough, I lift myself to face out my window. The grass below shows no sign of the wounded blue jay from yesterday.

Where did it go?

The gardener must have taken care of it.

The male nurse walks in, and I hand him the wires. As I watch him roll everything away, the room sways back and forth. My vision is fuzzier than usual. It's been a couple days since I've taken my medication, and now it's like my body and brain have detached from each other. I must be readjusting to the strength. Through my distorted state, I focus on getting through the day so I can spend another night with Gabriel.

The hours pass in one long blur. I go through all the motions on autopilot. It isn't until dinner that I finally feel like the fog is clearing from my head. I know yesterday my emotions were getting the best of me, but the strung-out haze I was lost in is worse today. I'd rather feel sorrow than a medicated nothing.

As I regain control of my emotions again, one is standing out: elation over seeing a cute boy at my window tonight. I decide to grab a book from the living room bookcase to entertain me until then. The collection Awana has is filled with self-help and spiritual healing reads. I guess they're fitting for a place like this, but I typically go for something with a bit more grit.

A worn hardcover missing its dust cover catches my eye. I pull it out from the bottom shelf and admire the navy blue cover with a striking gold emblem design. I open to the title page: *Selected Poems and Letters of Emily Dickinson.*

Perfect!

Emily Dickinson is an idol of mine: she loved birds and was another pioneer of those living with a brain you could call "disturbed." She spent most of her life in seclusion, some say because of her severe mental illness. But over her lifespan, she produced over 1,800 poems. I like to think that though Emily suffered adversity, it was the fuel of her ingenious craft. This was during a time when if a woman experienced any delirium, she was cast to spend a life alone. Writing may have been her only outlet, the one joy that kept her going. Little did anyone know back then that centuries later, her words would sit on a bookshelf in a center devoted to solving mental disorders.

I take my proud find and head to my room. With Lindsay being gone, the familiar feeling of seclusion reminds me of my past. When Olga found me, I was alone. Then I spent most of my life isolated from the world. I made friends with nature and the characters in the books I read. Olga worried I was creating imaginary friends, and that landed me another stay in a ward. But I don't think I was delusional; I was just lonely.

Grace comes in, and I close my book.

"How are you today, Grace?" I ask the older woman. I'm not sure if I've ever heard her voice.

"Fine," she mumbles stoically.

Aha! She speaks! And her voice is as cold as she is.

"Oh, that's good to hear. I'm so happy the rain stopped. I really do love the sunny days over the cloudy ones—"

"Take the medication, please," she interrupts my ramble.

"Oh, yeah. Sure." I pop the pills in, and after her inspection underneath my tongue, she leaves without another word.

I thought nurses were supposed to be considered caretakers for patients, yet, ironically, I feel some of them care the least about us. I'm sure it gets old dealing with the many antics the mentally ill bring, but an ounce of compassion could go a long way in making us feel like we're not such a nuisance to be around.

Without a question, I pop out the pills out and tuck them away with the rest. Seeing Gabriel is an easy choice now. He allows me to forget the world I'm in, even if it's just for a few secret moments.

As if I was a girl getting ready for an actual date, I put on my best outfit—well, the nicest pajamas I own, a nightgown Olga bought for me. I slip on the white satin baby-doll style dress, but I've outgrown it. The hem that used to come to my knees is now riding up my midthigh.

I crack open my window, then lie back in bed to lose myself in Emily's syntax and words that weave together like tiny masterpieces that bury themselves in your soul.

"To love is so startling, it leaves little time for anything else."

I ponder this line and what being in love could feel like. I imagine it's like a warm coat in the middle of winter, or maybe it's more like jumping in a pool of cold water—you're afraid to dive in, but when you finally find your courage, it's the most exhilarating experience.

A melody from outside distracts me in the sweetest way. I close my book and perch against my windowsill. The overwhelming sight of a boy and his harmonica brings me a thrilling shock.

"That's the girl I've been waiting days to see," Gabriel cheers, slipping his harmonica away, and I drop my chin to hide my warm cheeks. "How was your sleep study?"

"It was fine," I reply shortly, avoiding details.

"Glad to hear. I'm sure it's a lovely place to be."

"Where?" I angle my head and play with my hair seductively.

"In your dreams. I'd love to see what goes on in that mind."

I push my dark locks off my shoulder and sigh. "I don't think you would. My dreams are probably the furthest thing from pleasant."

"Who would have thought? I guess some of the darkest minds live behind the most beautiful eyes."

He's staring at me with such an intensity that for a moment, I have to avoid his gaze and sheepishly look up at the stars.

"There's a much better view out here." He points to the sky. "You're really missing out on this calm, clear evening we were gifted tonight." He spins in a circle with his arms held out, but I just shake my head. "What more can I do to convince you? Should I fall to my knees and beg you?"

"No, you don't have—" I start, but his knees hit the grass before I can finish.

"Please come lie with me, Natalia, and watch the stars. Please. *Please.*" His voice rises higher with each plea.

I shush him. "Fine, just please be quiet."

I give in so he'll stop making noise, but I hesitate. Can I really leave my room? What if someone sees? Is it worth risking never seeing him again if we potentially get caught?

He zips his smile closed with his fingers and stands under my window with his arms stretched out in front of him.

He's truly irresistible.

"Come on out," he urges.

"I'm not going to jump."

I look down at him with trepidation. It's not a huge drop, but it's enough to give me pause.

"How else will you get down? Come on, bring your legs out and push off the edge. I'll catch you, I promise."

Something in me brings each of my thighs onto the windowsill. Maybe it's his hypnotizing gaze or the fact that climbing out this window could defy all the times I've been kept away from boys, leaving me unable to form any sort of romantic relationship.

"Okay, Natalia. On the count of three. One… two…," he chants.

On "three," I push myself off the edge. My body falls perfectly in the curve of his arms, and it causes my heart to do cartwheels.

"I got you, babe," he whispers, and I adore his beaming eyes that rest under dark circles, probably because this boy doesn't get much rest.

"You can put me down now," I remind him.

"Oh, right. Sorry about that." He sets my feet on the grass, then slips off his red flannel and flattens it below us. Lying on it in his white shirt and beanie, he pats a small section of fabric left for me.

I lower myself and lie with my arm parallel against his. The warmth and adrenaline his skin brings me combats the cool wind around us.

We lie side by side, and I watch the endless twinkling lights above.

"One good thing about being out in the middle of nowhere is the way stars shine out here," Gabriel mentions.

I catch him staring at me from the corner of my eye.

"These are the only skies I know," I admit, keeping my focus upward. It's nerve-racking to look at him. He's just too damn cute.

"So, you grew up out in the boonies?"

I chuckle. He makes me feel like some sort of hillbilly with that term.

"Yeah. It's the only place I've ever lived—only a couple of hours from here."

"Growing up, I never lived anywhere where the stars outshine the city lights."

"Where are you from?" I ask, and he pauses for a moment.

"I don't think I have a definite place I can call home. Foster care doesn't really allow for that. I've lived in many different cities up and down California. But since I turned eighteen, I've spent the last three years traveling coast to coast in a van."

"A van?" I furrow my brow, confused. "Can I ask why?"

"Why not? It's a pretty decked-out van, I might add, with a memory foam mattress and Wi-Fi included. But yeah, I get that reaction a lot. Why would I choose to eat most of my meals cold and take showers at dirty truck stops? But I think it's because the nomad life is all I know. I don't think I know how to stay in one place. With my van, I can leave at my choice, not because I became too much for someone else to handle."

Is he reading my mind?

I know all too well the feeling of being "too much to handle" for those around you. I've never heard anyone else speak the words I've always thought. In that moment, I feel a kindship with Gabriel that I haven't experienced with anyone before, not even Lindsay.

"That makes sense," I tell him.

There's something about him that is so familiar, like I've known him forever.

"Does it? That means a lot coming from a girl who's only ever lived in one place."

He smirks for a moment, then turns back to the sky. His pensive expression shows me he's deep in a thought.

I don't know why he was in foster care, but I can only imagine it was because someone abandoned him, and though our upbringings ended up completely different, the start of ours is what's the same. Me being neglected as child is a fact that I had to grow up with, and a pain I felt was only mine—until tonight, I've never met someone else who's experienced something similar. It's a bittersweet connection, but one I'm grateful for.

Gabriel stretches his fingers out until our pinkies touch. He interlaces his with mine, and my heart releases sparks. I glance down at our interlocked hands, and what I see on his arms sends a sharp pain through me. Thick vertical scars run along his wrists, not mere scratches like the ones on my collarbones but the deep kind people don't survive. In this moment, I thank the stars that he did.

We both focus on the vastness above us, and I enjoy the sounds of the chirping crickets. As we lay, my body experiences something new lying next to his. There's a sense of refuge—a rarity for me.

I feel a gentle nudge.

"Well, Sleeping Beauty, I should probably let you get some sleep in a bed tonight."

It can't be time to go already. I'm not ready to leave him yet.

As much as I don't want this night to end, he's probably right. Getting caught would mean never being able to see him again, and if we stay out much longer, we'll be taking a huge risk.

He sits up, grabbing my other hand to help lift me. He ties the flannel around his waist and heads toward my window. Once underneath, he clasps his fingers over his knee, creating a step.

"Up you go," he demands.

"I can get back in myself."

"Come on, take the lift."

I narrow my eyes at him but stick my bare foot in his hands and rest my fingers on his shoulder. He hoists me up until I'm able to grab on to my window ledge. I pull myself in, landing on my bed.

"You have the grace of a ballerina," he boasts, and I roll my eyes. "When can I see you again?"

I rest my arms outside my window.

"How about tomorrow? Same place, same stars?" I ask.

His smile grows brighter than the moon above him.

"There's nothing I'd love more. Have a good night, Natalia." He waves, and I watch him until he disappears into the shadows of the night.

***

No nightmares, no nausea, just a sweet buzzing from the memory of last night spinning in my head. Focused on how amazing I feel, I'm startled by a knock, and Dr. Cassidy peeks her head in. And just when I thought the morning couldn't get any better, she gives me the most amazing update.

"Good news, Natalia! Lindsay will be returning tomorrow to stay with you in your room."

I shoot up in my bed and throw my covers off. "That's fantastic!"

"I want to discuss a few things. She's been under Dr. Beckham's care, and he did warn me that Lindsay has been a bit hostile lately. Would you be willing to let us know if you notice any changes in her behavior?"

I can't really blame the girl for any hostility. Who knows what's happened to her in the past several days?

"What sort of changes should I be looking for?" I ask cautiously.

I'm not sure I'm comfortable acting as their informant. I've never been one to speak up about past roommates' questionable behavior, even after I witnessed a bulimic hide vomit in her shoes. So, there's a slim chance that I would snitch on my closest friend here.

"Mood swings are normal, but please tell us if she experiences any outbursts, paranoia, or physical symptoms such as shaking or profuse sweating."

It's concerning that she'd even be experiencing such extreme changes. What the hell happened to her during isolation?

"Okay, yeah, sure," I agree, but something about this leaves me unsettled.

Could the drug rumor Kookie shared with me be true?

"Thank you. It's best we all work as a team here, and since we can't have eyes on Lindsay at all times, we could use an extra pair."

Dr. Cassidy leaves, and I use the time before breakfast to organize our room. I'm so happy to have Lindsay back, but it leaves me wondering what will happen to my nighttime visits with Gabriel. If I'm being asked to notify the staff if she acts out, what if they're asking the same of her? Do they have everyone in here serving as spies? Would she tell on me for sneaking out to see him? I'm hoping from what I know of Lindsay, she wouldn't.

Would she?

This is why I need to keep my mouth shut. I don't want to give Lindsay any reason to want to expose my new secret nightlife as some sort of revenge.

Abby hasn't said anything today, but I'm still a little weirded out by her, so I keep my distance. After breakfast, I grab some paint and a small canvas. I pick blue and yellow acrylics and use abstract strokes to try and recreate the beauty of the blue jay that lost its life in front of me. I paint its delicate wings flying toward a maroon sun. The finished painting brings a sense of relief.

Kookie and the ED girls giggle throughout yoga, leaving Abby and me out. I can't wait to have Lindsay back. I miss her laugh. I miss her jokes, even if they can be offensive. Most of all, I miss her friendship.

The sun stays out past dinner now that spring is in full effect. I spend the golden hour in my room and rest my painting on my dresser. Today has been one of my best days at Awana. I think it's because I just feel normal. Minus my current setting, obviously, but I'm just a girl who's excited to see her friend tomorrow, as well as the boy she's crushing on tonight. It's days like today that give me hope that I'm going to be okay, even if my sleep patterns are different than most.

Emily's poems keep me entertained until Grace comes in, and she leaves without the slightest suspicion that the pills she gave me are in a pile with the others, stuffed in my bra. I open my window and allow the crisp air to blow through, watching the glowing hues outside fade into a midnight sky as I count the minutes until 2:00 a.m.

It's a long wait, and I'm antsier than ever. My whole body feels like it's being pricked with a thousand pins and needles from the breeze, so I throw on a sweatshirt in the hopes that it will get rid of my shivers. My teeth are lightly chattering when I hear the soft melody of a harmonica calling to me.

With a skip in my step, I spring to the window.

My handsome suitor has arrived.

CHAPTER 9

For the first time in a while, I was able to get some sleep without my medication because, to my great disappointment, Gabriel wouldn't hang around long last night. My constant yawning and head that felt too heavy to hold up made him almost instantly send me back to bed. I can't say I blame him. He probably thought I was coming down with something and didn't want to catch it. Since there was no way I could hide my exhaustion from him, he only stayed for a quick song on his harmonica and a cigarette, then called it a night. But before he left, he did tell me to get some good rest because he has something he wants to show me tonight. The commotion in my head trying to imagine what that could be almost made it impossible sleep, but eventually I was able to get in a few hours in.

I want more of him, and it's not fair that I have to wait until the lights go out to see him. I turn off my alarm before it blares and look to the window to finish watching the last bit of the sunrise.

Without warning, a black bird crashes into the window, causing my whole body to jolt forward. It's the starling again. It's agitated and smacking the glass repeatedly.

Why is it so desperate to come in?

Before I can make my way over to shoo it away, my door springs opens, startling me yet again.

Lindsay waltzes in, wearing a bright yellow dress and shouts a loud greeting of "Hey, girl, hey!" She immediately springs onto my bed.

"The starling, Lindsay! It's back. Do you see it how angry it is?" I say, glancing back at the window, but the bird is gone.

Where did it go off to so quickly?

"Uh, I think I just missed it." Lindsay embraces me with open arms, but I'm too busy inspecting the bird feeder to hug her back. Yoo-hoo! Natalia?"

"Sorry. This bird out there keeps—"

"Glad to see nothing changed with you," she says, cutting me off. "Always concerned about the birds. I thought you'd be a little more excited to see me, though."

I snap out of my confusion and wrap my arms tightly around her.

"I am excited! Sorry, it's just early, I think. I missed you so much. Please tell me you're okay."

She squeezes me back even harder. "I missed you too. And I'm okay—now, at least."

"What happened? I mean, I heard rumors, but the doctors wouldn't explain anything." Lindsay gives me the side-eye. "Rumors? What did you hear?" Her tone is defensive.

Should I even bring this up?

"Well, I don't want to offend you, and it's really not my business—"

She puts her hands on her hips. "Spit it out, Natalia. What did you hear?"

I cross my legs and sit up to explain, worried she might not like what I have to say.

"Okay, well, Kookie said she overheard the doctors saying you had relapsed, and possibly someone from outside Awana brought you whatever it was you took. I didn't believe her, though."

Lindsay rolls her eyes and lets out a chuckle.

"Ha! Oh, Kookie. Leave it to her to eavesdrop and then try to smear me," she says nonchalantly, picking at the ends of her hair.

How is she completely unfazed by this?

"So, wait, is it true?"

"Well, yeah," she admits effortlessly.

Her casual reaction surprises me. "What? How?"

I don't want to be mad at her for having a relapse, but if she so seamlessly hid this from me, what else would she lie about or keep from me?

Before she answers, she stands up and heads to her dresser to open a drawer.

"Long story short, my boyfriend and I got in a fight. A stupid one… over Messenger when I was using the living room computer," she adds quickly. "I threatened to break up with him for good. But being the romantic he is, he came up here for a visit and brought me a thoughtful treat, and I couldn't refuse such a grand gesture."

She holds a dress up to her body, examining herself in the mirror.

"A thoughtful treat?" I pry, nervous to hear the answer.

She tosses the outfit onto her bed, then sits back next to me.

"Oxy, my favorite little pills! Any bad thought vanishes the moment it finds its way to your bloodstream," she says romantically. She runs two fingers along my arm to emphasize her point.

I pull my wrist away, totally shocked.

I can't believe Kookie was the one telling the truth and Lindsay had been hiding something from me. I thought friends are supposed to trust each other, and I don't want to become wary of Lindsay, but it does makes me wonder what else I don't know about her.

I try to shift my perspective. Maybe I need to cut her some slack. I have no idea the urges she deals with when it comes to feeding her addiction. My own sleep disorder can feel like a relapsing battle, and I know how desperately I want to sometimes hide those failures. I should give her some credit for her actual willingness to be open with me now. I guess it's better late than never.

"Can I ask you something?" I ask, recapturing her attention.

"Go for it."

She leans back against my pillow, picking at a loose thread on my comforter. Since she's being so honest right now, this could be the right time to ask the question that's been bothering me for days.

"What happened that day with Dr. Beckham? I was watching, and I don't think what he did was right."

Lindsay clenches her eyes shut for a moment, then shoots upright stiffly. Her relaxed demeanor disappears, and she leaves my bed to arrange hers.

Why is she so put off by my question?

"Nothing happened. He's just a dick," she grumbles, aggressively patting down a pillow.

"It didn't look like nothing. The amount of force he was using—"

"Let's drop it, okay?" she interrupts forcefully. "I'm gonna hop in the shower. See you at breakfast." She slams the bathroom door behind her.

Her reaction was abrupt. These must be the mood changes Dr. Cassidy talked about, but something still isn't sitting well with me. I decide to forgo waiting for the clear bathroom and head straight to the kitchen, hoping some food will settle some of my uneasiness.

After breakfast is devoured, Lindsay is back to her chatty ways, telling Abby and me a story about the summer she spent following a band. She went to thirty different cities across the States, and after the fifth city, the lead guitarist caught notice, and they dated until the tour was over. She said she could have dated any of them, but she thought the guitarist would know how to use his fingers the best. Typical Lindsay. I'm just happy to have her back and for things to feel normal again.

Dr. Cassidy walks into the dining hall and interrupts Lindsay's story, which I'm fine with because I think it was starting to take an X-rated turn I didn't exactly want to hear.

"Natalia, Dr. Beckham would like to have a quick session after breakfast, so make your way there after you're finished eating."

I clear my plate, and when I come back to say goodbye, Lindsay is already gone. I head down the hall and see light coming from Dr. Beckham's open door. I peer in, and he greets me with a quick wave.

"Come on in," he says.

I do as instructed and take a seat.

"That's a nervous habit." He points to my hands.

"Huh?"

I follow the direction of his gaze and notice that I'm pressing down on the skin of my thumb with my pointer fingernail. I move my hands under my legs to stop.

"Is something making you nervous?"

"Not that I can think of," I lie.

Shit. If they were able to catch Lindsay taking pills, he might catch me not taking mine.

"Well, good to hear. Your latest sleep study went well. You reached a full REM stage with no unusual brain activity. Which is exactly what we've been striving for. Also, Dr. Cassidy said you seemed to have a big appetite at breakfast. Is your nausea going away?"

"Oh, um, it comes and goes."

"Interesting," he states, jotting something on his notepad.

"It's nice having Lindsay back," I tell him, trying to steer the conversation.

"I'm glad you enjoy her companionship. She's a wild horse, that girl. Not easily broken."

Did he just use the term "broken" like he's training a horse?

His words put a pit in my stomach. He can't possibly mean that his goal is to literally break someone down to the point of submission. Though the physical force he displayed toward Lindsay is uncomfortably fitting. I return a nervous laugh at his strange analogy.

"You, though, Natalia, you have been very good. You're responding well to treatments and the medication," he praises.

"Does this mean I'll be able to go home soon?" I perk up at the thought.

"Not so fast. Good things take time," he answers, and any hope of freedom I had dissolves.

He goes into a long explanation about the reasoning for the multiple nights of sleep studies and how he compares each result. He loses me when my mind drifts to the memory of Gabriel and his perfect smile.

"Do you treat the boys here at Awana?"

Dr. Beckham raises a curious brow. "No, Dr. Cassidy and I only treat female patients. What makes you ask?"

"Oh, I was just curious," I say, obviously avoiding the real reason, wondering if maybe he could have worked with Gabriel too.

"Is someone having curious thoughts about the opposite sex?" he asks with a wry smile, and I wrinkle my nose. "Nothing to be ashamed of, Natalia. You're at an age where your hormones are blossoming. It's completely normal. The boys here are off-limits, but when you're out of here, you'll be able to explore those urges with whoever you please."

Somehow, my sex life is the topic of discussion again, and Dr. Beckham's version of sex education has me cringing inside. His eyes moving down my body isn't helping the situation.

"Are we done here?" I blurt out.

Seriously? There's no way that this older, married doctor is checking me out right now... is there?

I shake off the thought as completely improbable—although, his eyes linger a little longer than I'm comfortable with. He finally looks away from me to check his watch.

"Uh, yes. That will be all for today. Just wanted a quick check-in, but things seem to be going well. I'll see you at the end of the week for your study."

I awkwardly throw him a thumbs-up and head out of there as quickly as I can.

He may be good-looking, but his insistence on discussing "urges" and "hormones" is just weird.

I can feel myself distancing from Dr. Beckham. After our first few meetings I thought he might be the one doctor who understood me in a way that no other had before. I looked forward to seeing and opening up to him. Now all our sessions feel like an impersonal chore.

In the afternoon, Dr. Cassidy has something different planned for us instead of our typical yoga routine. The sun is high, and she brings our group over to the most stunning part of the otherwise plain exterior of Awana. The garden is blooming with tall wildflowers thanks to the perfect combination of rain and sun we've been having. Birds chirp in the distance, and butterflies' spotted wings flutter over sweet-scented lavender, creating a storybook ambience.

"Ladies, let's gather in a circle," Dr. Cassidy says from her seated position on the ground with her coiled curls blowing in the air.

The six of us join around her with our legs crossed.

"What are we doing? Some sort of séance? I'm sure Lindsay knows a spell or two," Kookie snickers, and the rest of the EDs giggle right after. The way they practically laugh on demand proves that Kookie is the twisted ringleader of this group.

"Great to see you, too, Kookie darling. Hope the pin I stuck in your voodoo doll this morning feels good," Lindsay mocks, then pops her middle finger up at her.

Kookie rolls her eyes and ignores the comment.

"Girls, no talking, please," Dr. Cassidy cuts in. "I want to try some guided imagery with you. It's a form of meditation that helps relieve anxiety and tap into emotions we might have hidden deep. Now, let's begin with everyone closing your eyes."

I keep my eyes open until all the girls have theirs closed. I don't want to be the only one taking this seriously.

"Now, start breathing in deep, all the way down to your belly button, and on the count of three, everyone exhale. One… two… release," she instructs in a soft, hypnotic tone.

I do as she says and allow air to expand in my rib cage, then gently blow it out of my mouth.

"Keep your eyes closed. I want everyone to envision a flower in your head. Now, really focus on the color of the flower and the shape of the petals."

My mind draws a blank, which is strange because if I opened my eyes, I could easily pick any of the flowers around me. I squeeze my eyelids harder until a silky white gardenia appears over the black canvas of my imagination.

"Now I want to go around and talk about which flower each of you sees, and I'll share with you some different meanings of why that flower could be the one you imagined."

"Me first!" Kookie shouts. I have a feeling this girl always feels entitled to put herself before others. "I picture a rose. A beautiful red one," she says proudly.

"A rose is a common flower that women choose. Mostly because a lot of us tend to keep a guard up as a defense to protect ourselves," Dr. Cassidy explains.

A rose perfectly describes Kookie. Pretty and soft from a distance, but boy, will her thorns prick you if you try to get too close.

Lindsay speaks up, "Or in other words, you picked the most basic flower. Just like you—a basic bitch."

When Lindsay lets out a sharp laugh, I worry that darts might shoot at her from Kookie's scornful eyes.

"Let's move along, ladies." Dr. Cassidy raises her voice among the group.

Abby is next, and since she's not vocally capable, or willing, she points to a sunflower in the garden.

"This tall yellow flower represents light and the ability to bring joy to others."

Although Dr. Cassidy's explanation is sweet, I can't say I fully agree with that one. Due to my recent experience at the dinner table, I've only come to find her a little strange and off-putting.

Dr. Cassidy then picks on one of Kookie's minions to share—Kat, the girl with highlighted blonde hair and braces.

"I guess I saw a lily," she mumbles, lacking any enthusiasm, as if she's bored out of her mind.

Dr. Cassidy doesn't let Kat's bad attitude deter her from dissecting her answer.

"Lilies are complex. They symbolize someone who has a wide range of emotions. This is why they're often given to others in times of both celebration and grief."

Kat shrugs, still acting like this is a waste of time.

The other ED, Cheryl, whose arms are covered in tattoos, is up next. She seems way more interested in this exercise than Kat. She describes a white orchid almost poetically. Her use of language shows me she's the sharpest of the three EDs.

"Orchids are aligned with their exotic and bold nature. It's been a well-liked flower throughout different cultures for centuries." Dr. Cassidy sums up the flower, and Cheryl's shoulders and smile lift with pride.

Maybe I would like Cheryl if I was given the chance to know her more, but it's hard when she's constantly hiding in Kookie's shadow.

Lindsay is up. I can tell she's been zoning out everyone else's explanation. I think it's hard for her to focus when she's not the center of the attention.

"I picked a tulip, because obviously they're the sexiest damn flower there is." She smirks and shimmies her chest. I can tell by her tone that she's joking, but I don't think the other girls do based off their annoyed scoffs.

"You're not that far off, Lindsay. Tulips represent femininity and a desire for love and beauty," Dr. Cassidy says, backing up Lindsay's somewhat conceited comment.

That's a perfect fit for Lindsay.

Lindsay's the most loving, beautiful person here, though I'm sure Kookie might argue that point.

Finally, it's my turn. I'm equally nervous and interested to hear what Dr. Cassidy will say.

"Uh, well, I saw a gardenia," I timidly tell her, and her eyebrows perk up.

"Aha. The gardenia can have a few different meanings, the main one being purity and gentleness, but it's also been identified with a secret love between two people," Dr. Cassidy explains, and my cheeks burn when Gabriel's face appears in my mind.

"I knew Lindsay and Natalia were secretly in love, but then again, Lindsay will get it on with just about anyone," Kookie sneers, and Kat bursts into laughter.

"You're just mad because you're a hungry virgin!" Lindsay snaps back.

Kookie's face hardens into a snarl. "Fuck you! I'd rather be a virgin than a walking, talking STD. How many guys have you actually fucked, Lindsay? Oh, right. I'm sure that number is way too large for your stupid ass to even count."

Lindsay condescendingly applauds her. "Oh, wow! Good one, Kookie. Maybe you should try choking on a dick sometime. I'm sure it tastes better than your fingers that you gag yourself with after every meal."

"Oh shit!" Cheryl says, placing a fist to her mouth, quickly trying to hide her smile after Kookie aggressively jabs her side with her elbow.

"Hey, now! That's enough from you two," Dr. Cassidy intervenes.

"Lindsay can't ever get enough. She wouldn't even know how to keep her fucking legs shut if she tried," Kookie says, still raising her voice.

"Bitch, please. Go eat the fucking sandwich that's hidden under your bed," Lindsay yells back, shooing her with her hand.

"Girls, please stop!" Dr. Cassidy snaps. "You're disrupting the peacefulness of this exercise."

They both shut up, and Kookie takes a deep breath and shakes her head like she's trying her best not to lose it while Lindsay pulls a finger trigger against her head.

Now that it's silent again, Dr. Cassidy continues. "Everyone, close your eyes again, and I want you to imagine a younger version of yourself. You can pick the age. Whatever comes to you."

Everyone simmers down and eventually closes their eyes. Though the tension between the other girls is still swirling, I take a deep breath and allow myself to try and stay present in Dr. Cassidy's instructions.

It's hard to picture yourself younger when you don't have a lot of photos of yourself as a child. Olga didn't take many pictures, probably because there weren't that many great moments worth documenting. But there's one photograph that is standing out vividly in my mind. It's the one Olga took of me in front of our cottage when we first arrived in America. I was three, maybe four. I stood stiffly with no smile and an ominous look filling my eyes that no child of that young age should convey. It's a strange sensation to not have a single recollection of that day, yet every time I see the photo, a sharp pain cuts deeps in my chest, almost as if someone is trying to carve out my heart with a cold knife.

"I want everyone to imagine yourself at this age holding the flower you first thought of, and now imagine holding it every year of your life until the age you are now."

She pauses for a moment, giving us time. The photograph and gardenia take turns flickering in my head like a broken film on repeat. The sorrow that little girl holds plunges right into me, causing the angst in my chest to ache even worse.

"Picture yourself today with the same flower, but how does it look now? Is it still the same? Has it blossomed more, or maybe it's missing petals, or wilted?"

I try to fast-forward time in my mind, but the vision of my younger self won't go away. Tears fill her big crystal eyes, and darkness is closing in all around her until together we are both sucked like quicksand down into an abyss. I can't move or see anything; I just hear her cries echoing around me. I scream and beg for her not to leave me. Her ghostly complexion reappears, sobbing and holding on to the white gardenia. The petals begin to wither as deep maroon pours out from the center, dripping down her small hands. Her tears turn into a choking hyperventilation as her bloody fingers grip her throat, and she struggles for air.

Someone help her! Why is no one helping her?

"Open your eyes, Natalia! Open them," a voice yells from afar, but my body won't obey.

I reach for the small child, ripping her hands from her neck. I cradle her in my arms and rock her. As she crouches into me, I shush her whimpering, trying to console her. Her cries soften as I run my fingers through her black hair, but she suddenly deteriorates, leaving me alone once again.

With a sharp gasp, I fight my eyes open. When reality flashes back into focus, Dr. Cassidy is above me, pinning my hands to my sides while Lindsay is holding on to my shoulders.

When Dr. Cassidy releases my arms, my body curls into the fetal position. Sweat and tears pour from me as I sob.

"Why does this happen to me?" I shout, unable to restrain my thoughts. "I just want to be normal."

My shallow breaths turn into racing pants.

"Kookie, go grab her some water," Dr. Cassidy commands. "Breathe slowly, Natalia, one breath at a time. In through the nose, out through the mouth."

As my gasps become more rapid, the garden flowers turn into a blur of colors spinning around me. I try to inhale deeply, but the air won't make it past my throat. I press my hands over my eyes, hoping to stop the dizziness. I can't catch a breath, and I'm afraid I might pass out. I cry out, pleading for it all to stop.

An embrace tightens around my body, grounding me. When I open my eyes again, I find myself lying on Lindsay's lap as her hand gently rubs my back.

"What's happening to her?" her frightened voice asks.

"This seems like a panic attack. It can happen with this particular exercise, when patients are relaxed and accessing the recessed areas of their mind that they typically don't tap into or have been suppressing. Nothing to worry about. Just keep taking slow, deliberate breaths, Natalia. You're okay. You're doing great," Dr. Cassidy says encouragingly.

I do as instructed and feel the crushing weight on my chest begin to diminish.

"There you go. Now you have some color in your cheeks. How are you feeling, Natalia? Can you hear me?"

A shiver crawls down my spine from the cool air breezing against my sweaty neck. Being able to regain control of my shaking queasy body feels like I was just poisoned, then given an antidote. The wrinkles around Dr. Cassidy's eyes become my focus as she hovers over me.

"I think I'm okay," I answer, feeling a hint of calm after taking a few more deep breaths.

"Okay, Lindsay, let's sit her up slowly," Dr. Cassidy commands.

Both of them place their arms under me to lift my limp body back up into a sitting position. Kookie hands me a bottle of water, and I take a small sip. After my dizziness subsides, I look around to find every girl in the circle staring at me with wide eyes. They all just witnessed my mental freak-out. I think the havoc in my head has lessened because of the pure embarrassment that's taken its place.

Great, now everybody knows how much of a fucking psycho I really am.

"All right, girls, that's enough for today. Go ahead and enjoy your leisure time early."

The rest of the girls jump up and head back to the main house, excited to have the extra free time, but Lindsay stays back with me.

"Lindsay, will you help Natalia back to your room? I think it's best that she gets some rest," Dr. Cassidy suggests.

Lindsay agrees and helps me stand. With her arm around my waist, she walks me back into the house. I assure her I'm fine, but she won't let me walk on my own until we're in our room.

"Girl, are you okay?" she asks, sitting with me on my bed.

I have no idea how to answer that question right now. Does someone who is "okay" have that type of reaction to a dumb exercise about a mere flower?

"I don't even know what happened exactly," I reply, omitting that it's a horrible feeling to not be able to take ahold of your own thoughts or movements.

"Well, we were all doing that metaphor thing, and all of a sudden, you—" She goes silent.

"What? What did I do?" I ask urgently.

The distress in her eyes shoots right into me.

"You were gasping for air, and then your whole body broke out in a shaking sweat. Like, within seconds, you were dripping wet. It was pretty terrifying, to be honest. I didn't know if you were having a seizure or being possessed by the devil himself, but you wouldn't open your eyes, and your whole body was convulsing. What were you imagining?"

Blood-soaked petals invade my mind. I clench my fists, trying to stop them. Lindsay takes notice and softens her tone.

"Whoa. It's okay, you don't have to tell me. But damn, girl, you scared me."

She pulls me in for a hug, and I let myself fall into her. I hate that I've lost control of myself yet again, and this time with an audience.

"I'm here for you for anything, okay? Don't forget that," she assures me as she lets go.

Her empathy soothes my anxiousness, and I slowly start to feel like myself again.

"Yeah, I don't really want to talk about it." I straighten up to brush back the hair off my face.

"I know what that's like," Lindsay says, biting a piece of skin on her lip. "Sometimes I wish I could wipe out certain thoughts or memories. The ugly ones, the ones that repulse you deep inside. But if we could do that, then I guess we wouldn't be here, would we?" She cracks a half smile.

"The weird thing is, sometimes I feel like I don't have memories," I confess.

It's hard to explain to someone how moments in your life can feel like they're being fast-forwarded, skipping you ahead in time. There's no way I can describe it unless you've felt the same eerie sensation before.

Lindsay tilts her head. "What? How is that possible?"

I do my best to put words to my experience.

"I mean, like, I have memories of all my ward stays and my life in America. But it's like anything before that is a void. It's almost like there are deleted bits."

"Maybe it's better that way. I wish I could delete scenes from my life."

"What sort of scenes?"

"Do you really want to know?" she asks.

"Of course." I nod.

She chews at her lip, then takes a deep breath.

"Growing up with a mother who's a drunk was hard, even harder when no one else realized she was one. She's not the kind you see in movies, where they just constantly fall down or sleep all the time. She's incredibly functioning, but I started to learn that when the vodka bottles went empty, she became vicious." Lindsay stops herself and lies back.

I've never encountered an alcoholic, but she's right—I usually picture someone fumbling down the streets with a bottle in their hands, spewing out nonsense.

"You don't have to keep going if you don't want to."

She lets out another lengthy exhale.

"No, no. It's fine. It's just, when she was drunk, she'd love to scream and tear me down, tell me I was worthless and pathetic, all the things you should never say to your child. Then in the morning, she'd act as if nothing ever happened, and I was just expected to forget too. I don't think she realized how much her words stuck with me, or that in my lowest moments, they still replay in the back of my mind."

Ugh, that's a horrible way to grow up.

It sounds like Lindsay's mother is more than just someone who overindulges in alcohol. She's an emotional abuser, and Lindsay, her own daughter, has been her punching bag. Behind Lindsay's charismatic confidence hides a bruised and damaged young child.

She shifts away from me. It's clear that her past still haunts and hurts her.

"That's horrible. How are you two now? Is it any better now that you're an adult?" I ask.

She turns back with water gathered in her eyes, then wipes her forming tears.

"With all my fuckups, I don't think I'll ever be redeemable to her. I forced myself to stop seeking her validation. The funny thing is, my mom is looked at as someone who loves an occasional Xanax and martini. Which is totally acceptable in the white-picket-fence, country-club world I grew up in, because they all love the expensive parties she throws. It's a glamorous way to mask her ugly truth. But when everyone leaves, and that morning sun shines down on her, I see her for who she really is. She's a toxic mess, yet no one can imagine where on earth *my* addiction issues come from or face the fact that maybe the apple doesn't fall far from the tree."

"I'm sorry." I reach for her hand and squeeze. "Maybe she sees too much of herself in you, and it's easier to ridicule you than face her own demons."

I know how hard it is to face the parts about yourself that you wish weren't there. But no one has the right to tear someone else down in order to make them feel better about their own flaws.

"God, you're probably right. All I've ever wanted was her love and acceptance. The therapists always tell me that's why I search for it in every boy I meet." Lindsay blows a strand of hair out of her eyes. "Well, I'll stop burdening you with my mommy issues, but I'm glad you're doing better." She swivels her wrist to check the time on her watch and sighs. "Unfortunately, I have to go to my session now, but I'll catch up with you later."

I wish I could console her more the way she does with me, but she dashes out the door before I get a chance.

Lindsay's childhood was far from the one I imagined for a privileged, popular girl. I wonder if her mother ever considered that Lindsay having to grow up around her substance abuse may have only normalized that type of destruction.

I bury my head in my pillow, but I can't stop wondering about the disturbing images that took over my head in the garden. I try to prevent myself from replaying them for fear of how awfully they affected me. Maybe it's just because I haven't been getting much sleep, and my body is starting to hate me for it. Whatever the reason, I wish they would go away and set me and my thoughts free.

I could barely speak at dinner. My whole mood has sunk since the guided imagery earlier. Out of everyone there, why was I the only one who had such an adverse reaction? Oh, right, probably because I have too many loose screws to count. My sleep deprivation is wearing on me, turning everything into a haze. I force myself to stay alert, though, because seeing Gabriel tonight is all I have to look forward to.

Later in our room, Lindsay seems to be in higher spirits as she reads a celebrity gossip magazine next to me. She keeps showing me photos of different guys, asking who I'd marry, fuck, or kill. Grace comes and goes, and I add the pills she gives me to my collection as if it's no big deal anymore.

"Wait, you're not taking your pills?" Lindsay puts down her magazine and gawks.

"No, not tonight. Today was hard enough. I just want to wake up without a medication hangover."

It's the semi-truth, at least.

I'm not sure why I'm too nervous to tell Lindsay about seeing Gabriel. Maybe because so far, it's just been us two against everyone else. I'm unsure how she'll react if she finds out I've been bonding with someone else.

"I get that. Shit, I'll take it if you don't want it." She sits all the way up. I shake my head at her, and she grins. "I'm kidding. Dr. Beckham might lock me up in isolation forever if he catches me on anything."

I almost forgot she was in insolation. I can't believe I didn't ask her more about the experience. I seem to be too distracted by all my own issues.

"What was it like?" I ask as Lindsay falls back onto her bed.

"I mean, I was pretty sick for the most part from my oxy withdrawals. They stuck me in a doctor's cabin, which was pretty nice, I'll admit, but I was locked in a separate room, so I really didn't get to see much other than four walls and occasionally Dr. Beckham, who took it upon himself to be my personal nurse. It was okay at first, until you're left alone too long with your own thoughts. Then it's like your own brain is out to get you."

My unconscious brain is always out to get me.

"Yeah, I know how that can be," I tell her.

I don't think humans—or any species, for that matter—are conditioned to be caged up, and yet for decades, it was the only solution for the mentally ill. And in many cases, it still is.

"Well, I'm so glad you're back, but, Lindsay, in all seriousness, this boyfriend who brought you drugs doesn't sound like a good guy at all."

She jerks her head in my direction. "Well, we broke up, so you don't have to worry about that," she snaps.

"I'm so sorry. I had no idea… That was a stupid thing for me to bring up anyways."

"It's okay. How were you to know?" She sniffles, and her eyes redden. She squeezes her hands into fists and is able to fight off her tears. "It's a bad situation—really fucked up. The worst part is, I'm afraid I'll never truly be able to escape him. I end things, but he has this control over me, and it's like he knows I'll come crawling back. I have before. But I have to be strong this time. I think I'll completely break if I allow him to hurt me again."

This guy sounds more like a monster than a boyfriend.

She needs to stay far away from him.

"Well, at least you don't have to ever see him while you're here. You're safe here," I remind her.

Lindsay looks at me, and when she forces a smile, the tears she was holding back stream down her face. I reach for her and wrap my arm around her.

"I'm not sure I'll be safe. He's awful. I think I might actually hate him now."

Why doesn't she feel safe? Is he some sort of stalker?

"Maybe you should tell someone here about him, if you're afraid of him."

I'm taken aback when a laugh slips out of her.

"Yeah, that will never happen. Plus, we're over now. I'm officially fucking done."

I'm not exactly sure why she's not willing to speak to a therapist about this. It's their job to help her through tough relationships and breakups. That's basically why we're here.

She digs her face in my chest, and I can feel the moisture from her tears as her shoulders tremble with each deep cry she lets out. I pat her back, trying to assure her that everything will be okay.

Hours later, Lindsay has officially cried herself to sleep. I've never felt the anguish that she's dealing with right now, so I don't exactly know what to say to make it better, but one thing is abundantly clear: a broken heart is one of the worst things in life. Whatever Lindsay is going through looks tortuous.

It's impossible to love without that risk of getting hurt, isn't it?

I wish I could do more for her, but some sleep is probably best for her right now. I slip my arms out from under her and gently pull the blanket over her, then tiptoe to my bed. I feel a little guilty, because while Lindsay is suffering with boy problems, I'm jumping for joy that it's almost time for Gabriel to be going on his nightly walk.

I open my window and wait for him.

Two o'clock rolls around, and almost instantly through the fog of the night, Gabriel appears. Dressed in a nice white button-up shirt that's untucked, he looks like a 1950s heartthrob with his long hair slicked back. He spots me and flashes his teeth that stand out against the night. He pulls out his harmonica, but I quickly press my finger to my lips to shush him. I peer back at Lindsay; she's facing her wall, breathing heavily. She's definitely out cold.

"Am I allowed to speak?" he whispers, walking under my window.

"Yeah, sorry. We've just got to keep it down," I softly reply.

"Well, are you going to come out here? Or do I need to come in there and get you?" He holds his arms out for me.

Without hesitation, I stick my legs out of the window. I give myself a little push off, and Gabriel catches me. Instead of setting me down, he holds me tight and spins me around in circles. I cover my mouth to stifle my laughter.

"Put me down," I tell him between giggles, but he keeps on spinning and laughing until he loses his footing, and we both tumble to the ground. My body is pressed under his, and his golden-brown hair falls forward, tickling my forehead. We both gaze into each other's eyes.

Kiss me, Gabriel.

I close my eyes in hopes his lips might brush against mine, but all I feel is his body rising off me.

"You okay? That was quite a fall."

I open my eyes to find him sitting next to me, wrestling his fingers through his hair.

"Yeah, I'm fine," I sigh.

"Well, good. You want to go for a walk?" he asks, rubbing dirt off his hands.

"Won't someone see us?"

I can't kick this fear that we're being watched. Abby did mention something about hearing us. What if she's been told to keep an eye on me?

"Take a risk, Natalia. Come on, follow me. I want to show you something." He walks off without me.

"Gabriel, it's too dark."

He stops, then walks back, reaching out a hand for mine.

"Don't be afraid, babe. Your eyes will adjust. Plus, I have this." He sparks his lighter, letting the flame illuminate his face.

I lace my fingers in his, and it gives me the courage to follow him through the grass.

"Where are we going?"

"Just trust me."

For some reason, I do.

He leads me to a familiar tree, the one Lindsay and I spend most of our afternoons under. He sits on the grass below it, and I sit next to him. His arm gently wraps around the small of my back. The view of the moon shines bright between the leaves above, and Gabriel shuts his lighter to look at me.

"I wanted to bring you to this tree because it's where I was first drawn to you. I watched you come here day after day before I accidentally stumbled across your bird feeder. The first time I noticed you was from inside. You were with your blue-haired friend, but it was *your* beauty that struck me. You, with your porcelain skin and long black hair." He brushes my cheek with his fingertips, and chills invade my skin. "I waited the same time every afternoon to see you. You've made the long days in here seem worthwhile, so thank you for that, but with the strict separation rule, I didn't think I'd ever get the chance to meet you, and you remained this distant daydream. But as fate would have it, on one of my worst nights, a night I was questioning my sanity, I went out for some air, and I just so happened to find the window of the girl who I couldn't stop thinking of."

This is a lot to process, but at the same time, it's better than anything I ever hoped he'd say.

How do I respond to the sweetest thing a boy has ever admitted to me?

His head leans in closer, and mine naturally gravitates toward his. "I hope this doesn't weird you out. I just want to get to know you. I want to be near you. You have this energy I can't explain that brings me a sense of peace, and with the chaos going on in my mind, it's so damn refreshing."

His eyes still won't leave mine. It's like he's able to see deep inside my soul.

His declaration mirrors my very thoughts about him. We have this undeniable connection, an explosive chemistry, but surrounding all these intense feelings, there's a relieving calmness. Can another person be your dwelling, shielding you from the mayhem that life brings? Is it dangerous to put that on another person, or is that what relationships are all about?

"Natalia, now would be a good time to let me know what's going on in that pretty head of yours."

I'm speechless.

My heart is racing, and my only instinct is to lean closer to his lips. Gabriel's fingers collapse into my hair, bringing my nose to his. I close my eyes and feel his breath on my skin. His lips hit mine, his electric touch igniting a passion in me I've never experienced before.

We break apart, and when I open my eyes, Gabriel tucks my hair behind my ear. "You're unbelievable."

Warmth infused with a lightheaded rush takes over my senses, the pleasant side effects of my very first kiss.

His fingers cup my chin to bring me back to his gaze.

"So, Natalia, you love birds, you grew up surrounded by nature... what else? I need to know more."

The transition in conversation brings me back down to earth, even though I wouldn't have minded staying on his lips in the clouds.

"I mean, I'm pretty ordinary, or a nerd as you called me before. I love art and poetry."

"You're anything but ordinary. It's a rarity to find girls your age who aren't obsessed with themselves, who refuse to pick up anything but a phone."

He crosses his ankles and readjusts his arms so one tucks behind me.

"I guess it's part of the way I was raised. Olga never prioritized those things for me, and being homeschooled, I didn't really have the social pressure to be online all the time."

"Who's Olga?"

That's normally a question I like to avoid, but I want Gabriel to know more of me, so I explain how Olga found me and how she's taken care of me ever since.

"Do you know if your parents are alive?" he asks.

"I have no clue. I don't even have a memory of them. Are your parents?" I return the question, and he takes a deep breath.

"They're alive, from what I know. I have no idea where they are now, though. All I know is that meth brought them more joy than their only son. I'm really sorry to hear that your parents left you. That's a tough reality to grapple. But in a weird way, I'm sort of envious that you have no memory of them. My last one was from over ten years ago. They had forgotten to take me to school for a week. They locked themselves in their room, and our power had been shut off. CPS busted down our doors. It was the first bit of sunlight I'd seen in days, and it was the last time I would see my parents."

He looks embarrassed to admit it, like I would somehow judge him for his parents' mistakes. I guess I'm not the only one with a complicated family history.

Maybe he's right. Maybe no memory is better than a miserable reality.

"I'm so sorry, Gabriel. I can't even imagine."

"It's okay. It's the life I was given, but I sometimes wonder if it's what's anchored this sadness inside me."

"Would you be willing to explain more?" I question, almost afraid to ask.

He retracts his arm from my waist and his shoulders curl over his chest, protectively.

"I get sad sometimes—really fucking sad. It's as if my mind likes to get really creative on ways to take me out." He looks up and points. "See this tree above us? Most people look at a tree and don't think much, but the first thing I think when I see that branch is 'Oh, what a great place for a noose.'" I can't stop my eyes from widening in shock, and I think he catches on to my stunned reaction. "I'm sorry. I know it's dark, and I know you're not supposed to show your crazy until the sixth or seventh date." He cracks a sarcastic smile.

I understand he's trying to make light of his situation, but this type of depression is no joke. In some cases, if left untreated, it can be devastatingly terminal. Years ago, there was a patient, Marianne, who checked into the same ward as me. We had group therapy together, but she didn't like sharing because she was riddled with these types of self-destructive thoughts. One day, she acted on them and never made it out alive. A morning nurse found her hanging in her room with bedsheets wrapped around her neck. She was only twelve years old. I can't fathom someone so young, with so much life ahead of them, having to deal with such a cruel disorder.

Gabriel breaks up my thoughts when he reaches an arm over my shoulder.

"What's your crazy, Natalia? What could someone as put together as you be doing in a place filled with broken minds?"

"Put together? Ha, you think so highly of me."

"How could I not?" he exclaims.

Gabriel has revealed the most intense parts about himself, and all it did was draw me to him more, making me feel safe enough to expose the fragmented bits about myself that I usually keep hidden.

"My sleep patterns have been a bit unusual my whole life," I confess, though not revealing the full weight of my story.

"Who? The girl who only sees me in the middle of night? Couldn't be," he says sarcastically. "Sorry, continue, please," he apologizes, tucking away his smirk.

What if I tell him and he thinks I'm a nutjob?

It's nail-biting having to admit my issues to someone I'm this attracted to. What if my flaws make him not like me in the ways he just professed?

I can't hide who I really am forever.

As hard as it is to accept, the realization settles over me that I'll never get close to him if I don't share my truth. And he's been brave enough to share his tough past with me; I think I owe him the same.

"My life has been filled with night terrors, some where my physical state has been... *compromised*," I say, trying to find the right words to explain my situation. "I sleepwalk, and in the past, I've hurt myself or others in the process. But I'm completely unaware, and I wake up hating myself when it happens. So, when it gets really bad, the only way I've learned to cope is to not sleep at all. Of course, doctors don't like that, but no one has found a cure for me."

Sharing this with Lindsay and now Gabriel makes it feel like the barrier I've built to protect myself from others' judgment is slowly starting to crumble. As nerve ridden as I am, there's something equally freeing about it all.

He grabs my hand and squeezes it, allowing my breath to release.

"So, that explains your sleep studies."

"Yes."

"How are they going?"

He's taking this all so well, no shocked expressions or timid body language, so I keep explaining.

"They're not going badly. The new medication they have me on seems to help. I sleep through the night whenever I take it, but the sickening side effects almost outweigh a bad dream."

"Whenever you take them? Shouldn't you be taking them regularly?" He looks perplexed.

"Uh, well, yeah. But sometimes I need a break from the violent migraines in the morning, so I just skip the pills once in a while. Don't judge me."

"I didn't know you had this rebellious side to you." He exaggerates a shocked gasp, and I playfully jab his arm.

"Yeah, like I said, don't judge."

"I wouldn't. I couldn't. I've been on medication my whole life, and it's been a constant battle to find one that numbs the sadness but doesn't numb every emotion inside me."

I couldn't say it better myself.

Our life experiences have been so different, yet there's still something so parallel about them.

"I know exactly what you mean," I tell him.

"We're just wounded creatures trying to blend in with the rest." He softly smiles.

He pulls me in closer to him, and my cheek finds his chest. I can hear his quickening heartbeat as I rest against him.

"So, I take it you didn't tell your roommate about our little rendezvous?" he infers while holding me.

"Yeah, no. She just broke up with her boyfriend and was really going through the thick of it tonight."

"That's too bad. But I get it. It's pretty hard to maintain relationships when you're stuck at these kinds of places."

"I wouldn't know. I've actually never been in a relationship," I admit, and he narrows his eyes at me. "I know, I'm weird."

I lower my chin, but he lifts it with his fingers.

"You're not weird at all. You've got this sweet, innocent aura to you, and I think that's something to be proud of."

I push my hair off my shoulder. "Maybe I don't want to be so innocent."

"Well, I can help you with that." Gabriel lifts his brows with a devilish smirk.

"That's not what I meant." I push his arm jokingly.

Typical guy with dirty thoughts.

"I just feel like sometimes there's this darkness inside me that doesn't match who I appear to be. Like, if I'm so pure, then why do I have such terrible night terrors or twisted images in my head?" I confess, because in Gabriel's presence, it's been easy to do so.

He tucks my blowing hair behind my ear and looks at me with tense eyes.

"I think we all have a bit of darkness inside us, and I think it stems from different places for everyone: trauma, pain, anger, abandonment. Darkness comes in many disguises, and no matter how deep you try to bury it, inevitably it'll creep through the cracks."

The gardenia tries to slip into my head, but I shield it from disturbing me. I won't allow the awful flashbacks to ruin this moment.

"But what if you just want the darkness to go away?" I sigh.

Gabriel clasps my fingers in his. "Well, love, I hate to break it to you, but sometimes darkness doesn't go away. It latches on to us, and we just have to learn to live with it, embrace it, or face it head-on."

I know in my heart that he's right. The fact that we can never truly escape the darkness in this world is something I'll never fully comprehend. Why does the human existence have to include so much suffering?

"I don't know where my darkness is even coming from," I admit, frustrated.

"Maybe it's trying to reveal itself to you."

An eternal conflict resides inside me: Part of me is desperate to know why I'm so mentally disturbed, yet the other part is resistant—terrified of the implications my darkness is trying to convey. A lifetime of doctors, pills, sleep studies, and psych wards has been imploring my murky waters to rise to the surface for years. But maybe I've been afraid that if I let them, they might overflow.

We go both silent, but our eyes stay engaged, as if we don't need words to express the similar links our lives have.

Like a magnetic force, his hand takes the back of my neck, and our lips touch. He leans me back on the grass, and the cold blades tickle my legs as his fingers slide into my hair and his tongue traces upward to my earlobe, causing my heart to pound in my chest. He undoes each button on his shirt, and his body is a sight that outdoes the stars. As we each explore the other's revealed skin, his fingertips stop at my collarbones.

My shoulders tense until he lightly kisses the remnants of the tiny cuts made by own fingernails before I came to Awana. He looks back at me questioningly.

"Did these happen in your sleep?"

I nod and bite my lip.

"Don't ever feel ashamed. Scars are just reminders of the toughest battles we've faced and won."

He places his wrist next to the scratches below my neck, now giving our healed slashes a new meaning.

I wrap my arms around his shoulders. Somehow, he's made my shameful wounds feel like a badge of honor. His lips find mine again. I can't keep my hands off his body as curiosity grows inside me. My fingers slide farther down his chest over his smooth stomach until he stops me.

"We gotta slow down," Gabriel warns between quick breaths. He pulls away from me, running his hands through his disheveled hair. "Damn, Natalia, you're going to make me run out of air." Breathless, he starts rebuttoning his shirt.

"Why did you stop?"

"I want to kiss you all night, don't question that. I'm just worried, though." My heart skips, nervous of what he might say, and he continues, "I'm worried about the feelings I have for you. They're getting deep now."

If he only knew how deeply I'm falling for him.

"What's wrong with that?" I ask.

"I have a lot of darkness inside me, and I would hate for any of it to bleed onto you."

Maybe this should scare me, but his vulnerability makes me want to cling to him more.

"You're the one who said you have to embrace darkness. What if I want to embrace yours?"

His tense eyes soften as he lifts the corners of his mouth. "Your heart really shines bright. I hope you know that. I think that light has helped getting out of bed seem worth it. Hell, today was the first in a long time I wore something besides pajamas. I'm not sure if you noticed," he boasts, straightening his collar.

This boy could put on a potato sack, and it would still be catalog worthy.

"I did actually, and you look great," I tell him.

"I didn't want my girlfriend to have to see me in rags once again."

"Girlfriend?"

The word causes my chest to buzz.

"Ah, damn. Yeah, Natalia. You dance in my head every day, and I count every second until I can see you again. I don't want to just see you at night. I want you in the daylight. I want to take you on a real date when I get out of this place. I wasn't expecting to want to experience life the way I want to with you." He shakes his head. "I hope this doesn't make me sound crazier than I already am."

His confession drives one out of me.

"I want to be your girlfriend, Gabriel. I want your darkness and your craziness. I want all the parts that make you, you."

"Then I'm all yours," he whispers in my ear.

Our eyes meet, and this time when we kiss, it's like the two of us are caught in this intense tornado, stirred in excitement and passion, knowing that our hearts officially belong to one another.

An amber glow fills the sky. Time flies in the presence of Gabriel King.

"Shit, we gotta get you back now, love. The sun is going to rise any minute," he says.

I reluctantly agree. I know that I need to get back inside before the sun threatens to cross any more of the horizon. But my room is the last place I want to be right now. There's something addicting about being able to share your deepest secrets and fears with someone else, and to do so without caution.

Gabriel offers me a helping hand up and flicks his lighter open to lead us through the damp grass to the light above my window. Once we arrive, he grabs my waist and brings me against the side of the house. With his arm perched above my head, his lips draw toward mine, and I stand on my toes to reach him more easily. The cool wind hits my skin, but it's his fingertips moving down my arms that gives me goose bumps.

"Until next time, my dream girl."

He brushes his thumb against my bottom lip, then plants his knee in the ground to give me a lift. I step up with my mud-covered foot and pull myself back into the warmth of my bed.

I turn around, and Gabriel points to the stars and presses on his wrist. I nod in agreement and send him off with a blown kiss.

The exhilaration from the night has my mind twirling like a ballerina in a jewelry box. But when my spinning head hits my pillow, the exhaustion sets in. My eyelids close, and my consciousness gives out within minutes.

CHAPTER 10

The two hours of sleep that felt like five seconds is ruined by our alarm. Lindsay sits up first and reaches over to shut it off. Her sleepy eyes dart open when she turns toward me.

"Why are you covered in mud?" she gasps.

What mud?

I look down and see my white nightgown is trashed. I must have been too wrapped up in the smitten tipsiness I feel when I'm around Gabriel to even notice. I have no idea what to say.

"Natalia, were you outside last night? Did you sneak out?"

Lindsay's face lights up, and I'm surprised she's not upset since I'm usually condemned for leaving my bed in the middle of the night.

"I might have," I admit bashfully.

"Oh my God, why?" she asks with eager curiosity.

I try to hold back my smile, but Lindsay catches me.

"Why are you smiling?" She narrows her eyes and then lets out a gasp. "I know that type of smile! Are you sneaking out to see a boy?"

My grin is uncontainable now.

"Natalia! You rebel, you! How the hell did you meet a boy locked in here?"

"Uh, it's kind of an interesting story."

"This is so exciting! You better tell me everything."

She sits on the edge of her bed, staring at me with wide eyes.

This whole spilling-my-secrets thing is becoming easier than I imagined. I suppose I can share one more with Lindsay.

"Fine, but you can't say anything to anyone. If the doctors find out…"

"I wouldn't ever say anything to anyone. I pinkie swear."

She reaches over and sticks out her finger. I've never confided in a friend about boyfriends, probably because in the past I've had neither, but Lindsay's giddiness for me is contagious, and I can't wait to share all the details. My past reservations—not telling her about Gabriel, thinking she might get jealous or upset—were completely foolish. She's only expressing happiness for me.

I curl my finger around hers, committing to my first ever pinkie promise.

"So, who is he? What's his name?" she asks, each word building in excitement.

"His name is Gabriel King, and he's staying in the other house. I heard him outside my window one night, smoking a cigarette, and we just sort of… hit it off."

I'm sure it sounds outlandish, but I'm grateful for the unusual meeting, and all the ones since.

"Gabriel King? Wow! What a name." She narrows her eyes. "Wait, so he's been coming to see you in the middle of the night?"

"Yeah, every night I haven't had a sleep study."

"So *that's* why you haven't been taking your medication! Wow, Natalia, this is cleverer than some shit I'd even think of."

That's a serious compliment coming from Lindsay.

I don't know if I should be, but I'm flattered that I've impressed her.

"And, most importantly, what's he look like?"

"Tall, tan, messy hair, a sweet smile," I tell her, falling into a daydream.

"He sounds hot. So, do you guys just, like, bang under the stars every night or what?"

My face flushes. "No. I mean, we've kissed, but he's a gentleman. We're taking things slow, but he did ask me to be his girlfriend," I confess.

"What? Oh my God!" Lindsay shouts, smacking me with a pillow. "You're over here making forbidden boyfriends. Who would have thought?"

It's relieving to finally be able to release this huge secret I've been keeping in, and Lindsay's ecstatic reaction is more than I could have asked for.

I press my lips together coyly. "I just wish I could see him more."

"Oh no." She shakes her head slowly.

"What?" I ask.

"I can see it in your eyes. You really like this guy."

I suck on my lower lip. She's right. I'm falling for him faster than I can comprehend.

"I mean, so far, things have been really good—like unbelievably good. He's so sweet," I try to convince her.

Lindsay sighs. "I'm not trying to sound jaded, but if a boy is here, it's probably for a reason. I know you have bad dreams or whatever, but you have a pretty damn good head on your shoulders, and I don't need some cigarette-smoking charmer to hurt my girl. Just promise me you won't dive headfirst into this."

I nod. "I'll try not to," I poorly assure her. But I'm worried it may be too late. Both my head and my heart have fallen into the waters of Gabriel King.

Once Lindsay leaves to take a shower, I glance out my window, and though it shows fickle skies that are dark and gray, my spirits are high and bright. I put on my favorite—and only—dress to match my mood.

After breakfast and yoga, everyone is spending their free time lounging inside the living room today. My mood shifts when Dr. Beckham pops in and calls my name, his finger curling in a "come here" motion. I follow him into his office, and my dread builds with each step. I'm starting to realize why Lindsay has always hated sessions. It's practically mandatory torture.

After he closes the door and I sit down, he jumps right in.

"Natalia, Dr. Cassidy informed me about what happened during the guided imagery exercise yesterday. This does bring me concern."

Oh God. What kind of concern?

"I want to know what triggered this attack. Can you explain any of it to me?"

Yes, of course. I know exactly why I broke down like a lunatic in front of every girl here. I have all the answers to everything. In fact, I think I'll give it another try because it was so much fun.

I'm sick of having to explain myself, especially to him. I can feel my built-up annoyance collapsing into anger.

"No, I really can't! And you're the doctor. Shouldn't you know?"

"No need for attitude," he interjects, sternly.

I squeeze my nails into my palm to calm my temper. I know he's just doing his job and is attempting to help me work through my issues, but sometimes I'd rather just push them aside. I know lashing out at him will only provoke him to pry more, so I rein myself in.

"I'm sorry. I just really don't want this to derail my progress. You even said my sleep studies have been going well."

"We need to examine this panic attack separately—" He stops himself, and I hear the sound of loud, blaring music. "Can you hold on just a minute?" He makes his way to the door and then rushes out into the hallway in a flash.

I sneak out the door, following him toward the ruckus in the living room.

Lindsay has her speaker on full blast and is standing on the coffee table. She's rubbing her body up and down provocatively, then pulls up her shirt and swings it around her head.

Cheryl and Kat giggle,

but the laughter is soon silenced when Dr. Beckham cuts the music off abruptly.

"Get down, you whore," Kookie yells, and Lindsay sticks her tongue out at her between two fingers.

"Lindsay, down, now," Dr. Beckham orders sternly with his nostrils flared.

"What?" Lindsay says, batting her eyelashes. "Dr. Beckham, you mad you missed the show? Don't worry, it's just begun."

Oh no, what is she going to do now?

She unclasps the back of her bra, revealing her breasts, causing all the girls to gasp at once. This doesn't stop her, as she carelessly tosses her bra in Dr. Beckham's direction.

"Get it, girl!" Cheryl hollers, laughing.

"Ew, no. She's so desperate for attention," Kookie says snidely.

Cheryl presses her lips shut.

I try to make eye contact with Lindsay, hoping I can convince her to cool it, but she's still dancing as if the coffee table is her private stage.

Dr. Beckham stomps over, yanks a blanket off the sofa, and throws it around her, pulling her down off the table. She lets out aggravated grunts as she repeatedly elbows and kicks him.

What is he trying to do to her?

"Not my problem," Kookie scoffs. Then she, Kat, and Cheryl look away, acting as if nothing is happening.

I can't ignore this. Lindsay may be acting erratically, but I need to make sure Dr. Beckham's not going to hurt her.

"Get off me, you prick!" she screams, but his arms won't release her flailing body.

"Lindsay, don't make a scene. You need to calm down, or I will do what I need to in order to properly make sure you do," he commands, using the blanket to wrap and restrain her now.

After his threat, his force becomes more aggressive, and I'm afraid what he did to her before could happen again. My defenses for Lindsay are starting to rage out of control. If he doesn't let go of her soon, I will make sure he does. I don't care what I have to do. She's not hurting anyone, so he has no right to put such rough hands on her like this.

Suddenly, Lindsay goes quiet as Dr. Beckham whispers something in her ear. All at once, her resisting body falls limp. She's lost all her will to fight against him. I have no idea what he said, or why she stopped, but he releases her. His hand moves to her shoulder as he guides her out of the living room. I quickly peer down the hall and find them walking together into his office before he slams the door.

"And that, ladies and gents, is what happens when you act like a slut," Kookie sneers.

"Shut up! You're not exactly perfect either, Kookie; otherwise, you wouldn't be locked up in here with the rest of us," I yell back and then head out the door to the yard. I know stripping on the table may not have been the best idea, and I'm unsure why Lindsay's acting out like this, but I am sick of Kookie's self-righteous commentary.

Whatever the reason, I hope this doesn't land Lindsay in isolation again.

I guess my session with Dr. Beckham is done for today—not like I care.

After a short, lonely doze by the willow tree, I head back into the house and find dinner is being served. I must have passed out for longer than I thought. Lindsay isn't at dinner, and I have a bad feeling that she might have gotten in big trouble. What if Dr. Beckham decides she's too much? She did tell me that she's been kicked out of places like this before. What if this was the final straw? It can't be. I can't lose her.

Abby sits across from me, pushing her salad around with a fork.

"He's going to hurt you," a low voice grumbles.

It's the same enigmatic voice I heard last time. I look up, and the only person at my table, once again, is Abby. She has her head down and is still scraping her plate.

"Abby, do you have something you want to tell me?" I hear my own agitation. My patience is wearing thin today.

She looks up at me blankly. I'm getting really tired of this whole I-only-keep-to-myself, innocent act this girl is trying to play.

"Don't go silent on me now. If you have something to say, then say it."

She doesn't answer. Her eyes move around the room like she's confused who I'm talking to.

Why is she doing this?

I'm not sure what here intentions are, but I'm onto her now.

"Okay, whatever," I say, pretending to be nonchalant.

Sick of her weird shit, I scoot my chair out and take my plate to the sink.

I head for my room, still irritated by Abby. When I open the door, my mood instantly lightens up. Lindsay is on her bed, bobbing her head to something from her earbuds. I hop on her bed, and she jumps.

"Gonna give me a heart attack," she gasps, pulling out each earbud.

She always plays up the dramatics, but it's such a lifted weight to see her.

"Sorry, I'm just happy you're here and didn't get in trouble."

"What for? Showing Dr. Beckham what he really wants to see? Luckily, Dr. Cassidy didn't find any harm in it. She's on my side and thinks the female body shouldn't be anything to be ashamed of."

Thank God for Dr. Cassidy. I'm beginning to think she's the only levelheaded doctor here.

"Well, I'm glad to hear that."

Lindsay gets up to change into her pajamas, and I stay quiet until Abby's bizarre words at dinner pop into my head.

"He's going to hurt you."

I can't be the only one who's caught her whispering strange, cryptic messages.

"Hey, Lindsay, does Abby ever say weird or random things to you?"

"Nope. The girl is the definition of a mute. Never heard her speak to anyone," she tells me while pulling off her shirt.

I've never encountered a mute at any other wards, but I'm beginning to think Abby's mutism is selective.

"She's spoken to me," I admit.

Lindsay's face appears from the collar of her blouse, and she looks puzzled.

"Really? Are you sure?"

"Yeah. She says vague things that don't make sense."

"Like what?"

"She told me at dinner, 'He's going to hurt you.'"

Her jaw drops. "Ew, what a creep. Well, shit, maybe her treatment is actually working. Or maybe she has a crush on you and is jealous of this Gabriel fellow."

The crush part is probably far-fetched, but I can't stop worrying that she knows more than she should, and that, since she's chatting so much these days, she might be willing to speak up and tell on us.

"But how? There's no way she'd even know about him." I try to rationalize my thoughts out loud.

Lindsay shrugs. "She does have a clear view of your window from hers."

Could all my suspicions of being watched be true?

"But don't let her get to you," she continues. "So, are you seeing him tonight?"

I imagine his striking gold eyes that lure me out of my window and into his arms.

"I'll take that grin as a yes. But are you really going to wear *that*?" She points to my dress.

"Well, I'd wear my nightgown, but it's covered in mud. What's wrong with this?" I glance down at my ankle-length maroon dress.

"I mean, if he's into *The Little House on the Prairie*, then by all means, go for it."

I pout at her rude remark and shake my billowy long sleeves. I don't let it offend me. She's just being her usual self, unable to hold back on what she's thinking.

Grace interrupts us to bring me my pills.

"Anything for me tonight, Gracie?" Lindsay mocks, but the nurse ignores her.

I slip the pills behind my upper lip and sip down the water. Grace leaves, and I spit them out into my hand.

"Only you could get away with that. Everyone here thinks you're such an angel, but I know the truth. You have some horns growing under that halo." Lindsay snickers.

I whip my hair back and forth, shaping my fingers into horns while shaking my hips.

"Such a tease." She laughs. "I have an idea."

She hops up to her dresser, shuffling a few things around, then yanks out a black silky camisole dress. "You need to wear this tonight."

I examine the low-cut, lacy ensemble that looks more like lingerie than something you could wear outside.

"Why do you even have that in here?" I ask, and Lindsay pauses for a moment.

"Don't worry about it. Just try it on."

She tosses me the small piece of black fabric. I do as she says, and when I slip it all the way on, Lindsay lets out a howl.

"Natalia has a body! Like a really nice one."

My face heats up as I walk over to the wall mirror, but what's in the reflection causes my jaw to hit the floor. I've never seen my body this way. The slinky dress hugs each of my curves provocatively. Seeing myself like this makes me a little nervous. I'm not sure if my mentality matches the mature woman staring back, almost as if my sheltered upbringing has stunted these types of notions. But after meeting Gabriel, and growing more intimate with him, there's an anticipation to keep exploring this new territory.

"It's too much," I tell her, trying to cover my exposed body with my hands.

"Not at all. I don't think Gabriel will think so either." She traces her lips with her tongue seductively.

I ignore her, feeling the embarrassment from the sexy article of clothing take over. I reach for the gray hoodie hanging on my bedpost and zip it up.

"Oh, come on!" Lindsay's voice rises in disappointment.

"What? It's cold tonight."

She rolls her eyes. "Let me at least put a little makeup on you," she insists, pulling a sparkly pink bag out from under her bed. "Come on, get over here."

I give in, sitting in front of her on her comforter.

"I've been wanting to do this forever." Carefully, taking her time, she brushes makeup over my eyes and cheeks. "You really don't need much," she says, applying some gloss to my lips.

Once she's done, she sits backs, speechless.

"How does it look?" I nervously ask.

"You're so lovely, Natalia. You're one of the only people I've met whose inner beauty actually matches the outward beauty."

"Um, can I see what it looks like?"

"Oh, right, of course." She hands me a small mirror.

I gaze into it, admiring my rosy cheeks and longer lashes. If there's one thing Lindsay is amazing at, it's her ability to boost one's confidence. I now feel ready to take on the night.

"Thank you. I love it." I hug her, and she holds me tight.

"I'm sure Gabriel will love it too," she says, releasing me. "Well, I'm exhausted. Fighting with Dr. Beckham all day really takes a lot out of a girl."

She climbs under her covers and curls up under the blanket.

"Don't you want to stay up and meet him?"

"Girl, I need my beauty sleep. We can't all be as naturally beautiful as you are when you're running on five minutes of sleep," she laughs, putting in her earbuds. "Have fun, and don't do anything I'd do." She winks before rolling over.

Lindsay is out without minutes. Her loud snore gives her away.

I do wish she'd meet him sometime. It would be nice to have my best friend's approval.

My eyelids are heavy, but I fight the urge to close them. I have my sleep study tomorrow, and a full night's rest sounds all too appealing, but tonight, I'd rather see Gabriel more than anything. To keep myself awake, I play a game where I name as many birds as I can that begin with each letter of the alphabet. I created it at my last ward to distract me from the frightening noises of the girl who would bang her head against the wall we shared.

Apostle, alpine robin, akekeee...

I make it all the way to *woodpecker* before I hear a small tap on my window. I sit up, and Gabriel's face is brightened by his cigarette ember. He's kicking around some dirt with his shoe until he notices me, and his lips move upward.

I crank open my window, and he tosses his cigarette, standing beneath me with open arms. I climb over the ledge before glancing back at Lindsay, whose pillow is covered in drool. In one swoop, I push out of the window, and Gabriel's warm body nestles me. Our lips gently touch, and my legs stay wrapped around his waist. His tongue tastes like ash, but it's something I've gotten used to.

Our lust builds as he pushes me against the wall under the light outside my window, his body keeping mine propped up while his hands cup my face.

"You're stunning," he whispers between exhales.

I'm caught up in desire, but I finally take notice of a white bandage wrapped around his wrist. Sadness dims the flame between us. I set my feet on the ground. The placement of his covered wound is one I've only seen on those who have attempted to take their own lives.

"What happened?" I ask, disheartened.

He follows my eyes to his forearm and tugs his flannel sleeve down.

"It's nothing," he grunts, walking away to light another cigarette.

"That doesn't look like nothing."

He blows out smoke, and his hollowed eyes hold more despair than I've ever seen before. He slumps down with his back against the house.

I need to change my approach.

I slide down next to him, asking him gentler this time, "What happened, Gabriel?"

A cloud from his heavy exhale releases into the air. His melancholy-filled eyes drift away from me, but just when I think he's too reluctant to share, he speaks in a low voice.

"I don't know. I wish I had a clear answer for you. I'm not exactly sure why I get so low in my mind. Maybe it's the shitty weather. It never seems to help my depression. But it was only one cut, and I didn't mean for it to bleed as much as it did."

He tries to act like one cut makes this situation any less severe.

"Why didn't you tell anyone? How did you even find something to do it with?"

What if that one cut went deeper than he intended? What if that one cut had cost him his own life?

I try not to bombard him with all my worried internal questions.

"How do you get away with not taking your pills? Same reason. They don't pay attention here. The only reason my doctors found out was because the cleaning crew found a bloody towel under my bed while I was at dinner."

He's right. Sadly, not just here but in many mental hospitals, especially the overcrowded ones, it's impossible to know every little thing that goes on. But in cases like Gabriel's, I pray he's not overlooked.

"Are you in trouble?" I ask.

"No, but I'm not sure how many months it will cost me in here."

"Why, though, Gabriel? You've been in such a good place every time I've seen you."

I can't help but want more of an explanation from him.

Was there something I could have done to prevent this?

"I don't know why I'd expect you to understand," he says sharply, flicking his cigarette.

"Well, help me to." I grab his hand, careful of the bandage.

He shrugs. "It's hard to explain. It's like there's always a whisper in the back of your head reminding you that the world would be better off without you. Most of the time, you're able to ignore it, but when that nagging noise turns into a raging scream, it becomes hard to not believe it. The physical pain from the blade is the only form of relief I've found that numbs the unbearable self-hatred, and as fucked up as it sounds, it's comforting to know it's a way out if I allow myself to take it that far."

Ugh.

He has no idea how much it hurts to hear this. Losing him is a heart-wrenching thought that I don't even want to have to imagine. I know how terrible my self-loathing can be at times, but it's never gone this far. I want to understand more so I can help him.

Suddenly, his breath becomes unsteady as he covers his face with his shaking hands. He's trying to hide his cries, but the sound of his sorrow is unconcealable. Watching this brilliant boy fall into shambles is killing me. I rest my cheek on his shoulder and try my best to comfort him.

"I wish I could take away all your horrible thoughts, because they are the furthest thing from the truth. But I know what they feel like… to some degree. It's poison in the mind. And it's cruel that it happens to someone as incredible as you. But also, Gabriel, you're the one who taught me about our scars and our battles. You must keep fighting the war in your head. I promise, I'll help you through it as much I possibly can. Just please don't give up now."

His defeated eyes rise to meet mine with a speck of hope. "You have no idea how much strength you just gave me."

A loud rumble strikes the sky, and I jump, latching on to him.

"Just a little thunder, darling. Even the sky has to let out some pain from time to time," he whispers, scooting me closer to him.

We spend the rest of our time in stillness, looking out to the sky as it roars in anger. Our bodies stay tucked in each other's warmth. He goes in for a kiss, but when he does, the sky suddenly opens up, and buckets of rain begin pouring down on us. We both leap to our feet. He tugs his flannel over our heads and steals back the kiss the skies took from us.

"I think we oughta call it a night."

He pulls away with a laugh and guides me to a small awning near my window to shield us. My sweatshirt is heavy and damp. I slide down the zipper to remove it, and my cheeks flush with warmth when I see the forgotten sexy dress clinging to the outline of my body.

Gabriel's mouth partly opens, intrigue widening his eyes.

I quickly zip it back up.

"Yeah, I probably should go," I agree, feeling the embarrassment from my revealing outfit linger. "I won't be able to see you tomorrow, so please take care of yourself."

"I will, don't worry about me. Hopefully this rain will have let up by then," he says, taking off his beanie to shake out his hair.

How could I not worry?

If one day he were to just suddenly disappear, I don't think I'd be able to handle the heartache and grief.

"But before I go, make me one promise, Gabriel." I reach out for his hands.

"Anything," he says, lacing his fingers through mine.

I stand up tall, so our gazes are inches from each other.

"When you feel like you want to cut yourself, or hurt yourself in any way, please just remember that there are people out there who care about you and couldn't bear it if something happened to you… *I* couldn't bear it."

He nods his head, then pulls me in for a tight hug. His lips against my forehead allow me to feel slightly relieved.

We say our goodbyes, and I give him one last kiss before I'm back in my window. Lindsay is still fast asleep, tucked toward her wall. I close the window so the rain will stop trickling in, then take off my wet clothes before sneaking back under my warm blanket.

Tonight, I saw a different side of Gabriel, an up close and unfiltered glimpse into his dark parts. Why are some people born with overwhelming urges to inflict pain onto themselves or to want to end their own existence? It just seems so unfair that someone should have to feel so helpless in life that the only solution is death. It's a burden I can't imagine and wouldn't wish on anyone, not even my worst enemy.

It does scare me, but I'd be a hypocrite to judge anyone who has a mind that's different, or riddled with unexplainable dark holes that we can lose ourselves in.

I'll never stop trying to convince Gabriel of his worth in this world and how much he matters to me. I truly believe that every single person on this earth is here for a reason, no matter who we are, our past, or our fears of the future. Every soul deserves to live. Even in the darkest depths of despair, there's always a sliver of light; we just need to give ourselves the chance to find it.

Ironically, Gabriel, who deems himself unworthy, is my beaming ray. While this illness tries to convince its sufferers differently, he proves that the ones who hold the most darkness can shine the brightest. I just wish he could see all the love and joy that he radiates, or that those with a similar type of sadness would realize they're part of the million candle lights covering the globe, and each time one blows out, the world becomes darker for everyone around them.

The weight of my eyelids takes over my heavy thoughts, and I soon give in to the sleep my body has been begging me for.

CHAPTER 11

A hailstorm falls over me as I'm pinned to the grass below my window. Rainwater flows into my mouth, causing me to gag. The turbulent sky breaks into a hundred starlings, circling above me, waiting to attack their prey—me. In a synchronized swarm, they turn their attention downward and descend. As I lie defenseless, stunned in sheer horror, their wings and beaks slam against me, screeching and clawing as they tear my skin to shreds. I scream as they peck and pull chunks of bloody flesh off my bones.

"Natalia! What's wrong?"

My eyes open to Lindsay standing above me, and when I turn to my window, the aggressive birds are still present, slamming themselves psychotically against the glass, transforming the clear view into a blood-splattered mess.

"The birds! The starlings! They're trying to get me!" I scream, disoriented by the threatening creatures trying to break in.

Please leave me alone. Please leave me alone.

"Natalia, there are no birds! Calm down! Please!" she cries.

I shut my eyes tightly, but tears sneak through. When I reopen them, there's a peaceful window showing the sunny morning sky.

Lindsay is kneeling at my bedside, squeezing my hand.

"Are you all right? Did you have a nightmare?" she asks, panicked.

I nod and wipe the moisture from my cheeks.

"Yeah, but I'm fine," I tell her, although my full-body twitches might say differently.

"Girl, are you sure? You were thrashing around. The same as during the guided imagery."

"I'm fine, I swear. It was just a dream." I try to remain calm to soothe her worried frown.

"Maybe you shouldn't be skipping your pills so much."

As much as I hate to admit it, Lindsay might be right. The frequency of my nightmares is increasing, and they only seem to happen when I'm not on my medication. But there's no way I can just stop not taking them now, especially after seeing the state Gabriel was in last night. As much as I need sleep, the need to see him is far greater.

"Well, I won't be skipping them tonight. I have my sleep study," I assure her.

A medicated good night's rest is probably exactly what I need to alleviate these terrifying dreams. I'll also be refreshed and as good as new for when I see Gabriel again.

"Okay, good. My roommate screaming bloody murder is not how I usually enjoy being woken up." She lets out a light laugh, though I can still see a bit of concern in her eyes.

"I'm sorry. I wish I could stop it."

Dammit. My sadistic dreams aren't only disturbing me.

"Don't worry about it. I'm sorry you had a nightmare. I thought you liked birds, though, but it sounds like they were attacking you or something."

"It's the starling. Ever since I saw it, I can't get it out of my head."

"The bird you were upset about a while ago?"

I nod.

"Well, it's not here, so let's forget about the stupid thing."

After I agree, she offers her palms to help me out of bed. I place my hands in hers, and she lifts me up, supporting me until I'm steady on my feet.

I head for the bathroom. The mirror shows a face of smudged makeup. I scrub at it, but the dark circles don't wash away. The whites of my eyes are covered in tiny veins, a familiar look for me when I previously had bouts of insomnia. I need this study more than anything tonight. Every moment spent with Gabriel is one without sleep. I'm afraid of what might happen if I lose any more.

I'm on edge all day. Every sound causes me to jump. Yoga felt like physical torture, and every surface looks like a comfortable place to rest my head.

After dinner, Dr. Cassidy and Dr. Beckham have a surprise planned for us, and I hope it doesn't involve too much effort. We're taken closer to the doctors' cabins, where a fire is lit with few wooden benches surrounding it. I have to admit, the dimming sun mixed with the smell of burning wood is a nice change of scenery.

Next to the firepit is our surprise: two women and a man, all probably in their twenties. They're dressed in trendy attire with acoustic guitars and a tambourine. Lindsay shrieks, then grabs my hand, brushing past the ED girls and Dr. Beckham. She sits us directly in front of the guy with a beard and a nose piercing as he towers over the lead mic.

Dr. Cassidy gives an introduction.

"Dr. Beckham and I thought you guys could use some entertainment. This is Torn Canvas. They came all the way from

San Francisco to play you a private concert tonight. Now let's give them a round of applause."

Everyone claps, and the guy speaks into his mic.

"I'm Lance, and this is Shana and Bell. Thanks for having us, Awana."

We continue clapping to cheer them on. Lindsay cheers the loudest, and Dr. Beckham's sharp eyes watch her every move. I'm sure he's worried hot male musicians are a trigger for her.

The long-haired blonde girl shakes her tambourine while the other girl strums the guitar. The bearded young man sings into the mic. His voice is serene, and the melody of their songs blends perfectly with the crackling fire. Everyone is swaying to the rhythm except Dr. Beckham, who doesn't look too impressed. He's standing rigid with his arms crossed. Lindsay is the exact opposite, bouncing around like a giddy puppy. I don't have the energy to match her enthusiasm, but I'm enjoying listening.

They play a few more folk-style songs, and it's obvious Lance is taking an interest in Lindsay. They're mere feet apart and keep longingly gazing at each other throughout the entire concert.

Lance speaks into the mic during a song break. "I'm so happy to be playing for you all tonight. I was a patient here two summers ago, and I'm extremely grateful for this place. A special shout-out to Dr. Cassidy."

She blushes and waves.

"This is our last song for the night. Thank you. You guys were a great crowd."

Lindsay howls, and Lance shoots her a grin. The way Lindsay is biting her lip and moving her hips, and the way Lance watches her while he runs his hands through his hair, there's some thick sexual tension going on. I'm sure if we weren't at a mental facility, these two would be getting it on.

Dr. Beckham catches on and forces his way between Lindsay and me, standing firmly at her side, breaking the eye flirting between them. Lindsay goes still, and Lance looks elsewhere in the crowd. Dr. Beckham grips her wrist, and she squirms.

Did someone else catch that?

I look to see if anyone did, but even Dr. Cassidy is enjoying herself in a dancing frenzy and doesn't notice. When I look back, Lindsay's arm is free, but her lively spirit has disappeared. Dr. Beckham has pinned himself to her side like a watchful guard.

The song ends, and everyone cheers. The band members begin packing up their instruments. The music has left an uplifted energy breezing through the wind. The fresh air and impromptu concert seem to have all the girls buzzing in delight—except one. Lindsay uncrosses her arms and throws them to her sides, letting out a frustrated grunt. She's the first to leave, heading back to the house.

Before I can follow her, a deep voice stops me. I turn back and see that it's Lance.

"Hey, do you think you could give your friend this? She left before I got the chance." He hands me a piece of paper with his number and a heart.

"Sure." I smile at the cute gesture, but when I go to grab it, Dr. Beckham snatches it from his hand.

"We appreciate the concert, Lance, and I'm glad to see you're doing well, but this isn't the place for you to catch a date. We strictly separate our female patients from the male patients for this very reason, as you well know, and I don't need you ruining someone's treatment here because you want a groupie," Dr. Beckham says inches from Lance's face.

"Is there a problem here?" Dr. Cassidy intervenes.

"Nope, no problem now. I've taken care of it." Dr. Beckham replaces his scowl with a grin. He steps back as Dr. Cassidy swoops in, gushing to Lance about how great the band was.

"I'll be seeing you in an hour," Dr. Beckham says to me.

I force a weak smile in response.

He walks away to a distant cabin, and I release my breath.

Dr. Beckham is becoming harder to like every time I see him.

I reach our bedroom and find a quiet Lindsay staring blankly at the ceiling with no music or distractions.

"This place fucking sucks," she says in a somber tone.

I plop onto my bed across from her. "I'm sorry. I saw what happened. Can I just mention that I don't like the way Dr. Beckham gets physical with you?"

Lindsay jerks her head up. "What do you mean?" she asks, as if I've caught her by surprise.

"I saw the way he grabbed your wrist at the bonfire."

She slides back down on her bed.

"Yeah, he's a prick," she whispers dismissively, but then her voice rises again. "But he's the doctor who dictates when I'm ready to be let out into the real world, so there's not much I can do." She sighs, tucking her knees up to her chest, distress evident on her face.

I know that pain. I know the feeling of your fate being in the hands of doctors, and sometimes their means of helping you feels more like a violation than anything.

"Well, if it makes you feel better, Lance totally came up to me after the concert and wanted me to give you his number."

Lindsay lifts her head, and her eyes light up. "What, really? Did you get it from him?"

"Almost, but of course, Dr. Beckham didn't let it happen. He reprimanded the poor guy in front of everyone."

"Fucking cockblocker," she huffs.

"Why don't you turn on some music?" I suggest, trying to lighten the mood.

She stretches up to turn on her speaker and plays a hard rock song filled with angst and anger and abrasive power cords, then curls back toward her wall. I don't question her song choice and just lie back, doing my best to not fall asleep.

Grace brings the monitor in, which Dr. Beckham usually does. After handing me my pills, which make their way down my throat this time, she begins to stick on the wires.

"Where's Dr. Beckham?" I ask her.

"He had some things to tend to. He'll be in after you fall asleep to check on things."

Grace leaves after attaching me to the monitor. Lindsay is still facing her wall. I can tell she doesn't want to be bothered, so I let my drowsiness overtake me.

The room gets fuzzier, and everything seems to be slowing down. My lightheaded buzz feels like I'm being rocked to sleep.

I hear a door slam. My body is heavy, and my mouth is too lazy to speak. The lights shut off. My eyes close, and I lose all strength to open them. Hearing is my last sense that hasn't left me.

Footsteps walk over, and a hand touches the wires stuck to my chest. An exchange of mumbled voices forces me to hold on to my last bit of consciousness.

"You said you would leave me alone. You said this was over." I hear the strain in my best friend's tone beside me.

"You can't do those types of things in front of me. It's not good for your treatment." A man speaks.

"My treatment? Or for you? I'm not yours. I'm not your property…"

Lindsay's words become contorted and mix in with the daze of my wavering conscious mind.

Did I just hear that right? I feel so loopy. This must be a dream.

"You're talking nonsense again."

The familiar deep voice of my doctor becomes clear and is the last thing I hear before everything fades.

CHAPTER 12

An intense stabbing between my eyes wakes me. I press my palm to my forehead, trying to soothe the ache. My stomach roars, and in my groggy state, I pull myself up to grab the nausea pills on my bedside to prevent anything in my frenzied gut from coming up. A searing bolt of lightning-like pain strikes my brain as the alarm screams in outrage. I rip the cord out of the wall so the snooze button can't attack me again, then rest my head between my knees as I try to nurse myself.

"You good?" Lindsay checks.

"Just the price I have to pay for a good night's sleep," I grumble and lie back in bed.

"Damn, girl, I'm sorry. Hold on a second, let me grab you something."

She leaves but quickly comes back and presses a cold, wet washcloth against my throbbing head.

"This always helped me when I used to have gnarly hangovers. That's one thing I do not miss about my party days."

She reaches over me to close the curtains, which are letting in the glaring light.

I thank her and sit in the darkness while she gets ready for breakfast. The meds start to kick in; my pain is easing, and I'm beginning to be able to focus. The vague memory of last night comes to mind, including the strange conversation. The intimate nature of their private dialogue is alarming. I force myself up because I need answers.

"Lindsay, what were you and Dr. Beckham talking about last night when he was in our room?"

She stops swirling makeup onto her cheeks and glares at me.

"Nothing. I was pretty much passed out by the time he came in, and I'm pretty sure you were too." Her voice rises callously.

"I don't think so. I swear I heard you two fighting. You were saying something about how it's over and you're not his property," I say, trying to remember the exact words.

"I think you were just having one of your weird dreams." She slams her compact shut. "Well, I'm starving. I'm going to get a head start on breakfast."

The only thing weird here is her disregarding the conversation she was having with Dr. Beckham last night. I'm almost positive of what I heard—almost—and her trying to use my disorder to cover up her lie would be a low blow, but she's fast out the door before I can get another word in.

Having a strange dream is definitely not an uncommon occurrence for me. But one thing I know for certain is when I take this medication, it seems to prevent me from dreaming at all. So I'm not sure why Lindsay would lie to me. Or maybe I've got this all wrong. I was half-asleep and highly medicated, so what if it *was* just some weird side effect? But it felt so real. I hate that I can't completely trust myself to decipher reality.

The door opens, and Dr. Cassidy pops her head in.

"Good morning, Natalia. I have some great news for you. Dr. Beckham and I think it would be a good time in your treatment to have a visitor. Olga will be coming tomorrow, and we can all sit down for a discussion about your progress."

"That's great news," I tell her, because it's what I should say, but it's not my true feelings about the situation.

Dr. Cassidy leaves with a smile.

Normally, I'd be ecstatic to see Olga, but this time, my excitement is dampened, almost like I don't care whether she comes or not, which is the furthest from how I usually feel. I always miss her when I'm gone, sometimes manically. I can remember being little when she'd drop me off at an institution. I'd beg for her not to leave, and when they ripped us apart, I'd cry and panic, sometimes to the point of throwing up. I think it killed her inside, but it was always difficult to tell with her hard exterior. Her toughness began to rub off on me as I got older, though, and that's when I learned how to force myself to be brave.

Awana has been the easiest place to be apart from her. It's also the first time I've made deep connections with people other than her. I'm afraid seeing her would make me fall right back into my deep dependency on her, and I won't be able to focus on anything else but the nauseating homesickness I feel when she visits. I swallow the bittersweet taste on my tongue about Olga's arrival and try my best to be happy about seeing her for the first time in weeks.

Lindsay has been short with me all day, so it makes sense that she didn't show up to our spot during free time. It's frustrating to have your friend act distant with you, especially when you're not exactly sure why.

Is she trying to avoid me so I can't mention the confrontation we had earlier?

It hasn't rained since last night, but the sun is still hiding behind the clouds. The dreary weather doesn't stop me from enjoying the fresh air outside. I lie under the usual tree, picturing a life with Gabriel outside Awana, and realize how desperate I am to experience it. We could go to the movies or on dinner dates like normal couples do. He'd meet Olga, and she'd love him—it's hard not to with his charisma.

"Quit daydreaming, Natalia." The voice kills the romance going on in my head.

I sit up to find Lindsay holding a bouquet of mixed flowers.

"I brought you a gift. All handpicked from our very own garden." She holds them out.

"What for?"

"For being kind of a dick this morning." She takes a seat next to me. "I don't know why I'm being rude to the one person who I actually enjoy in this place. I think I'm just having a bad week, and I could really use you to help cheer me up."

Her ruffled hair and appearance prove she's not feeling her best.

"Thanks, but don't worry about it. We all have our moments," I assure her and give her a gentle squeeze around her shoulders.

My mood shifts, and I change my mind about bringing up the conversation I heard last night. She apologized for acting weird about it, and I don't want to upset her more, as she already seems down in the dumps and is now relying on me to make her feel better.

"So, what's this Gabriel guy like? If he's going to steal my best friend away from her bed at night, I'd like to know a little more about him."

I can't help but pause on Lindsay calling me her best friend. I've considered her mine since shortly after we met, but she doesn't have much competition. Hearing her announce me as hers feels like I've won a huge trophy.

"Well, he's intelligent, handsome…"

"I want the real stuff, not just the pleasant adjectives. Why is he in Awana?"

Her bluntness is something I'll never get used to.

"I mean, that's sort of a difficult question. He's been in foster care his whole life, and I think that's brought on a great deal of depression."

"He's suicidal?" she guessed before I had to say it.

"I'm afraid so."

She blows out a long breath. "Damn, that's a tough demon to battle. But I've been there, and it's not an easy low to climb up from. Do you ever worry?"

Lindsay's never opened up about being suicidal before. She's mentioned overdoses in the past, but it stings wondering if they might have been intentional.

"Worry about what?" I ask her.

"Falling in love with someone who can one day just off themselves without any warning?"

I glare at her. *How can she be so insensitive?*

"He's not going to just off himself. That's a horrible thing to say!"

Her usual inability to bite her tongue isn't cute right now and is starting to tick me off.

"Natalia, I'm not trying to be mean," she says more gently. "It's just a harsh reality you have to face when you fall for someone with that type of flaw."

This is one of those rare times when I feel like I could slap someone. I never would, but my defenses for Gabriel are higher than ever.

"Why are you so damn negative all the time?" I say with a snarl.

A fury rushes to my head, and I throw the flowers on the ground and walk away without another word. How could she say something so wrong on so many levels? For someone who's dealt with her own hardships with mental health, her view on it is insensitive. You should never assume someone will take their own life.

Too annoyed to engage her again, I keep my distance from Lindsay for the rest of the day, and when she comes into our room at night, I turn toward my window with a book. I think she takes the hint, because I soon hear muffled music coming from her side of the room.

When Grace comes in, Lindsay and I finally make eye contact for the first time. After Grace leaves, I spit out my pills. Lindsay rolls her eyes at me and faces her wall like I've done something that's bothered her.

What's her problem?

I'm the only one who has a right to be mad based on her rude comment about Gabriel earlier. I choose to ignore her and try to focus on my book until the time comes to look out my window, but the words on the page blur, and my eyes are irritated and strained. I know my body wants to shut down to revitalize itself, but I can't allow it.

I tiptoe to the bathroom to splash some water on my face, hoping it will help, but the cold rush doesn't hide the fact that I look like a zombie. The shadows under my eyes are only worsening, making it look like I lost a fight, and the skin on my face is translucent and peeling. Gabriel should be here soon, so I don't have time to try and fix my lackluster appearance.

I ditch the mirror for my window, and when I peer out, the adrenaline rush from seeing Gabriel outside with his legs stretched out on the grass instantly wakes me up. He nods and pushes back his hair that's blowing freely.

The chilly air creeps in as I open the window, and I turn back to check on Lindsay. She pulls up her blanket but doesn't open an eye.

Gabriel stands up, walking toward me until he meets my dangling legs. His soft hands slide up my thighs, stopping where my nightgown ends, sending chills farther up. After he helps me down, his hands move to my cheekbones, and he kisses me hard.

"Hello, gorgeous," he greets as he releases me.

"I don't feel gorgeous tonight. I think my sleep deprivation is starting to show," I confess.

"Do you want to do this another night? I'd hate for you to not feel your best because of me."

"No, seeing you has made me feel better already."

I press up onto my toes so I can reach his lips. He kisses me back, and when he pulls away, he grabs my hand, signaling with the other to follow. He stays in the glow of the floodlight on the house, which beams a perfect path through the grass to the river. The sounds of the water strengthen with each step closer to the black trees ahead.

"Ouch!" I call out, the sudden pain making me fall to the ground.

Gabriel drops down to me and brings his lighter out. I check under my heel and see something has cut open my bare foot. Blood pours out of my porcelain flesh, and Gabriel wraps his hand around the gash, trying to contain the dripping.

Once the bleeding lessens, he helps me stand, but the pressure on my foot causes me to cry out again.

"Let me help you." He scoops me into his arms, and I wrap mine around his neck while he carries me the rest of the way.

He brings me through the bulky trees to a clear area of dirt above the river. The light from the main house is faint now, but my eyes soon adjust to the blinding darkness. Gabriel sets me down, removing his flannel to wrap around my shivering arms, and I move between his legs.

"Isn't it beautiful?" he asks, bringing me closer to his chest. "The water makes me miss the coast. The ocean mostly."

"I've never been."

He gasps. "To the ocean? That's a tragedy."

"I mean, I guess. Olga hates the water. Like the way someone hates snakes or spiders. It terrifies her, so I'm just used to living life without it."

"That's really a shame. The ocean waves are my favorite form of therapy. I'd love to take you someday."

"I'd love that too," I murmur, imagining all the places I'd love to explore with him.

Nestling his chin on my shoulder and wrapping his arms tighter around my waist, he talks in my ear, but my eyes can't leave the water. The strange familiarity I felt when I first arrived at Awana returns, overcoming me as the river thrashes violently, sending tree branches rocketing down its powerful stream.

Has Olga somehow passed her phobia on to me?

Fear stabs its daggers into me as my repetitive nightmares become reality. The water below breaks like a dam that has suddenly been let loose, sending a rapid flow of water in our direction. Before I can move a muscle, I'm engulfed in a disastrous flood that is tearing Gabriel and me apart.

A hand grips my convulsing body, pulling me out from the dark waters in my head. I retch and choke, but nothing comes out. My fingers reflexively reach for my throat, and I'm surprised to find that they're dry. I sit up on my elbows and see we're still lying in the dirt above the streaming river, which didn't actually rise up.

I'm no longer struggling to stay afloat in my imagination, but the panic that has enveloped me evolves into an unexplainable sorrow, as if there's something I've left behind, and I need go back to those terrifying waters to find it.

I remove my laser focus from the river to find Gabriel next to me, eyes struck with horror.

"Natalia, what's wrong? You're scaring me!"

I can't answer. My confusion and inability to figure what just happened migrates into sharp, hyperventilating gasps.

"Breathe, Natalia! Breathe!" he calls out.

I blow out slow, orchestrated breaths like Dr. Cassidy taught me, and the disarray slowly dissolves.

Once I gain control of my body and surroundings, I turn to Gabriel for answers.

"What happened?" I ask, fearful of what he saw.

"My God, you tell me. I think you had some sort of attack. You completely left me, you went limp, and your eyes were vacant. Your body started shaking out of control. I thought I was going to have to get help."

I'm mortified that I completely freaked out in front of the boy I adore. My shame leaves me without words. I know what happened. This is a repeat of the garden exercise—the shortness of breath and the all-consuming fear both mirror the same type of episode.

"Are these the bad images you told me about, the darkness that worries you?" Gabriel asks, tucking himself closer to me.

I slowly nod. I can't rid myself of the fact that my panic attacks and dreams all have a worrisome similarity. Why do dangerous waters keep haunting my mind to the point that my body is physically reacting?

He brings his hand behind my head, pulling me toward me his lips so he can kiss and comfort me.

"You don't need to be afraid as long as I'm here. I'll never let anything bad happen to you," he whispers in my ear. His words bring me safety and peace, the way he always makes me feel whenever he's near.

He dusts off the dirt that managed to get all over my legs.

"I'm sorry I'm like this," I say in a low tone.

"You don't need to apologize."

"There's just something about the river…"

How can a place I've haven't been until now seem so familiar? It doesn't make sense.

The rough, choppy waves breaking against the bank make my neck hairs stand like nails screeching down a chalkboard.

I turn my head, trying to avoid the water in my peripheral vision, because staring at it too long seems to have determinantal effects on me that I can't get a grip on.

"You don't have to explain if you don't want to."

"Actually, I wish I *could* explain, but it seems to be something I haven't figured out myself."

"We don't have to stay here. Come on, let's go back," he suggests.

My nervous lips move up into a comforted smile as he scoops me up. I close my eyes and rest against his chest. His beating heart matches the rhythm of his legs as they carry me through the field. His gentleness could rock me to sleep if I allowed it.

When we come to a stop, we're back by my window.

"I don't want the night to end yet," I tell him when he sets me down.

"It's been a bit of a rough night for you. Maybe you need some rest," he says, glancing at my foot.

"It doesn't hurt anymore. I'm fine."

He sighs and rakes his fingers through his hair.

"Natalia, I think you may need rest for other reasons. I'm worried that keeping you out at night might not be the best thing for you right now." His eyes still carry the worry in them from the incident by the riverbank.

"That's not true," I retort, raising my voice.

I know he might have a fair point, but what he doesn't realize is seeing him feels better than sleep or any medication.

He's becoming the only cure to all my madness.

He covers my mouth with his finger and kisses my cheek.

"Babe, you need to get some rest. Maybe let's take some time until you feel better."

Is he actually suggesting time apart? Why? Is he afraid me of me now? Did my stupid psychotic episode freak him out?

I try to rationalize with him. "I feel fine. What do you mean? Do you not want to see me anymore? It was just a little panic attack—nothing to even think twice about."

He quiets me with his lips, but I pull away.

"I just want you to be as healthy as you can be," he explains. "Let's take the rest of the week off. That way you can get some good rest. I promise I'll be here at the same time next week, okay?"

There's no point in trying to argue with him. He's made up his mind, and I feel defeated. He wants a break from me, and it's a terrible truth to face.

His eyes soothe me as they look down into mine, and as much as I hate the idea, it doesn't seem like I'm left with a choice.

"Fine," I give in, even if it's the last thing I want to do, lifting my head to kiss him good night.

He offers to help me through my window, but I refuse it, using all the strength in my arms to lift me in. Once I'm on my bed, the frustration builds. I lie down, not saying a final goodbye to him because I'm too hurt by his decision, but before my eyes close, my heart pulls me back up for one last look. My aching chest takes another blow when all I see is empty grass where he'd been standing only a moment ago.

Today has been undeniably awful. My best friend and I had our first fight. Now, my boyfriend has cast me away because of my mental state, which triggers the relentless worry that no one will ever want to get close to me because of my screwed-up head. I don't know what I'll do if he doesn't show up in a week like he promised. My hope in everyone is wearing thin, and that's a miserable feeling to have to fall asleep with.

CHAPTER 13

As much as my body desperately needed sleep last night, my brain decided to sabotage me. My thoughts wouldn't shut off: I was weighed down by the anticipation of seeing Olga, the worry that Gabriel saw a side of me that scared him off, and Lindsay and Dr. Beckham's strange behavior that she wrote off as a delusion.

What if it was *a delusion? What is happening to me? I'm not sleeping. My nightmares and panic attacks are getting worse. Is this all proving that I'm just a delusional, sleepless wreck?*

My deepest fear has always been to lose control of mind, and I'm worried it's slipping away from me now.

Lindsay stretches up when the alarm rings.

"What are you doing?" she asks between yawns.

I take the skin of my thumb out of my mouth to answer and notice my nail beds are sore and raw.

"I couldn't sleep," I answer. Even though I'm still a little mad at her, I could use her as a distraction.

"Your eyes look shot. Did you see him last night?"

"Yes."

"He's the one keeping you awake. Did you ever think of that?" she says condescendingly.

"Well, I'm sure you'd love to hear that he doesn't want to see me for a week now, and I'm worried 'a week' really meant 'never again.'" I try to fire back some sass, but the reality of my words ends up only hurting myself. "I think I messed up." I drop my chin to my chest.

"What happened?" Her voice softens. "Did you get into a fight?"

"No, not really. I think there's just something wrong with me," I confess with heavy conviction.

Lindsay sits up all the way and narrows her eyes on me. "Natalia, there's nothing wrong with you. If he doesn't want to see you, then there's something wrong with *him*. Don't ever let a man make you feel inferior. It's not a healthy place to be. Trust me."

I shrug. Though her words were nice, they don't make me feel any better.

She lets out a light sigh. "Cheer up, babe. I don't like seeing you like this. I'm sorry if what I said yesterday put a damper on anything."

Her sympathy and apology both seem sincere.

"I really do appreciate that. I'll be better later. Olga is coming to visit me today."

"Lucky! I don't think I'll be able to see anyone I know until I leave this place. 'Troublemakers don't get rewards,' as Dr. Beckham says," she says in a low voice, imitating him, and my lips curl up. "So, we're good?"

"Yeah, we're good."

She jumps out of bed and holds me, and I think I need it, because her embrace eases my stressed state.

"You only deserve the best," she whispers in my ear before pulling away.

I hoped the day would get better knowing Olga will be here soon, but my gloominess won't leave me. I'm headed to meet Dr. Beckham now so when Olga arrives, the three of us can have a meeting. His door is open, and when I walk in, his cologne makes me want to gag.

"Good afternoon, Natalia. I'm sure today is an exciting one for you."

It would be if I didn't feel like garbage.

I make a poor attempt at a smile and take a seat, trying to conceal the fact that I'm sleep-deprived and having the worst day I've ever had at Awana.

The door opens, and Dr. Cassidy walks in with the announcement that someone is here to see me.

When petite Olga appears behind Dr. Cassidy's curves, the nostalgia hits. Olga runs to me, wrapping her arms around me tightly. I nestle myself into her, taking in her scent. She smells like the only home I've ever known, and it causes my eyes to water.

She grabs the sides of my face and wipes the tear that's slipped.

"I hope those are happy tears," she murmurs. Soft wrinkles surround her luminous eyes.

I'm not sure what prompted my tearful reaction. It's probably because I've missed her. But in a way, being in her presence hurts. She knows all of my terrible flaws, and even if she doesn't mean to be, she's a reminder of them.

Before I get in a word, she gasps.

"Your hair! It's shorter."

"Yes. Please don't be mad," I say.

Oh no. She's going to think I purposely cut it behind her back and be pissed.

Our hair is no longer the same length. In many ways, I think Olga likes us to be alike. She wants me to follow in every one of her footsteps, and I usually do, but here at Awana, I'm finding myself wandering further from her carefully planned path more than ever.

"I'm not mad. I just didn't know haircuts were an added service here."

Her response surprises me. She's way more relaxed about my new look than I expected her to be. I'm grateful it didn't throw her into an uproar.

"They aren't," Dr. Beckham adds. "Natalia's lucked out that her roommate is an aspiring cosmetologist."

"Ah, I see. Well, she should stick with it. It suits her."

Olga flips my hair over my shoulders, and I'm relieved by her acceptance.

"Please have a seat, Ms. Sokolov. Or is it Mrs.?" Dr. Beckham grins, pulling out a chair for her.

Is he really trying to flirt with Olga right now?

"Ms. But I don't think my title is the topic of concern right now." Olga shoots him down, and I'm not surprised. She gets hit on all the time, and I don't think men realize it only makes her resent their gender more.

Dr. Beckham clears his throat before sitting back down and shuffling through his notes.

"Natalia has been showing great improvement. She hasn't shown any signs of severe parasomnia while being here, only mild nightmares, which we have kept a close eye on. But the majority of her days here have been good."

"Is that true?" Olga's eyes fill with hope.

"Yes," I reply timidly.

I know it's not entirely true, but for once, I just want to give her the answer she's always wanted to hear. Plus, I can't mention my triggering episode at the river last night in front of Dr. Beckham without exposing my unmedicated late nights with Gabriel.

"I think the medication we have her on and our daily therapeutic routines attribute to it. Both will allow Natalia to lead a normal life outside Awana, hopefully for a very long time."

"This is wonderful news," Olga exclaims, but the thought of being on that medication for the rest of my life forces me to break her enthusiasm.

"Yeah, it all sounds great, but you haven't brought up the fact that those pills make me horribly sick every morning. Dr. Beckham, I thought you said we could explore another option."

He reads through his papers and lifts his head with a pensive look.

"Hmm, I know you've reported nausea and headaches when you first started the medication, but I also have it noted that you said you've been feeling better. Has this changed?"

Oh shit.

Without realizing what I was saying, I almost outed myself. I don't need to give Dr. Beckham any more hints to why my side effects may be fluctuating.

"I mean, it comes and goes, I guess," I reply casually, knowing the real reason it goes away.

"Exploring another medication would require more tests and more time."

"Natalia, sometimes we have to make sacrifices," Olga chimes in. "An upset stomach sounds like a small price to pay for a life free of worry for both of us."

She has no idea what it feels like to wake up bedridden and be violently ill as often as I've been here. I hate how easily she can disregard the quality of my life.

"Both of us?" I ask.

"Yes, both of us. Every night I worry about this strange disease that could accidentally cause you to kill yourself in some sort of sleep trance. If this medication is going to cure you, then you better take it."

Her response shoots down any defense I could have. She's right. Olga has spent her most her life worrying for me, and if I can do something to change that, then I have to, not only for my benefit but hers as well.

"Well, this medication isn't a cure-all. Since she still has had some nightmares and one panic attack, we would like Natalia to attend therapy outside Awana," Dr. Beckham states.

More therapy? How shocking, Doctor.

You'd think the last decade of therapy might have something to show for itself, but here I am, still dealing with the same problems I've always had.

"Panic attack?" Olga interjects, clearly unsettled.

"It was hardly that," I'm quick to assure her.

I do not need to give her any reason to doubt that I'm not well enough to come home.

"It's not uncommon for patients to have panic attacks while under our care. It can be good to confront deep-rooted emotions," Dr. Beckham speaks up, and I'm thankful that he seems to have my back. "Which brings me to another recommendation for Natalia. Pinpointing parasomnias is a tough surface to scratch in the small amount of time she's been with us. Since the first few years of her life are unknown, I suggest we spend some of her treatment here in hypnotherapy to figure them out. Dr. Cassidy is masterfully trained in hypnosis. The first few years of one's life are crucial in mental development. It could help dig into some of her unknown memories before she was in your care."

I've never been hypnotized, but it seems that a part of my mind is hiding itself from me. What if he's onto something here? Could hypnosis be the answer to shedding light on the shadows?

"Absolutely not." Olga's quick response catches me off guard. "I know you guys are a new-age facility, but there are good reasons why I've only placed her in medical settings before. They stick with science and facts. They don't dangle watches in front of her eyes. I don't need any of that experimental crap messing up her head even more."

"Hey!" I yell at her insult.

For someone who has been willing to try extensive and, at times, traumatizing measures to control my illness, it's confusing why she'd hastily write this one off.

"Sorry, Natalia. That came out wrong." She squeezes her eyes shut for a moment, and when she opens them, her attitude changes. "Just agree to take the medication. Please. So we can get you out of this place and back home where you belong." It's clear in Olga's voice that she's fighting back pain, and it forces me to agree.

"I'll take the medication and continue therapy after this," I announce in a monotone.

Once again, Olga wins, and I'm left apathetically complacent.

"There you have it, Doctor. So, when is her discharge date?" she asks.

Dr. Beckham looks stunned at Olga's tenacity but quickly hides his expression. "I'd say three weeks, as long as her nightmares don't escalate and we have no hiccups during her sleep studies."

I perk up. The words *three weeks* have bells ringing in my head. The light is finally shining at the end of the tunnel.

"I don't see why there would be. You said yourself that she's doing great." Olga picks back up her defensive attitude toward him once again. She lifts her left hand and admires what looks like a fresh coat of nail polish, clearly sending him a message that she's uninterested in anything else he has to say.

"This is true. She's very well behaved and hasn't caused any trouble during her stay here," he says, staring at me intently.

Ew.

I don't like the way his tongue subtly moistened his lower lip, all without breaking eye contact. Either that was creepy, or someone should seriously get this man some Chapstick.

Olga finally lifts her head and scrunches her nose.

"Are you describing a dog or a patient?" she says in jest, but Dr. Beckham doesn't return a laugh. She continues, "Since we've all agreed on Natalia s outpatient treatment and discharge date, is there anything else we need to go over?"

This is one of the few moments that I appreciate Olga's ability to command a room and anyone in it. Dr. Beckham loves to hand out his own demands, and it's about time someone dishes one or two back to him.

"Nothing else for now."

"Great! Now, can I get some alone time with her? I haven't seen her in weeks and would love some privacy."

"Oh, uh, sure. Of course," Dr. Beckham says, then stands up, offering a hand for Olga to shake, but she turns her nose up at his gesture. "I'll leave you two to it, then." He tries to slyly slide his denied hand back into his pocket, and when he turns around, he knocks right into his chair, causing him to trip. He quickly leaves without another word.

Ha! Well played, Olga. That was fun to watch.

She chuckles, then rolls closer to me and holds my hand. "The girls at the studio miss you. I miss you. Every bird that flies in the sky reminds me of you." Olga pushes the hair out of my face. "What's wrong? You look tired. Have you been getting good rest here?"

"Yes, I'm completely fine," I lie.

I can't tell her that the real reason why I'm tired is because I've been sneaking out at night to see a boy, or that my nightmares are more haunting than they've ever been in my life.

We make small talk about Awana's impressive meals and my newfound yoga hobby, but our conversation feels forced and contrived. Soon enough, Olga checks her watch and decides it's time for her to go.

We hug and say our goodbyes, but her leaving doesn't prompt the usual response from me. I'm not left with the empty feeling I usually have every time she does, or the fear of her not wanting to deal with me anymore. Maybe we're growing apart, or maybe I don't need to rely on her as desperately as I once did. Either way, things are changing between Olga and me, and I'm not sure how to feel about it yet.

CHAPTER 14

I have two weeks left at Awana, but the last week felt like a month. I've been taking my medication every night since Gabriel insisted we take a break from each other. My body aches from the side effects as usual, but the thought of seeing him tomorrow makes getting out of bed a little easier today. The nights spent without him made the days mundane with little to look forward to. At least I had Lindsay, but as much as I appreciate her, she doesn't quite satisfy my craving for his company.

The sun is bright, and the warm air means summer is near. The sunny season is my favorite, even if my skin tone might say different. Though, the glowing daylight isn't why I love this season. It's the warm nights that allow for great stargazing and a comfortable temperature for my late-night walks when I've had my bouts of insomnia or, in the worst case, when I've woken up outside. Sometimes I try to picture my complicated relationship with the night not as a mental flaw but more of being wired differently, nocturnal, like an owl or a nighthawk. Maybe I'm just meant to experience the world after midnight.

Yoga in the rising heat today had everyone in a sweat. Lindsay and I head back to the room before our usual cloud watching to change into something cooler. I slip into my *Little House on the Prairie* dress while Lindsay opts for something a bit more revealing—a white halter dress that makes her skin and blue hair stand out strikingly.

As I meticulously rub sunscreen over my body, Lindsay spreads some olive oil she stole from the pantry over hers. We both slide on sandals and head to our sunbathing tree, spreading out our bathroom towels on the grass to lie on. Days like today, I like to pretend Lindsay and I aren't where we really are. Instead, we're just two friends on a beach vacation or at a summer camp— both things I've never experienced.

I've never been on vacation. Olga's attitude about it has never been pleasant, almost like we don't deserve one. Whenever I've asked her about going somewhere new for leisure or to explore, she's always told me, "From where we escaped, our life now is a vacation."

I'm sure she's right, in a way, but I've also wondered if she's just afraid. I may not know the exact details of her life in Russia, but whatever happened caused her to seek safety somewhere extremely remote. I don't think it's the traveling that terrifies her but more who will be at the destinations. In her mind, strangers are unpredictable, and that's where the fear really lies.

A car engine disturbs my daydreams of being on a Caribbean beach. A shiny, new black minivan heads up the dirt driveway. A slender woman in her thirties with perfectly curled hair hops out as she pulls on her modest linen dress. When she opens the back door, two blond preteen boys slide out with tablets in their hands.

Dr. Beckham walks out from the front door of Awana and greets the family with kisses. I jab Lindsay to watch, and when she takes off her sunglasses to look, she rolls her eyes.

"Oh, how sweet. A family reunion," she says sarcastically.

She sticks her finger in her mouth and gags then turns over to tan her backside.

The wife looks over at us. Lindsay raises her torso and waves. She unties her halter top, slowly moving it down, stopping right before her breasts would be exposed, causing the boys to lift from their screens and gawk. The wife loosely waves back, and her nose wrinkles as if she caught a whiff of something bad. Dr. Beckham shoots us a stern scowl. After he pushes the boys into the back seat, he hops into the car, and they all drive off.

"Wait, my sleep study is tonight. Is he going to be coming back?"

"Don't you worry. His family trips only last a few hours. It's kind of sad to me actually. I don't understand how you can have a family you only see a few times a month."

"Yeah, that's weird. Makes you wonder why someone married with kids would choose to live here full-time. Maybe the pay is good?"

She flares her nostrils. "Yeah, or you just shouldn't have a family if you're never going to be around."

Lindsay pushes herself up abruptly, scanning Awana's yard. She stands up, grabbing my hand to help lift me.

"Come on. Follow me. Quick."

"Where are we going?"

She doesn't answer me, but I follow her behind the main building, past the firepit where four cabins sit. She walks closer toward the off-limits area, but I stop behind her.

"Lindsay, I don't think we're supposed to be back here," I call out.

"Oh please. You break the rules for Gabriel every night, but you won't trust your best friend?" she says, clearly trying to guilt me into submission, and it works. I look around, but no one is in sight, so I cautiously proceed after her.

She beelines to the farthest cabin on the left, and I'm forced to chase after her. Once we make it to the quaint wooden bungalow, she jiggles the doorknob and groans when it doesn't open. A cracked window catches my eye, and I know I should ignore it, but instead, I tap Lindsay's shoulder to show her what I've found.

"What's up with you and windows?" she snickers, then reaches in and cranks the window open. "Help me up," she commands, and I bring my hands to my knee, hoisting her up the way Gabriel does with me.

Once she's inside, she opens the front door to let me in. I take one last glance back at Awana's main campus, but Lindsay pulls me forward, into the cabin.

The small two-bedroom cabin is nicely decorated with leather furnishings and green indoor plants. Lindsay sits on the sofa and turns on the TV as if she lives here.

"What is this place? Is this where you stayed when you were in isolation?" I ask.

"No, this is Dr. Beckham's cabin. I stayed in Dr. Cassidy's, but you'd think it was his by how often he checked on me."

How does she know her way around this place?

"Have you been in here before?"

"Once." She quickly changes the subject by jumping up and heading to the small kitchenette, opening the fridge.

"Lindsay, we should go," I suggest nervously.

"Come on. Live a little." She pulls out two glass beer bottles and searches the kitchen drawers until she shouts, "Aha!" and holds up a bottle opener. She cracks off the top and takes a long sip. "God, that's refreshing."

"Lindsay!"

She wipes her mouth and tries to hand me the other bottle, but I refuse.

"No way. Won't he notice?"

She opens the fridge to show me it's filled with beer bottles. Then she opens a cabinet next to the fridge and reveals various half-empty liquor bottles.

"He doesn't keep track. A little secret about Dr. Beckham: he loves his liquor. I've smelled alcohol on his breath more than once."

Has Lindsay drunk from his stash before? She does have a way of getting her hands on things she's not supposed to. It's a sizable collection of hard alcohol, bottles of all shapes and sizes filled with clear and amber liquids. Maybe Dr. Beckham has a drinking problem. That would explain his off-putting nature.

"One beer isn't going to kill me. Come on, have one with me. Just one and then we'll leave."

"Lindsay!"

Does she not realize stealing booze and risking our asses is not my idea of fun?

"Natalia!" she imitates my voice. "You're twenty-one! It's time to act like it and live a little." She takes a long chug.

I should ignore her, but her taunting remark gets to me. She's right. Maybe sneaking a beer is exactly what someone my age would do. I snatch the bottle from her and take a sip. The cold carbonation hits my tongue and tastes like stale bread.

People drink this gross shit purposely?

"There! Are you happy?" I say once I swallow.

"See? That wasn't so hard, and you weren't struck down by lightning either."

I roll my eyes at her. This is the first time alcohol has ever touched my lips. Olga doesn't drink, and I just assumed I never would either because she didn't. Not that I'm ready to become a lush, but I'm beginning to realize there are a lot of things in this world I'd like to experience, even if it might displease her.

Lindsay taps our bottles together, and the desire to explore this foreign drink brings it back to my mouth.

After a few more sips, I'm taken aback by a bright flash.

"Say cheese!" Lindsay giggles, ripping a photo from a vintage camera. As she shakes it, I snatch it from her.

"Give me that. This is how we'll get caught," I scold her, and she sticks her tongue out at me.

I pour water on the photograph and crumple it so it'll fit in my pocket.

We head for the sofa and turn the TV to a black-and-white movie.

"I love this movie!" I cheer.

"What is it?"

I scoff. "Are you kidding me? *Breakfast at Tiffany's*. A classic romance!"

My body melts into the couch, and my eyes stay glued to the screen.

Before I know it, I've finished my stale-bread beer and have lost time in the movie. I notice Lindsay isn't next to me anymore. I look to the fridge, and there she is with her lips wrapped around the top of a bottle, the dark golden liquid quickly disappearing into her mouth.

"Lindsay! Stop!"

I hop up and have to physically rip the bottle from her. The alcohol spills onto my hands and smells like gasoline.

"Lindsay, how much did you drink? This smells strong," I say, putting the bottle's mouth up to my nose.

"It's just a little bourbon, baby doll." Her voice is higher than before, and she lets out a loud hiccup. Her eyes are fighting to stay open as she struggles to stand straight.

"We should get back."

"No, let's stay! Let's have a dance party!" she yells, twirling around until she trips, falling to the floor in laughter.

"Lindsay, please come on!"

Why did I possibly think it was okay to let an addict have "one drink"? I have no idea how long we've been in here. Dr. Beckham will probably show up any minute. We'll both get caught and banished into isolation. I do not need any more reasons to not see Gabriel right now.

Lindsay stays on her back, rolling back and forth on the floor, loudly singing a horrible attempt at "Old MacDonald."

How on earth am I going to get this grown girl who is now acting like a giggling toddler out of here?

I grab her hands and struggle to pull her up as she wraps her arms around me, almost knocking me down.

"Are you wasted?"

"Nah, just feeling good!" But her slurred voice further confirms it.

"We can't let anyone see you."

"Fuck 'em all." She lifts her middle finger in the air.

I make her sit on the couch while I clean up the mess.

"Sit here. Do not move! I'm cleaning everything up so Dr. Beckham won't know we were here, and then we're getting out of here and never coming back!"

I clean the spilled liquor and discard the beer bottles, shoving them to the bottom of the garbage can where he won't see them.

Then I straighten the pillows on the sofa and turn off the TV. I peer out the window, and once it's clear, I wrap Lindsay's arm around my shoulders since she now can't walk on her own.

"One foot at a time, left, then right. You got this." I carefully instruct Lindsay and her wobbly legs out of the cabin.

Somehow, Lindsay manages to escape my grip, and half-assed cartwheels become her choice of transportation through the field back to the house. I chase after her and grab her before she has a chance to dive into the hard dirt and snap her neck.

"Please, just follow me," I say, lifting her up again.

Finally, she listens, and I gain enough control of my friend, who's wiggling around like an intoxicated jellyfish, to lead her toward our room.

As we get closer, I see Kookie and the ED girls bunched together on the grass. I dodge them by walking around the other side of the house to our window that I thankfully left open to air out our room from Lindsay's hair bleaching that she did earlier that day. It isn't easy, but I push her helpless deadweight up through our window and then pull myself in after her.

She plops onto my bed, her eyes drifting off. This is my first time dealing with a drunk, but from what I've seen on TV, hydration is key. I grab a glass from the bathroom and fill it with water. When I get back, she's attempting to rip her dress over her head, but her arms are tangled in the fabric.

"Whoa, Lindsay. Leave your clothes on, please!"

With one eye shut, she sways back and forth, trying to free herself from what looks like a self-imposed straitjacket.

"Are you ready for me, Bennett?" she slurs, running her fingers through her hair as she arches her back and moans.

"What?"

She lies down and rubs her curves.

"I've been a good girl. I promise," she says, sticking her chest out.

Okay, so the booze has clearly brought out her sexual side.

"Lindsay, snap out of it."

I rush toward her to hand her the water. I press it to her lips, but she shoves me away, and it spills over both of us.

"Get the fuck off me, you fucking creep!" she yells and tries knocking the glass out of my hand. Her glossed-over eyes grow wide with panic. "Don't fucking touch me," she screams as she aggressively rips at her hair.

I grip her shoulders, trying to snap her out of her rage. She thumps down to the floor onto her knees, disheveled and dazed.

"Lindsay, it's just me. Please, keep it down. I don't want you to get in trouble."

She quiets down, and when she focuses on me, it's like she slips back into reality. Her strained eyes soften. After I help her back up to my bed, she tucks into me with whimpers, and her body starts to relax. I rub her head while she cuddles up in my lap. Her tears don't end until she slowly falls asleep.

I have no idea what just happened. Lindsay quickly went from a mumbling drunk to a seductress, then morphed into someone who seemed petrified. As much as I hate to leave her like this, I think rest is the best thing for her right now.

I leave Lindsay in my bed and head to the living room until dinner. All the other girls are outside enjoying the last bit of free time in the sun, and the quiet room is the exact solace I need after dealing with Lindsay's antics. I'm concerned about her drinking. Dr. Cassidy did explicitly tell me to report any unusual behavior, and I'm sure this more than counts. But I can't betray her like that.

If there's one thing I know about friendship, betrayal is the fastest way to ruin one. It's almost like she had an episode like one of mine, but hers was probably exaggerated by the alcohol. All I know is whenever I've had a panic attack, Lindsay has always been there, judgment free, so I should do the same for her. I just wish I hadn't been the idiot to enable her. I've always known about her alcohol issues, and I let them fly out the window because I wanted to try a stupid beer and have a little fun.

To stop myself from overanalyzing Lindsay and to pass the time until the same place and stars, I decide to choose another book from the shelf. A small paperback with a shirtless guy on the cover, biting his lip above glistening abs, catches my attention. *Seduction in Seattle.* Maybe it's the long-awaited anticipation of seeing Gabriel tonight, but a little romance is exactly what I need. I sprawl on the couch and am quickly immersed in the story.

I've never heard so many different ways to describe the private parts of a male. The erotic read seems a little out of place for a treatment center for those who struggle with sexual addiction. As much as I'd love to stay and read the predictable ending, dinner is soon, and I better check on Lindsay. Unable to find the motivation to peel myself off the couch yet, though, I hear two voices come through the front door. Dr. Cassidy walks in first.

"I told you, Bennett, the girls' moods instantly improve with the sun."

Right behind her, Dr. Beckham walks in and closes the door behind him.

"What? Like a bunch of flowers, all they need is water and sun?" His laugh jars me and causes my stomach to flinch like someone knocked the wind out of me.

Dr. Cassidy just called him Bennett. Was Lindsay referring to Dr. Beckman when she was undressing herself? It can't be a coincidence.

The pieces fit all too well together. A horrible feeling hits my gut like I just swallowed a rock.

They both go quiet when they spot me and stop walking when they pass the sofa.

"Oh, hi, Natalia. Why are you cooped up inside? The weather is spectacular outside," Dr. Cassidy asks.

"My shoulders were starting to burn," I quickly come up with a lie.

"I'll go tell Grace to bring you some aloe with your medication tonight."

"That would be nice. Thanks."

Dr. Cassidy heads down the hallway, but Dr. Beckham stays hovered over me with his arms crossed behind his back.

Does he always have to awkwardly linger?

"Where's your partner in crime?" he asks.

"Uh, just changing before dinner," I lie again.

"Very well. I'll be seeing you both tonight. Don't forget, you have the sleep study this evening."

I stretch my lips in a fake smile until he walks away.

When Dr. Beckham is gone, I'm reminded of the altercation between him and Lindsay when I was falling asleep during my last sleep study. The exact words are cloudy, but the emotion was clear. The angst Lindsay had toward him was undeniable. Almost like the way you'd act toward an ex-lover. All the strange little moments between them I disregarded before are now clues compiling a sinister story that I can't let go of and don't know how to wrap my head around.

Could there really be something romantic between them? If so, Lindsay has done a damn good job at hiding it from me. But I won't allow her to anymore. If there's the chance that Dr. Beckham is not the trusted doctor he's supposed to be, then I'll be devasted, not just for me but for Lindsay and every girl here. How could he possibly engage in any type of relationship with her beyond the professional one that's required of him?

My face is burning with growing aggravation, and I don't think I'll be able to cool off until I find out the truth.

Tonight, I have to get to the bottom of this. I need to find out if Dr. Beckham is the creep Lindsay mentioned while in her drunken haze, and if he is, I won't allow either of

them to keep this hidden any longer.

CHAPTER 15

Lindsay slept through dinner, but thankfully no one noticed. It was the solitude I needed to come up with a plan on how to properly address this disturbing revelation. Back in the room, I find her in her own bed with the lights off and the blinds drawn, a pillow over her head.

"I brought you some orange juice and bread from dinner," I whisper.

She reaches out and points to her bedside table. Once I set them down, she peeks an eye open.

"You okay?" I ask.

"I feel like shit," she mumbles into her pillow.

"Well, you sure did drink a lot. I'm not here to judge you, but you can't ever do that again. You're so lucky no one saw us or suspected something. But besides getting caught, I'm worried about you. I don't want to ever be the reason you relapse, and I think me naively drinking with you was fueling that fire."

"Ugh, sorry. I'll never drink again." She uncovers her face. Mascara is smudged under her bloodshot eyes.

"You say that now 'cause you feel awful, but what about in the real world where temptation is everywhere?"

"I know, I know," she groans.

"Why did you do that?"

"What?" She raises her head.

"Drink so recklessly."

Lindsay sits up to gulp down the juice and then lies back down without looking at me. She stares up at the ceiling pensively.

"Great question. Maybe if I solved that mystery, I wouldn't be here," she snaps but then lightens up. "Sorry, I'm extra irritable when I'm hungover." She sighs and turns her head to face me. "I don't know. I guess being intoxicated is an escape for me. A way to forget who I am and where I am for a moment."

"Why do you need to forget who you are? I think you're great!" I cheer, trying to boost her spirits.

"Ha. Thanks. I wish everyone in my life felt that way."

"I'm sure they do. Maybe they just don't know how to say it. A lot of people suck at communicating."

She breaks eye contact and rubs her fingers against her temples.

"They don't. My parents can't stand me. All my friends from home dropped like flies when I told them I had to be sober. I found out the hard way that the people closest to me were only ever drinking buddies. And my love life is a fucking joke. Everyone spits me out like I'm gum that's lost its flavor. And I'm sure if you give it enough time, you'll find a reason to too."

"Don't say that. You're the only friend I've ever had." I place my hand on her shoulder.

"Well, if that's true, then I feel sorry for you." She curls away from me.

I jerk my hand away like I've been burned. "That's a shit reply, Lindsay. How can anyone be close to you if you push them away like that?"

209

I know the type of protective barrier Lindsay has built because I created a similar one. What she doesn't realize is that she was the first person I felt safe enough with to break down some of those walls, and as her true friend, I'd hope she feels comfortable enough to do so with me.

Her brows furrow in resignation. "You're right. I'm not trying to push you away. Coming down from alcohol just gets me down sometimes. You're the only good thing in my life right now, so thank you. I promise I'm not always this messy."

"Messy and low days happen, but they pass. Trust me."

Her face perks up, and her grimace breaks into a soft smile. "Thank you, Natalia."

She sits up to sip the last of the orange juice, then retreats back under her covers. This isn't the right time to bring up Dr. Beckham. Lindsay is fragile, and I'm sure she can't handle any prying questions. As much as I want the answers, the right thing for me to do is to wait until she's in a better headspace.

Grace comes in at her usual time and hands me my medication. I place it in my mouth, and after she shuts the door, I head to the bathroom. I spit the pills into my hand, but instead of stashing them with the rest, I put them in my pajama bottoms pocket.

I can't not take them, because Dr. Beckham will clearly see my sleep patterns change in the sleep study, but if I wait until a little later, it'll buy me some time before it kicks in. Lindsay hasn't given me the information that I need, and I'm starting to doubt she ever will. It's time to take matters into my own hands.

Lindsay goes into the bathroom after me, and when she comes back out, her raccoon eyes are cleaned up and her matted hair is brushed out smoothly. She's done a great job at concealing the fact that she was a hungover mess earlier.

She keeps her earbuds in, and I lie in bed with my nose in a book until the time comes for Dr. Beckham to show up. When the door opens, he's behind the machine this time, pushing it into the room with his sleeves rolled up like he's ready to get to work. I turn my head away from him and sneak the pills into my mouth while faking a yawn, swallowing them dry.

I can't fully rely on Lindsay to tell me the truth, even if I'd rather directly have it from her. I'm afraid she'll continue to deny everything. She's had a bad track record with secrets, and I have a strong suspicion that she's been keeping a huge one from me. The last time I witnessed inappropriate behavior between her and Dr. Beckham, I was too drugged to trust my own judgment, and Lindsay used that to her advantage. By delaying my pills, I'll be aware just long enough before the disorienting side effects kick in.

"Good evening, ladies."

"Good evening," I reply, trying to make my voice sound sleepy. I rub my eyes with my fists the way little kids do when they're tired and ready for bed. I want them both to assume that I'll be passing out any moment now.

Lindsay ignores his entrance.

Dr. Beckham comes to my bedside to prep the machine. I slide down my top for the stickered wire, and Lindsay's eyes seem to fixate on his hands touching my skin. The first wave of sleepiness hits me, but it's nothing like it usually would be if I had taken my pills when Grace first came in. To keep up pretenses, I close my eyes as if it's hard to keep them open any longer and deepen my breaths.

"Good night, Natalia," he says.

My acting skills convinced him, but to my disappointment, I hear his footsteps and then the door shut. I peek an eye open. Dr. Beckham is nowhere to be seen.

Am I reading way too much into this? Has my imagination been running as wild as my nightmares?

Time passes, and my eyelids become heavier as my muscles relax. I'm close to drifting off, but the sound of the door opening sets off a small alarm in my head. I fight off the unconsciousness threatening to black out my brain.

I squint, allowing myself a sliver view of Lindsay's bed. A dark silhouette of a man approaches and pulls down her blanket, moving onto her body. My hazy eyes fight for focus, and when they do, my heart races, causing the machine to beep rapidly. Dr. Beckham jerks his head in my direction, and I clench my eyes shut.

"Is she awake?" Lindsay whispers.

"No, no. She can't be. It's probably a dream," he says confidently.

I take deep breaths so the beeping slows back down. My eyes are shut, but I can hear everything.

"I told you I don't want to do this anymore. Why are you here?" Lindsay asks, her discomfort evident.

"I know you were in my cabin. My $200 whiskey didn't just drink itself."

"And it was damn good. Okay, so now what? Are you going to isolate me again?" Her tone is filled with defiance.

"I can keep this one between us, but only if I can have you again."

This validates my deepest fears. Controlling my breaths is almost impossible now, but I force myself to keep my composure because I can't blow my cover.

"I saw you with your wife and kids again today, Bennett. You're obviously still with her, while I remain one of your disturbed patients to her and everyone else. I can't be your dirty secret anymore. I won't. It's killing me," she whispers low and in defeat.

The voices stop, but an exchange of kissing and heavy breaths continues.

With my last bit of consciousness, I force an eye open and get a clear view of Lindsay's hands pinned above her head and Dr. Beckham passionately kissing her neck. I'm desperately trying to fight the drug's influence, but its weight is pulling me past the point of my control.

Lindsay's detached, sad eyes staring at the ceiling are the last thing I see.

CHAPTER 16

I blink my groggy eyes open to an empty bed beside me and a clock that shows I've overslept. I ignore the nagging ache in my head and look around the room. Lindsay is nowhere to be found. I know the truth now, and the memory of last night makes me want to vomit.

All my suspicions have been confirmed. There's no denying it: Dr. Beckham is a predator—a disgusting one for preying on his patient, especially one with a disease that makes her vulnerable to men like him. Any irritation with Lindsay for keeping this from me is replaced with utter sorrow for her. All my anger falls directly onto Dr. Beckham. He abused his authority by coercing her into whatever sick dynamic he has going on with her. I heard and witnessed everything. She was trying to end things, and all he did was physically throw himself on her. I have no idea how long this has been going on, but I wish I'd known sooner so I could have tried to protect her. I'm gutted that she's been dealing with this all on her own and for whatever reason felt too afraid to turn to me.

I don't even change, just head straight down the hallway with tight fists, not sure how I'll react if I see either of them. Breakfast is almost over, but I don't think I could eat right now anyway.

Lindsay is rinsing her plate in the sink. After she shuts the garbage disposal off, she turns around. When her eyes meet mine, she twitches.

"Whoa, you scared me. Glad to see you're awake, finally."

I've drawn a blank. How do I approach her about this? A big part of me wants to find Dr. Beckham, slap him across the face, and announce to everyone that he's a pervert, but Lindsay's in this, too, and I care for her. I decide to tread lightly.

"We're making stained glass today. Should I save you a seat?" she asks.

"No, I'll go with you. I'm not hungry."

She thinks nothing of it as I follow her to the crafts table covered in supplies Dr. Cassidy laid out. We normally have free rein during arts and crafts, but Dr. Cassidy has been talking about this project for over a week now. I know now isn't the best time to bombard Lindsay with questions, so I'll just have to wait.

Dr. Cassidy shows off the finished example she made of a stained-glass sunset. It's small in size, but the various gem-colored pieces melded together perfectly replicates the hues of a setting sun. She leads us through the steps, and it's the first time we've been trusted with something sharper than what you'd give elementary students. She has us trace our designs with a pencil first. Some of the girls draw sunsets or flowers. Abby creates an intricate butterfly, and I decide on a canary.

Once most of the girls have finished, I look at Lindsay's design. She hasn't drawn anything but a few scribbles that she's now erasing. She's blowing out air and can't hold still.

"I can't fucking do this." She elevates her voice, ripping the paper in two.

Dr. Cassidy kneels at her side and calmly asks what's wrong.

"This shit is a fucking waste of time." Lindsay raises her voice louder, which causes the circle of girls to draw their attention toward her. "My parents don't pay you so I can make glass sunsets. They're paying you so you can fix me and to do it fucking fast so I can get the fuck out of here and go back to my real life. I'm sick of all the bullshit!" she howls and furiously pushes her chair backward, creating a loud screech on the hardwood floors. She tugs at her sweatshirt sleeves, letting out a final huff before she swipes her paper and pencil off the table and storms out of the room. Dr. Cassidy leaps to her feet and chases after her.

"God, what's her problem? Can they just kick her out yet?" Kookie sneers, reaching down and grabs Lindsay's unfinished design off the floor. She crumples it into a ball.

Why does this girl always have to run her mouth at the worst possible times?

"Mind your own business. You don't need to know everything about everyone all the time," I snap, feeling defensive of Lindsay once again. Kookie wrinkles her nose.

Hearing commotion from the hallway, I scoot out from the table. Lindsay's yelling from our room down the hall. I march forward as a door opens in front of me and Dr. Beckham comes out of his office, blocking me. I try to push past him, but he grips my shoulders.

"You stay," he demands, towering over me.

"I'm not a dog. Get your hands off me!" I yell back.

I know exactly who he is now, and it's made me lose any last bit of respect I had for him. He's a sleazy perv who has put my friend in such distress that she can't even sit through a simple craft project. My teeth grit and my shoulders shake as I try to hold back the real words I want to scream at him.

"Natalia, now is not a good time. I don't want you to get in trouble because of her. I wouldn't want this to affect your release day."

He's trying to emphasize the power he has over me. I stare up into his cold eyes defiantly, proving I'm not afraid of him.

"Let go of me," I say firmly.

He releases my arms, but as soon as I'm free from his restraint, Dr. Cassidy comes out of our room, closing the door behind her.

"Her emotions are high. She just needs some time alone."

"Is *she* high?" Dr. Beckham asks with a hint of sarcasm.

Dr. Cassidy raises her brows at his crass remark. "Dr. Beckham, I need Natalia back with the others."

"Oh, right." He abruptly changes his tone. "Yes, Natalia. You shouldn't be here."

"All I wanted to do was quickly check on Lindsay," I interject, "since something or *someone* obviously has her very upset."

As I reach for the doorknob, Dr. Beckham firmly pulls away my hand

"I told you to stay away! Why won't you listen?" he scolds, cracking his poised act.

A gasp slips from Dr. Cassidy, and she sternly shakes her head at him.

Dr. Beckham, your true colors are showing. You're not as handsome and charming as you like everyone to think you are.

"Come on, Natalia. You did nothing wrong. Let's go finish our art project. Dr. Beckham, we can have a word later."

Dr. Cassidy leads me away with a gentle hand on my back.

Dr. Beckham has no idea how lucky he is that I didn't just out him right then and there to Dr. Cassidy. As much as I wanted to, Lindsay is my top priority, and I still need to hear her truth and her side of the story. I shoot him a look of contempt before I pivot and leave with Dr. Cassidy.

After our stained-glass projects are prepared to be baked, lunch is ready, though Lindsay hasn't showed up. My stomach is growling, but I need to see her. I ditch Abby and head to our room, where Lindsay is lying on her bed in only her bra and underwear. Her puffy eyes are empty as she huddles into herself.

She's crumbling right before me.

"Lindsay, I think we need to talk."

She blows a tuft of hair out of her eyes. "What? Did Kookie say something? Fuck her."

"No. Well, I mean, doesn't she always have something to say?" I add. Lindsay cracks a tiny smirk. "I don't want to upset you because I can tell things are… heavy right now. But I need to talk to you about something."

"Let's hear it," she demands, stretching her hands out to admire her nails.

"This isn't easy at all for me to bring up, but I just want you to know I love you, and I'm here for you no matter what you decide to tell me."

She glances at me with a lost expression. I swallow a big gulp and realize confronting her is harder than I thought, but I have to do it.

"I saw you and Dr. Beckham last night. He was kissing you, and don't tell me I'm imagining things because I know you know what I saw is the truth."

Her eyes stretch open.

"Please tell me what the hell is going on there."

"You can't say anything to anyone! It will ruin everything for me," she begs.

"Why? What's going on? Please tell me. I won't say anything. I just want to be there for you."

She bites her lower lip as her eyes move around the room.

"I need a cigarette." She disappears into the bathroom. "I swear someone has been smoking all my fucking cigarettes. How the hell do I only have one left?" she yells.

She comes back and sits on my bed to unwind the window. She lights the stick, pressing her lips around it with a deep inhale.

"Dr. Beckham is a fucking creep. Let me start by telling you that," she says, blowing out smoke. "But I love him. Insanely."

Those three words stun me. That was the last thing I expected her to confess.

"How? Since when?"

How could she possibly love someone who I watched blatantly take advantage of her?

"Oh God, Natalia. The moment he laid eyes on me, I wanted him. His superiority complex, his dominance. It would be like taking home the biggest prize in a fair game nobody wins. At first, it started off innocent. Every session I'd test him. I'd wear more revealing clothes. He'd ask me about my previous sexual encounters, and I'd describe them in a way that made his pants tighten."

She stops to puff some more on her cigarette. I'm hanging on her every word, but I try to give her the space and time she needs.

"Eventually, he couldn't resist me, and that's when he pounced on me. I thought I had finally won, but boy, did the gold polish on that trophy tarnish quick. But by that time, it was too late. I had already fallen too hard." She slowly blows out smoke. "I learned that loving him is a double-edged sword. It felt good that this intelligent doctor wanted me, and at first, I enjoyed being his fun little secret he'd hook up with behind closed doors. But then our feelings for each other grew stronger, and while I fell helplessly in love, his motives became dark and obsessive. It's almost like he got off on punishing me when I didn't show him the type of affection he felt he deserved. In a normal situation, I would break things off, but not here. I can't get away from him here because he's in my face every day. All he has to do is report whatever bad behavior he chooses, and I'll be stuck here even longer. He loves to hold that over me. But the most fucked-up part of it all, even after all the awful things he's done, is that I somehow still want him, and I know that makes me sound fucking crazy."

Her shaky breath stops her words.

"Lindsay, this isn't good at all. You're doing exactly what your illness would have you do. His very job is to recognize that and resist you. He broke his oath as a doctor and violated every code a therapist should stand by."

She presses her lips tight together. I can tell she's struggling with this, so I try to soften the conversation. "I thought you had a boyfriend when you came here. What happened there?"

"My last boyfriend was well over a year ago. I was always talking about Bennett... Dr. Beckham. I'm sorry I lied." She coughs, flicking ash out of the window.

I'm so confused. Didn't she just have a boyfriend?

Is Dr. Beckham the guy Lindsay was gushing about when I first arrived at Awana?

"But what about the boyfriend who brought you drugs? Was that a lie too?"

"No, that's true. Except the drugs weren't brought from outside here. They were given by our very own prescribing doctor. I guess you could call him my boyfriend in some twisted way."

Right when I thought I couldn't hate him more, I find out he willingly gave an addict pills. Was it a way to force himself on her?

"Dr. Beckham gave you drugs? Was it because you were resisting him… sex wise?" I ask as delicately as possible.

"No. The sex was always consensual."

She takes her longest inhale from the cigarette before tossing it outside.

It's clear now that she doesn't see the full reality of this fucked-up situation. She needs to know how wrong this is on so many levels. I have to break it her, but I need to do it gently.

"Lindsay, you may think it was consensual because you wanted it, but you are in here to treat your sex addiction, and this man is your doctor. You are not in a position to give consent. He's abusing his power."

She closes her eyes for a moment, and after they reopen, I see the pain they hold. I think this may be the first time she's ever considered this to be true. She covers her mouth with her hand as a tear slowly rolls down her cheek.

"God, you're right. I think he knew drugs were the one thing that would keep me indebted to him. And I'm fucking weak and fell for it."

So, Dr. Beckham's manipulations are methodical and layered. And the more I learn about his tactics, the scarier it's all becoming. Feeding an addict drugs so they're dependent on you is about as low as you can go.

"What happened with the drugs? Why did he give you them?" I ask softly.

"Because I refused to be with him romantically anymore. Yes, he still forced me into weekly group therapy sessions, but during them, I wouldn't speak. I could hardly glance in his direction because I knew deep down inside what we were doing was all kinds of wrong. It was probably the only time I had my senses straight. But low and behold, he offered me my favorite drug of choice. Two weeks went by on my oxy haze, but the cost to keep my high alive wasn't worth it anymore. I was so over it. Giving my body to him whenever he pleased was taking my soul too. I had to break it off. I refused any more drugs and had a terrible comedown. But after he put me in isolation, that's when he nursed me back to life, and I fell back in love all over again."

"How could you be in love with a monster like that?" I cry, throwing my hands in the air in frustration.

I manage to restrain my temper even though it feels nearly impossible amid the disturbing revelations about Dr. Beckham's character.

"You don't get it. When it's just us, he has his softest moments. He held me in his arms for hours when I was in my lowest of lows. He'd rock me to sleep telling me all the things he adored about me and all the future plans he had for us. He told me I was everything to him, and I've never had someone love me with that sort of intensity. But I should have known better. He told me he left his wife, and as we both saw, he didn't. That's why I freaked out yesterday."

What a slimy bastard!

All this time, this man has been conning her, lying to her, and using her, both physically and emotionally.

"That's not love! That's manipulation! His whole career is built on getting inside people's heads. He loved having control over you. A man like that doesn't love anyone but himself." My blood rises to my head, and right when I could boil over, Lindsay cowers in my lap, the wetness coming from her eyes soaking my jeans.

"You deserve so much better than this—than all the horrible things he put you through. We have to do something. Tell someone, at least."

I stroke her hair, trying to soothe her but also talk some sense into her. This isn't going to go away on its own. She has to speak up and put a stop to it.

"You think I haven't thought of that before?" She sits up and crosses her arms and legs. "They won't believe me. Dr. Beckham already made that clear, and he's right. Not with my history. They'll just think I tried to seduce him, and after he rejected my advances, I vengefully came up with a story to get even with him."

"You need to at least try. You need to tell someone. You can't let him do this to you. It's not right," I insist.

I've never experienced anything close to what she's dealing with right now, so I'm trying not to be a preachy critic, but she needs an advocate to fight for her—especially if she's not ready to fight for herself.

"You don't get it. I've seen this all play out before. Society has shown they don't like believing a woman, especially one with a slippery past like mine. It's my word against his. He's a doctor, and I'm just the girl who will fuck anyone for an ounce of attention. You don't know all the stones that will be thrown my way once my promiscuous nature is brought into the debate."

I narrow my brows. As much as I hate to admit it, she has some valid points, but not enough to keep her stuck in this stranglehold.

"But it's not just your word anymore. It's mine too. I witnessed what he's done. We can take him down together."

I rise to my feet with an overwhelming feeling of vengeance, ready to run and tell the world right now what a deviant Dr.

Beckham is. There's a fire inside me that I have never felt before, and I'll use it to burn that man's world to the ground. Never again should he get away with taking advantage of vulnerable patients and young girls. Lindsay and I could make sure of it, together. There's strength in numbers, and we need to expose every lie he has ever told. Hopefully when we're done, he'll have lost everything—his reputation, his career, his family—and be placed behind bars.

Lindsay grabs my arm and pulls me back down to the bed. She gently puts her hand in mine.

"The last thing I want to do is offend you, but you have a questionable history, too, because of your sleep disorder," she says in a soft voice to disarm me. "Dr. Beckham could easily write you off as mentally unstable. He has you highly medicated half the time you're here, and that alone would allow him to cast doubt on your sanity and your ability to think clearly. Plus, they all know we're best friends and have seen you stick up for me even when I've been in the wrong. They'll think you're lying for me."

It feels as if all the air has been sucked from our room. Could she be right that no one would believe us if we tried to bring this forward because of their preconceived judgments about our mental health?

Does the world really deem me too "crazy" to believe?

Lindsay's words hit me with a gravity that feels like I've been slammed against the floor. It's completely unfair, but a harrowing truth. I've been in and out of mental institutions my whole life, much of which has been spent sedated on various drugs to curb my nighttime behaviors. Even with us speaking up together, we could be dismissed and disregarded and even penalized for making "false" accusations.

I can't help but wonder, if a cancer patient spoke against a doctor, would they be treated the same way? Someone's mental illness should not diminish their creditability when they cry out for help. I can't even formulate words of protest because I know what she said is probably a fact, and it guts me.

"I just need to get out of here. I'm only a few weeks away. Please don't ruin that for me. I just want to put this all behind me, so please promise me. I've confided so much in you, and I need you to have my back on this." She squeezes my hands and stares at me with pleading eyes.

I'm truly torn. I know I have my secrets too. She's never judged me for hiding my medication or seeing Gabriel. And what if she's right, and we actually make the situation worse by saying something? It kills me to concede, but the choices in every direction are impossible.

"Fine, but you have to promise me you won't fall into him again. No late-night kisses, no secret cabin visits. You'll never move on from him if you keep giving him the power."

"How did you know about the cabin visits?"

"You knew his cabin like the back of your hand, and now that I put everything together, there were so many signs. The jealous fit he threw when that lead singer asked for your number, the way his eyes are always on you, his concern with every little thing you do."

"Well, you make it sound romantic," she jokes, sniffling and wiping away the last of her tears.

"It's not romantic at all. It's possessive and creepy. Now promise me," I demand without a smile.

"I promise you. It's over. It has to be," she says with a sigh.

I can't believe we both have to sit on this. Dr. Beckham is still in charge of us and every female in this place, and there's not a damn thing we can do about it. At least not right *now*.

We may not be able to do anything now while we're trapped here under his thumb, but we won't have anything to lose once we're out of this place.

"Lindsay," I say with renewed enthusiasm, "please keep an open mind about exposing him down the road. I know you have little faith in this system, but once we're out of here and no longer at his mercy, it'll be easier. Wouldn't you hate if this happened to someone else?"

She pauses and gazes out the window.

"Yeah, I guess you're right," she says sadly and nods.

It's comforting to know she's at least considering it. I pull her in for a hug, and her shoulders relax. I hope some of the weight from this heavy burden has been released from her, but now I feel part of it has been hefted onto me.

It's hard to find balanced thoughts after Lindsay's confession. Every strange inkling I've had about Dr. Beckham is true. That asshole might have the sickest head in this place. I want nothing more than to expose him, but I made a promise to Lindsay, even if I'm not sure it was the right one. I pray that one day she finds the strength to do so on her own, no matter how it's received, and if she does, I will be right there to back her up.

I try to continue the rest our day in our normal fashion, which I think Lindsay appreciates. During free time, we lie side by side under the tree. She's back to telling me her quick-witted jokes, and as I watch her giggle behind her big sunglasses, I'm reminded of everything she's forced to hold inside. Day in and day out, she's had to mask her suffering, and somehow, she's done it with grace.

No one should ever have to do that, but why do so many of us still do? I may not know everything Lindsay has dealt with, but I do know what it's like to minimize my pain because I'm afraid if I show it, it will only cause a bigger disaster than what I'm already dealing with.

As nighttime rolls around, Grace comes in and then leaves. For the first time in a week, I hide my pills. Even with all the intense drama of the day, Gabriel's face is burning in my mind. It's been seven days, and that might not seem that long for some, but some days in Awana can feel like eternities.

Lindsay is already dozing off, and I don't blame her. Today was a lot. Normally, she's a living earthquake, her strong presence felt by everyone around her, but tonight, I see her in a different light as she's snuggled on her bed holding on to her pillow like a small child.

It kills me to see how vulnerable and fragile she is right now.

I open the window, and a warm wind blows into my hair. The air smells like musk and pine. The scent confirms summer is here. I close my eyes, losing myself to the nighttime sounds of buzzing bugs and a swirling breeze. The melody intensifies when the soft notes of a harmonica join in.

My eyes open to Gabriel's face a few feet away, half in the darkness and half illuminated by the light of the moon. His smile hits me like a dizzying rush. He walks over, reaching out for me, and my body falls into him like a rag doll. Once I'm in his arms, my lips find his. The strands of his hair tickle my nose, and I push them away to fully see him.

"I've missed those eyes more than you'll ever know," he whispers.

I might have an idea. Awana becomes tortuous without him. Today was incredibly draining and defeating, yet somehow being reunited makes all the misery of the last week disappear.

After a moment of holding each other tight, I get a good look at him. His flannel is unbuttoned, and his face has a glow to it that's recognizable even in the dark night.

"I have something for you," he says, reaching for my fingers.

His presence is more than enough. I don't think there's anything he could possibly have that would be better than solely being with him.

I lace my fingers in his and follow him, knowing I'd go anywhere with him right now.

He takes us through the grass, and flickering light catches my eye. The closer we walk toward it, the more I see. Lit small glass candles are glowing around the tree trunk, showcasing a blanket spread out in front with rose petals scattered across it.

I stop in my tracks, astounded.

"Is this all for me?" I ask in disbelief.

He nods, flashing his charming grin.

I place both hands on my chest. This romantic setup is the nicest thing anyone has ever done for me. Gabriel showing up tonight was already a huge relief. I thought he might not ever want to see me again after my complete freak-out by the river last week.

He's still into me.

"Yes. It's a small way of trying to show you how sorry I am."

He helps me down onto the spread-out blanket, then nestles himself against my side.

"Sorry for what exactly?" I ask incredulously.

"Sorry for ditching you last week. I left you when you probably needed me the most. I was afraid I was making you stay out too much, and that the fear I saw wash over you at the river was my fault somehow. I'd hate myself if me keeping you out at night was doing you more harm than good."

He has this all wrong. My panic attack had nothing to do with him, but I do appreciate his concern. As hard as it was not seeing him, I'm beginning to understand his reasonings. And maybe if we hadn't taken our break, I'd have been too distracted to find out everything going with Lindsay. It may have been a blessing in disguise.

"It wasn't your fault at all, and I don't think you realize how much good you do bring me," I assure him.

"I'm sorry if I made you feel like you did something wrong. I get what it's like to have anxiety take hold like that. I guess in that moment, I didn't know how to explain myself well."

"Thank you. That really means a lot."

It's not just his apology that feels goods. It's the confirmation that he accepts all of me, even the sides that I wish he never had to witness.

I plant a kiss on his cheek, and he straightens his shoulders.

"Now, I know it's not a fancy restaurant, but I thought this was the closest thing to a proper date," he says, pointing to the picnic setup he put together for us.

"Wow, this is so proper."

I pick up some red petals and blow them in the air above, and they fall around us like silky rubies of confetti.

"Only the best for my girl. So, how was your week?"

An absolute hell between not seeing you and the bombshell dropped about Dr. Beckham and Lindsay.

As much as venting could feel good, I'm too emotionally spent to go into detail, and I just want to enjoy my time with him.

"A bit of a whirlwind. To be honest, it would take the whole night to dive into it all, and I really don't feel like going there right now."

"We don't have to. Let's not focus on the bad. Why don't you tell me something good that happened?"

As I admire the flickering candles around us, he swings an arm around my waist, and I melt into his side. It's hard to concentrate on anything other than the Dr. Beckham fiasco, but I rewind to a few days before when Olga came to see me.

"Hmm, well, I saw Olga earlier in the week. That was good."

"Ah, a visitor. Sounds fun! Did you happen to mention me?" He wiggles his brows.

"Uh, no."

He scoffs, then grins. "Well, why not?"

Probably because she thinks men are a waste of time.

"Well, our relationship is technically forbidden here, and as you know, she's a firm believer in playing by the rules. Plus, I've actually never had one before you, so I've never had that conversation with her before. I didn't know how she would react."

"I mean, I'd say I was shocked because you're so damn beautiful, Natalia, but from what you told me, you've been pretty secluded most of your life. It makes sense."

Ugh, he always knows just what to say.

I bite back my giddy smile. There's no way I'm his first relationship.

"I'm sure you've had plenty of girlfriends before me."

He squeezes me into him and laughs.

"I love that you think I'm some desirable bachelor, but you got me all wrong. I've only had one girlfriend. We met at a group home I lived in when I was sixteen."

One ex-girlfriend is enough to make me insecure, but I keep that hidden.

"Why did it end?" I curiously pry.

He pulls his hand away from mine to tug through his hair.

"After a suicide attempt. My first one." His voice and eyes lower.

My breath goes weak.

How many times has he tried before?

I hate that Gabriel's suffering was so severe that it led him down the darkest route. But I'm so thankful his attempts were just that and they didn't take him from the world, because then he'd never exist in mine.

"We don't have to go there if you'd rather not."

"No, it's fine. It's probably best you know. The attempt was too much for her to handle. She said I never would have tried if I truly loved her. She felt I had betrayed her, and I get that viewpoint, but it wasn't true. In reality, it had very little to do with her at all. It was my fucked-up thoughts that wanted to ruin me."

I understand if she was worried about him—I constantly am—but I'd never want to put that kind of blame and pressure on someone who is already struggling to live.

"I'm so sorry. I can only imagine a breakup when you're already feeling so low. I'm sure it only made matters worse."

He sighs. "It was for the best. I wasn't in the right mind to give myself to someone else. My mental state was destroyed, and nobody wants to be given something broken. My worry is that I'll never be whole enough for someone else, even you."

He gravely focuses on the ground. I can tell distraught thoughts are creeping in all around him.

"Don't say that!" I tilt his chin up. "Two broken pieces are better than one. With all the cracks and dents in our minds, the two of us next to each other create something abstract, and abstract has always been more beautiful to me."

The corners of his mouth lift, and his sad eyes brighten. He slides his hands against the sides of my head, bringing my nose to his.

"Natalia, if love at first sight exits, then there's no doubt I fell in love with you the moment I saw you. Normally, I'm too much of a pessimist to ever admit that. But not tonight! Tonight, I can truly say my collapsed heart has found a beat again, and every part of you is now coursing through my veins. You're in me now, whether we wanted this or not." The feel of his fingertips and nose against my cold skin and the intense words he softly spoke under his breath send every one of my nerve endings into overdrive. He peers right into my eyes before tracing his lips up to my ear. "I'm so in love with you, if you haven't already noticed."

My world is spinning like I'm on a sped-up merry-go-round, and if Gabriel wasn't holding me, I think I'd fly off. A new sensation is taking hold of me, an erratic heartbeat mixed with a pleasant buzzing. All the physical reactions of falling in love are consuming me faster than I can comprehend.

The words pour out with such passion, I have to close my eyes.

"I'm in love with you too," I confess, and it's as if a needle is threading through our chests, sewing our tattered hearts together.

His lips find mine, and his arms gently lay me underneath him. Our skin, our bones, and our souls align under the galaxy above, and our professed love is sending me soaring higher than any star in the sky. I stay in his arms for as long as the night allows me.

***

Though my eyes are closed, I couldn't sleep, not after a night like that. Kissing Gabriel until the sun almost broke has me on a high I never want to come down from. I'm levitating in another dimension with the familiar smell of Gabriel's smoke blowing around me.

"Natalia! Are you smoking one of my cigarettes?"

Lindsay's yelling drops me through the imagined cloud I'm floating on.

Startled by the lit stick between my fingers, I throw it on the bed.

What the hell am I doing?

"Put it out! You're going to light yourself on fire." She waves away the smoke.

After she stomps the bud and tosses it, she immediately comes back to my bed.

"What is going on? I know you're not a smoker. Wait, did this Gabriel kid get you addicted?"

"I don't know. Honestly, I didn't even know I was smoking it," I admit, worry flushing my cheeks.

The leftover smoke in the air is pungent and makes me want to gag.

Why on earth was I smoking a cigarette? Where did it even come from?

"Wait, have you been the one smoking all my cigarettes?"

"No!" I shout defensively.

I know she's complained before about them going missing, but it couldn't have been me. I've never smoked a cigarette a day in my life.

Right?

"Then where the hell else did they go?" she shouts back, causing me to crouch into myself. She wraps her arm around my rocking body. "I'm sorry. I didn't mean to come off mad. It just scared me."

"It scares me too," I mumble, almost unable to get the words out.

I'm normally used to my body acting out on its own accord, but it's never been while I'm awake. This is the first time something like this has occurred, and it's deeply unsettling that I've lost total control of my memory and movements.

What is happening to me?

She squeezes me against her. "Maybe you just need some breakfast."

"Yeah, maybe," I agree with a deep gulp.

I think what I need is a nap. I didn't get any sleep last night, and it's obviously making me delirious.

I can't ignore the unrelenting fear that I truly might be losing my mind. But I won't ever admit that. I'm going to blame this on my sleeplessness. I don't need to add anything else to my long list of insane behaviors. If someone other than Lindsay had caught me in a stupor, not knowing what I was doing or why, they'd probably tell on me, and it would be a whole new issue for doctors to take all the time in the world to try and identify. Not now, though. I won't allow it, not when I'm so close to leaving this place.

Once in the bathroom, I scrub my tongue to get rid of the ashy taste, then slap my cheek.

Snap out of it, Natalia. Do you ever want to live a life outside confined walls and timed medication? I ask myself, repeating Olga's words on my first day here.

After splashing water on my face, I straighten out my hair and shoulders, hoping that imitating sanity will get me through the day.

My stomach is growling by the time I make it from my room into the kitchen. Abby is at the table sipping on juice, and her eyes follow me until I sit down. I squint back and wonder if she has more strange things to say to me.

Could she have heard Lindsay and me this morning talking about Gabriel or me smoking?

I do not need her deciding to break her vow of silence to rat me out. If Dr. Beckham finds out about any of the things I've been up to lately, I will be supremely screwed.

Lindsay breaks our stare-down, and as soon she joins the table, Abby leaves. Lindsay grabs an orange from the fruit basket. Her nails sink into the peel, slowly picking it away without saying a word.

After breakfast, Lindsay is off to a session and heads down the hall. I can't stop yawning. I thought breakfast would give me more energy, but every one of my muscles is throbbing. My bed is the only place my tired limbs will take me.

Once in my room, I lie down and shut my eyes in the hope that I'll get some sleep. I still can't shake off what happened earlier this morning. It's strange because I don't usually do things unconsciously unless I'm actually unconscious.

What if my disease starts to control all my movements, even my waking ones?

All I need is ten minutes of rest.

Please.

A yellow daisy appears in the black expanse behind my eyelids. I slide the silky petals between my fingertips and pluck each one out slowly.

He loves me. He loves me not.

Each petal falls to the rhythm of a harmonica, which sounds as if it's right beside me. My eyes open to Gabriel's haunting stare outside my window.

Why is he here in broad daylight?

The door slams, and the hairs on my neck stand on end. I rub my eyes and turn back to my window, but there's nothing there, not a single trace of him.

Okay, now my mind is definitely playing tricks on me.

Knowing I better get some rest before things escalate any further, I bury my face in my pillow, trying to do everything in my power to shut off my overimaginative brain.

CHAPTER 17

Every night this week has been the exact same, and it doesn't bother me one bit. Gabriel meets me in the middle of the night, we kiss, we talk for hours, and then I climb back in my window. Everything is perfect, except one little thing, one tiny detail that would make Olga or Dr. Beckham frown. I haven't been able to fall back asleep after my visits with Gabriel. It's not like I don't try. I shut my eyes, I count sheep, I meditate, but for some reason, when the moon is out and alive, so is my mind. I figured since I can't sleep anyway, why not spend the restless nights in the arms of the boy I love.

I'm fighting through the days to get to the nights. Luckily, I've been able to sneak in some midday power naps during free time. They're probably what's keeping my organs from shutting down. I know deep down that thirty minutes of sleep here and there's not going to be enough to keep me going. My body is longing for a full night to recover. Not taking my medication is also partly to blame for my insomnia, but I want just one more night tonight with Gabriel, and then tomorrow I'll take my pills for my sleep study. My body will get the rest it deserves, and everything will be just fine.

Sleep is overrated anyway. I'll sleep when I'm dead.

Getting out of bed today feels like I'm trying to move with a bag of boulders strapped to my back. Lindsay steps out of the bathroom, singing and full of energy. I'd stay in my pajamas all day if I could, but that might give a hint to my exhaustion. Any time Dr. Cassidy or Dr. Beckham interacts with me, I have to scrape up all the energy I have to plaster on an awake face and engage with a lively attitude. I know it seems like I'm going to extremes, but I guess the saying is true: love will make you do crazy things.

"I'm headed to breakfast," Lindsay informs me.

I give her a nod while I struggle to pull up my jeans, but my arms and legs are so weak they shake. Even putting on clothes is a taxing exercise.

She tsks. "Oh, girl, you look dead."

"Jeez, thanks."

"I'm just saying, if you don't want to get caught not taking your medication, your appearance is going to give you away real quick."

I check myself out in our small dresser mirror and see she's right. My sunken eyes and bluish reflection could land me a role as a monster in a horror film.

"Come on. Let me help you."

She pulls me onto her bed, then grabs a plastic cylinder out of her makeup bag.

"A little concealer will fix those black under-eyes right up." She slathers the liquid under my lower lashes and stands back, squinting. "One more thing." She pulls out some blush, dabs some pink powder onto the brush, and begins sweeping it across my cheeks. "Let's bring some life back into that complexion. There ya go. Take a look."

She hands me a compact mirror.

"Whoa, that's amazing," I rave, staring at my skin that now looks rested and supple.

"Cosmetology school did teach me a few things. Always came in handy for me when I had to hide a comedown. If I didn't know you better, I'd be wondering which drug you were coming down from right now."

Does Gabriel King count?

With my makeup mask, I now feel ready to face the day.

After breakfast, we find out that today is Kookie's last day at Awana. Balloons and streamers hang around the house alongside a "We will miss you!" banner the ED girls made during arts and crafts.

I don't think Lindsay and I can relate to that sign. With Kookie gone, it'll be one less nuisance for Lindsay, which I think she really needs.

After a brutal yoga session due to my weakened muscles, I want nothing more than to lie under the willow tree and daydream of Gabriel, but as I head in that direction, Lindsay grabs my hand.

"I'm not going to let you go stare off into oblivion by that damn tree. Come on, follow me."

"Only if you promise we're staying far away from Dr. Beckham's liquor stash."

"Ha, fine!" She sticks her tongue out at me. "But seriously, I want to take you somewhere I used to go when I felt like this place got too overwhelming. I think it could help both of us right now."

I follow her past the garden toward a cluster of tall redwoods I've never been to. We walk farther into the woods, Awana getting smaller behind us.

"Do you really know where you're going?" I ask tentatively.

"Yes. Come on, just a little farther."

My legs are stiff, but I continue to follow Lindsay up the rough terrain of branches and leaves fallen on the ground.

After our hike is over, we stop at a big rock. Lindsay takes her time climbing up, and when she makes it to the top, she signals for me. Not sure I'll make it, I carefully climb up step by step until Lindsay holds her fingers out for me to grab. After she pulls me up and I settle in next to her, the view at the top captures me. Below us is a large canyon filled with trees, making the tips of massive redwoods look tiny in comparison to us.

"This view is incredible," I gush.

"I need to have a difficult conversation with you," Lindsay says with trepidation.

My anxiety spikes. "What about?"

She grabs my hand tenderly, positioning herself closer to me on the rough rock we're sitting on.

"You confronted me when you suspected something was wrong between Dr. Beckham and me. I feel I owe you the same. I don't know if Gabriel is right for you."

I'm blindsided.

Where is this all coming from?

I sharply retract my arm, and our hands break apart. "That's not fair. You don't know him at all. You never even tried to meet him. Why would you even say that?"

"I know this is the guy who makes you practically a zombie until you're able to see him again. I mean, you have to quit taking your medication in order to see him, for God's sake. And I think not taking your medication is really having an effect on you, and not in a good way. The panic attacks, the cigarettes, the black bird you claim to see out your window—"

"*Claim* to see?" I repeat defensively.

Where the hell is she going with this?

She presses her lips tightly, choosing her words before she speaks again. "I don't know if the black bird was ever even there. I hate to tell you this, but I think you might have been imagining it."

Her words slice my heart. It's terrible that she doesn't think I'm capable to decipher what's real—or even worse, the idea that my own eyes are betraying me.

Could this really be true? No. It can't be.

"That's bullshit," I snap.

"I'm sorry. I didn't mean to upset you."

Why is she doing this to me now? I'm already at my weakest physically. Is she trying to completely break me mentally too?

I try to balance my wavering emotions, but anger rises to the top. The blood rushes to my head, causing my defenses to flare.

"You don't know what you're talking about. Who are you to judge me or my love life when yours is a complete mess?" I spit out, instantly regretting my harshness.

She whips her head back with her mouth partly open in shock.

"Oh, I'm sorry. I forgot there's no possible way you could possibly be as fucked up as me. Well, shit, maybe you're right. Why would someone as perfect as you want to believe anything I have to say?" Her voice is now high and distressed.

She uncrosses her legs to stand and shrugs.

"No, that's not what I—"

Lindsay's eyes water, and before I can finish, she leaps from the rock and drops to the ground. When her feet thump onto the dirt, she takes off without me.

"Lindsay, I'm sorry! That came out wrong!" I call out for her, but she doesn't turn around.

There I go again, speaking my mind when I should have just shut the hell up. But she was the one person I thought would never write me off as some sort of lunatic. She has this all wrong. I may have a long list of issues, but being delusional has never been one.

A strong breeze gives me goose bumps while the clouds move over the sun. I climb down the rock and wander through the tall trees back to Awana.

When I arrive, my chest burns from the long hike. Lindsay is nowhere to be found. I'm apathetic. I don't want to do anything, not even the things I normally love like read or look for birds in the sky.

I retreat to the quiet living room for some peace and solace after that travesty. I focus my sight upward, counting the wooden planks in the high beamed ceilings until my eyelids can no longer stay open, and I allow myself to drift off into a doze.

My nap is quickly ruined, as all the ED girls rush through the sliding door, ignoring me to grab some water from the kitchen.

After a few moments, Lindsay pops in and lingers near the sofa, creating a painfully awkward silence. When we finally lock eyes, she throws her arms at her sides and sinks down onto the sofa next to me.

"I hate fighting with you. Can we just squash all that shit earlier? You're literally the best friend I've ever had. I'm sorry. I promise I was only being protective, and I probably just didn't look hard enough for the black bird the way you did."

Though her apology is one I needed, I feel like I was the one who took it too far.

"Thank you for saying that. I'm sorry, too, for getting so defensive. I had no right to say that about your love life."

"Well, you weren't too far off. It is messy as fuck." She laughs lightly. "It just hurts to be reminded of it sometimes." Her smile falls.

"I'm truly sorry for that," I tell her.

"It's okay. I'm not a doctor and shouldn't be analyzing you like one."

"Thanks. Yeah, we get enough of that already, don't we?"

We both grin and latch on to each other in a truce. I never want to have an argument with her ever again.

Giggling echoes from the kitchen. I tune it out, but Lindsay shifts away, squinting her

eyes and trying to focus on the cackling voices.

"What is it?" I ask.

She puts her pointer finger against her lips to shush me.

"Listen. Who is Kookie talking about?"

"I don't know. Who cares?" I say, leaning farther into a cushion.

"Shhh. Listen!" she hushes me once more.

I focus, and Kookie's high-pitched voice isn't hard to miss.

"Now that I'm out, he says he's going to leave his wife. He even wants us to get our own apartment. We were thinking of wine country," I hear Kookie boast.

When I look at Lindsay, her face is flushed, and her fists are knotted into tight balls. Something Kookie said has triggered heated flames in her eyes. Before I can ask, she bolts up and marches right into the kitchen. I peel my aching body off the sofa and chase after her, afraid of what might go down next.

"Who the hell are you talking about?" Lindsay yells, startling the girls, who aren't happy that she's been eavesdropping on their conversation.

"Mind your own fucking business," Kookie squawks back with a hand on her hip.

Lindsay takes a few stalking steps forward and is inches from Kookie.

"Who's gonna leave his wife for you, huh? Who?" Lindsay's anger has fully possessed her, as she's now nose to nose with Kookie, screaming right into her face. "Well, if it's who I think it is, your little secret boyfriend just came into my room a couple nights ago and fucked my brains out!"

Oh shit. This isn't going to end well.

Everyone's shocked jaws drop, including mine. That sounded like a catalyst for a war.

"You're psychotic! Nobody here would touch you with a ten-foot pole," Kookie spits back at her.

Kookie lunges at Lindsay and pushes her back with her palms. Lindsay stands her ground but loses full control of her temper. She jumps on Kookie, screaming at the top of her lungs and knocking her down to the hardwood floors. Lindsay climbs on top of Kookie, who is now lying her back, and straddles her. Kookie claws up at Lindsay, trying to pull any part of her that she can grab, but Lindsay blocks every attempt, frantically slapping her hands away.

"This whole time, you made me out to be a slut to everyone here when it was actually you fucking everybody!" Lindsay rips at Kookie's hair, yanking a large clump as Kookie screams in pain.

"*Ow!* Someone get this crazy bitch off me!" Kookie cries, unable to escape the chaotic force that is Lindsay.

Cheryl and I lean over their entangled bodies, trying to loosen Lindsay's death grip, but it's impossible to pull the two of them apart. Kat screams out for help, and within seconds Dr. Beckham rushes in.

"Lindsay! What is wrong with you? Get away from her now!"

He hovers above them and pries open Lindsay's locked fingers to release a chunk of Kookie's hair. He picks Lindsay up by her waist and turns her around, holding tight to her shoulders.

Just when I think Dr. Beckham's restraint has calmed Lindsay down, she looks up at him with a spiteful scowl, and her anger redirects.

"You're fucking her, aren't you? You're fucking Kookie! You're a disgusting piece of shit! What happened to all that talk about how much you loved me and how I'm the only one for you?" She pounds her fists against his chest repeatedly. The anger morphs into a look of angst and betrayal as tears begin streaming down her face. "All you care about is getting your dick wet. Are you fucking all your patients?"

Wrath washes over his eyes, and his pupils grow as he digs his fingertips deeper into her arms.

"You better watch what you say," he growls.

The veins in his arms bulge as he takes her wrists and forces them behind her, causing her to cry out in pain.

The beast has officially been unleashed.

"Stop, you're hurting her!" I yell, concerned for her safety. He's twice her size and could easily snap her bones like a twig if he wanted.

Kookie scoots backward on her butt and quietly retreats from the madness. Cheryl and Kat freeze and stare apprehensively, but an audience doesn't stop him. With white knuckles, he twists Lindsay's body so that her backside is pressed against his groin.

"Isolation? Is that what you want?" he barks, speaking directly in her ear, though loud enough so we can all hear.

"Go ahead, lock me away. It won't prevent me from telling everyone all about the sick fuck you really are!" she threatens him back, still squirming in his arms.

"No one is ever going to believe anything from the mouth of a pathological whore, so you're better off keeping yours shut!"

His harsh words resound around the room, and they cause Lindsay to wilt like a dead flower, losing all her will to fight back. When her restrained body weakens, the chaos stills.

I look around for anyone's reaction, but Cheryl and Kat sheepishly avoid eye contact with me.

Why are they acting like they didn't just see this asshole completely lose it?

"She should be in a room with padded walls. I'm glad I'll never have to see her again," Kookie cries out from her huddled position in the corner of the room. The girls run to her side to console her.

"Are you okay?" Cheryl and Kat both ask repeatedly while rubbing Kookie's back.

Lindsay finally lifts her head up to say, "Oh please, Kookie, quit acting like a fucking victim."

Dr. Beckham still has ahold of her arm and tugs on her to leave.

"Lindsay, I'll escort you to your room. Your free time is over," Dr. Beckham says in a calm manner. He's somehow managed to completely switch his demeanor, as if he wasn't just a hotheaded, seething menace a second ago.

Maybe someone should have him checked for a split-personality disorder.

I try to follow them, but Dr. Beckham stops me. "Natalia, you can return to your room after dinner. Lindsay needs some time to herself right now."

"You better not fucking touch her, you dirtbag," I warn him under my breath as he walks her away.

"What was that, Natalia?" he asks sharply, glancing back.

"Oh, I think you heard me."

He sends a callous glare in my direction, then continues to push Lindsay forward down the hall.

Everything about this has me radioactive—not just Dr. Beckham's behavior that further validates how horribly abusive he is, but also the possibility that there's something going on between him and Kookie. If that's the case, then this whole situation has taken an even more disturbing left turn. If he has two girls enamored enough that they're willing to fight over him, it proves he's terrorizing more patients than just Lindsay. *This* is exactly why she needs to speak up.

How many other girls have been involved with him, and how many more will have to suffer at his hands until he gets caught?

I know I promised her I'd keep quiet, but I don't know how much longer I'll be able to hold something this heinous inside.

I can't stand the sound of Kookie's whimpering, so I head outside and lie in the shade of the tree. The intense adrenaline rush is wearing off, sending me back into my exhausted state. I curl up in the grass, trying to process everything that just went down, but my eyes roll into the back of head as my body desperately seeks sleep.

A gust of wind causes a small branch to fall next to me, startling me back into consciousness. The sun tucking behind the trees indicates how much time has passed—dinner is probably ready. When I walk in, all the food is almost cleared, and the sink is filled with dirty dishes. The clock shows that I'm thirty minutes late.

I enjoy the hazy silence of dinner by myself and then head back to my room.

I turn the doorknob, and when I walk in, I'm shocked at what I find. Lindsay's hair is almost all gone, with just a few inches of choppy pieces left. Her blue locks sit on the floor like a pool of chopped societal beauty standards.

"What do you think?" she asks, forming her bangs into spikes with hair products.

I wait a moment to take in her new look. It's edgy, but at the same time, it perfectly contrasts her soft features.

"Actually, it looks really good. It suits you."

This haircut might have been rash, but I'm just so happy to see she's not been locked away in a doctor's cabin.

"Thanks. I knew the craft scissors would continue to come in handy." She chomps the scissor blades together with her shoulders lifted and proud.

If only we could use them to cut Dr. Beckham out of our lives.

My mind has been on autopilot, and her new look almost distracted me from addressing all the craziness that went down today. "Okay, wait. Are you okay? That was insane earlier."

Lindsay grunts and tugs at her new haircut in the mirror.

"It's so fucked up!" She lets out an aggravated roar, squeezing her temples with her palms. I stay quiet, giving her a moment to let it all out. "Ugh, sorry, thanks for asking. I'm starting to believe you're the only person in my life who actually gives a shit about me," she says, calmer now, sweeping her fallen hair to the side of the room with her foot.

I reach out for a hug, but she pulls away. I don't take it personally. I can tell she's too defeated right now to return the embrace. As she moves to curl under her blanket, I sit across from her on mine.

"He's seeing Kookie. He's fucking seeing Kookie!" she screams, then lowers her voice, taking it down a notch. "I should have known I'm not the first patient he's fucked around with. She said he's going to leave his wife for her and that he wants to get an apartment in wine country with her. That's exactly, word for word, what he said to me. We had those plans, Natalia. He said it could be our escape. No wonder Kookie hates me so much. She loves him, too, and she has to hate all the extra attention he gives me. God, what a fucking snake he is!"

Lindsay is talking a mile a minute, and my half-working brain struggles to fit the pieces together.

"Well, isn't this good, in a way? We have proof now that he's been messing around with other patients and have witnesses. Cheryl and Kat saw everything."

Lindsay chuckles. "Yeah, right! Kookie is obviously obsessed with him and would never speak against him, and do you really think her devoted followers wouldn't have her back? This doesn't change anything. He's still in control, and this just validates that he can get away with whatever he fucking pleases."

"That's not fair!" I pound my fist on the mattress.

"Life isn't fair, Natalia. I know you've been sheltered from most of the world, but this is the reality. Humanity has failed girls like you and me. We're here because people say we're mentally ill and a danger to society, then give men like Dr. Beckham gold stickers for just having a degree and a dick in his pants."

Lindsay gruffly puts in her earbuds and closes her eyes.

She's instilled a sense of doubt in me. I've constantly been controlled, disregarded, and labeled insane by men in a white coat. But this fiery rage in me is uncontainable now and refuses to believe that they can revoke all our power. While Lindsay is losing hers, I won't let Dr. Beckham steal mine.

Grace comes in, and every part of me is pleading to just take the damn pills tonight except my heart. My heart wants to see Gabriel. My heart needs to see him. He's become my haven, and after the hurricane events of today, I could use him more than anything, even sleep.

As another night goes without medication, I decide to sneak out a little earlier than our usual meeting time, needing the fresh air. I climb out and sit against the wall beneath my window with my legs crossed. The wind is whistling, and my mind drifts to the white noise of nature.

"Natalia, wake up," a voice softly says.

My once-asleep body contorts, and the awning light blinds me as I blink my eyes open. When I can focus, I find myself curled on Gabriel's lap.

"You're okay. It's just me," he whispers. I stretch up, and he kisses my forehead. "Are you sure you want to stay out ton—"

"Yes," I answer with a yawn.

"I mean, you were passed out on the dirt when I showed up. Don't you think you should get some sleep in your bed?"

"It's fine. Trust me." I try to heighten my pitch to get rid of my groggy voice. I won't let my lack of sleep hinder my favorite part of the day.

We walk to the weeping willow, but something about tonight is unusual. Gabriel's hardly saying a word or making eye contact, just pulling pieces of bark off the trunk. I hope me being passed out didn't scare him earlier.

As I look up to the night sky, I'm reminded that this has been the backdrop during our whole relationship, a relationship that's been kept hidden in the dark.

"Are you okay?" I ask him.

He tosses a piece of bark to the ground and folds his legs down to sit on the grass, but I stay standing.

"I'm sorry. I'm just in a low place tonight." He pauses, pressing his lips tight together.

"What is it? What's going on?"

"It's just…" He sighs. "It's just that I've been trying to stay hopeful for us and our future, but truthfully, it's been so damn hard these last couple days."

My heart is pounding rapidly. His answer was not what I was expecting.

"What do you mean exactly?"

I move in front of him, but he won't glance up in my direction. His voice and head stays lowered.

"My depression has always kept me stagnant. Why look to the future if it's not guaranteed? Being excited for the future has always been foreign to me, and I'm not sure if I quite understand how to grasp that feeling yet." He rips his beanie off and tugs at his hair. "I just don't see how this can all work—how *we* will work—if I constantly feel this way."

Wait, is he breaking up me?

My legs go weak, and he reaches for me when my knees hit the ground, but his embrace doesn't soothe the heartache slowly crushing me.

He whispers in my ear, "I'm so sorry, Natalia. But there are these voices in my head telling me we'll never work because I'll never make it out of this place. You'll leave here soon enough, and you deserve to get out of here."

"I'll wait for you! I don't mind."

"I don't know if you even should. Whether I'm here another six months or six days, my sadness seems to just grow deeper. You're better off living a life without me," he confesses.

251

"That's not true!" I cry out.

It's becoming hard to swallow or breathe. He can't do this. He can't be ending this.

He squeezes his eyes shut briefly as he struggles to get out the words.

"You don't get it. I'm afraid this sadness or darkness or whatever it is will take over the last bit of me, and I don't want you to ever have to be there when this rotting bridge collapses."

His head falls between his knees, and it's the first time I've ever seen him weep.

I wrap my arms around his shaking shoulders and hold him as tight as I can. I'm trying to not make this all about me, because clearly it's not. It's hard to think of the right things to say to someone dealing with so much pain, but I try.

"Gabriel, you're not your illness or any of the awful things it tries to tell you that you are. Even after your lowest nights, there will always be a new day. Take it from someone who knows. I've dealt with some pretty horrific nights. You just have to give yourself the chance to make it to the sunrise."

He lifts his head and gazes at me. Tears slide down his cheek, but his lips lift for a moment, and it makes me adore him. His ability to smile in the midst of devastation gives me hope, not only for him but for us.

A light turns on above the sliding door of the boys' house, and a voice yells out, "Is someone out there?"

My pulse stops. Gabriel looks at me with a finger to his lips until the light shuts off, then whispers, "We better go. Here, take this and go first." He hands me his lighter to guide myself back.

As much as I don't want to leave, we can't get caught now. I do what he says and head back to the house. Mustering my last bit of strength, I struggle as I climb through my window.

After I fall like deadweight onto my sheets, I try to unravel our conversation. Did Gabriel just break things off? I'm still so unsure about what he meant. He basically said he doesn't see a future with me because he doesn't know if he'll even exist in one. I should have never brought anything up. Did I just destroy the best thing that's ever happened to me?

As my heart falls into pieces, I push myself up to the sill once more, hoping Gabriel stayed because he has to be as fraught as I am.

But he's gone.

All that's left outside is the tormenting sounds of the river that are growing louder every second. I cup my palms over my ears, hoping the water—and the pain of uncertainty—will stop taking turns beating me down.

CHAPTER 18

The growing light of the morning creeps over my bed. I watch specks of dust float around, sleep-deprived and my heart wrung out. I didn't get a second of rest.

How could I? Gabriel tried to end things, and I'm honestly not sure if I was able to talk him out of it. Now I have no clue where we stand.

The misery in Gabriel's eyes is haunting me, and the only thing I have to hold on to is his broken smile before he left me. It's my only reassurance that there's still hope for us.

Having to go through the motions today has been the hardest it's ever been. Lindsay caught on to my bad mood, but I couldn't bring myself to tell her why. She has enough to deal with on her own, and it would just prove her theory that Gabriel is having a poor effect on me.

The evening couldn't come fast enough. Nothing could distract me from my despair, but being asleep and not having to think about it for a while could be exactly what I need right now.

The sun finally sets, and Grace comes in with my medication. The sharp feeling of it sliding down my throat reminds me that I won't see Gabriel tonight. Tonight, rest wins whether I want it to or not.

Dr. Beckham comes in, and Lindsay turns her head to make eye contact with him. If only looks could kill. She rolls back toward the wall, tugging the blanket over her head.

"How are you feeling tonight, Natalia?" Dr. Beckham asks, placing the wires in their usual spots.

"Good," I lie. As much as I despise him right now, I have to play it cool.

"Well, this is our last sleep study. You're a week away from being able to sleep in your own bed with no more wires. I'm sure that has to feel nice."

"A week?"

"Yes, haven't you been counting the days?"

I nod, but I really haven't. It's almost like I've been living in a continuous dream.

It hits me suddenly, almost violently, like a whiplash, that I'll be leaving so soon. Normally, I'd be filled with excitement at the prospect of going home, but the only thing dominating my emotions is dread. I don't want to leave Gabriel—not with the type of heaviness he was experiencing and being so unsure of where we stand.

The beeping monitor slows down, and so do my thoughts. My resisting heart and head are finally overruled by my exhausted body, and the view of Dr. Beckham's eyes fades into nothing.

***

My consciousness comes back, but I can't move. My arms and legs feel stretched and stapled down. My eyes fly open. I anxiously inspect my surroundings, and I'm horrified at what I find: my worst nightmare. Leather straps are tightly restrained around my ankles and wrists, pinning me, spread eagle, to my bed. My body breaks out in a shivering sweat as the memories of being repeatedly tied down strike me like lashes on bare flesh—the dark hospital rooms, the raw lacerations on my skin from the rough buckles, the degrading loss of consent over my body, the crying and pleading for help but overtly being ignored.

"Let me go! Please!" I thrash and scream until someone else's hands release the ties. My shaky vision finally focuses on Lindsay's watering eyes.

"I'm so sorry. This is all my fault," she cries, fully removing the straps.

My limbs are free, but my chaotic state is not. I pant and cry out, unable to calm down.

Lindsay is at my side, brushing the hair off my face, trying to gently hush me.

Our door flies open, and Dr. Beckham runs in. "What is all the commotion?"

"Why did you do this?" My strained voice attempts to wail at him, but it's too hoarse to be effective.

Dr. Beckham stands in a wide stance with crossed arms, unfazed by my panic.

"You were showing active signs of your parasomnia during your sleep study. This was for your and everyone else's safety. I don't want you to put yourself at risk of ruining your discharge date. So please calm down or it will."

"Fuck my discharge date," I spit out fiercely, and his cold eyes narrow.

"She's calming down. How would you react if you woke up tied down like a fucking animal?" Lindsay shouts at him.

"I'll give you two a moment, as your emotions seem to be running high. But, Natalia, the discussion of your behavior is not over."

Lindsay is digging her teeth into her lower lip, and I can see the physical strength it's taking her to not go ballistic.

Once the door slams behind Dr. Beckham, she grabs me, and my emotions spiral out of control. The mental wound I thought was scabbed and scarred over has been split open, oozing out my past fear and pain. I clench the sides of my head, trying to keep it together.

"I'm so sorry," she cries.

"Why would he do that to me? I told him that's the one thing I couldn't deal with. I spent three months of my life pinned to my bed every night. It's a deeply vulnerable and violating experience that no human should have to ever endure."

Lindsay's tears pour harder than mine as she chokes out, "I told him that you know what's going on between him and me, that you saw us together. I think this is his sadistic way of sending you a threat. I shouldn't have told him. I shouldn't have gotten you involved. I'm so sorry. I just thought it might get him to leave me alone if he found out someone else knew."

As if he couldn't go any lower. Strapping me down was his reminder that he has all the power here.

It's scary that Dr. Beckham is now using physical tactics to instill fear in both Lindsay and me, but I put on a brave face for her.

"Don't be sorry for that at all. Dr. Beckham is the only person I could hate right now."

I channel my emotions into a boiling rage aimed solely at him.

"I really want you to know that I just love you so much," she says, nestling her head on my shoulder.

"I love you too." I lean my head against hers.

My anger dampens into a simmer. I still think Lindsay somehow thinks this is her fault. Her lips perk up, but tears are still building in her eyes.

"It's going to be okay. I promise. We have each other, and that's all that matters," I assure her, pulling her closer.

"I just need a break from this place... from him. I don't think I can handle any more of his fucked-up antics. Can I lie with you for a little?"

"Of course."

As we lie together side by side, Lindsay plays with my hair. It causes every one of my tense muscles to relax and reminds me how important she is to me. Just moments ago, she found me in my worst possible state and instantly came to my rescue. I've never had that before—that kind of devotion and support in my most miserable times. Even if Awana has stripped us of our freedom and placed us under the thumb of a corrupt doctor, I'm still thankful it brought me our unbreakable, rare bond.

I close my eyes, comforted, and allow myself to fall into a much-needed slumber.

***

My body jars awake from my nap, but Lindsay is no longer next to me. I sit myself up, and vertigo hits me with the nauseating sensation of a carnival ride. The side effects must be kicking in late. I hold on to my stomach and run to the bathroom, trying to keep its contents down. The door is closed, so I rapidly knock.

"Lindsay, can I come in?"

I wait for a few seconds, but there's no answer.

"Lindsay, please. I'm going to be sick!"

I don't want to intrude on her privacy, but my rumbling queasiness forces me to turn the knob and enter. I crack open the door, and what lies ahead steals my breath from me.

Lindsay is sprawled motionless on the floor with my bra that had been filled with pills next to her hand.

I rush to kneel beside her and cradle her head. After inspecting every inch to make sure she didn't hit it on something on her way down, I rest her cheek on my knee. I pick up the leftover pills scattered around us with my trembling hand and flush them down the toilet.

"How many did you take?" I yell at her. Her eyes are rolling back. I try to prop her head higher.

"Two. Three… maybe four. Those really fucked me up…," she mumbles, barely conscious.

I lightly tap her forehead to keep her aware, but it's not working. I set her head down and turn on the faucet above us, taking sprinkles from the running water to splash on her face.

"Come on, wake up, Lindsay. Try to remember how many pills for me. Please. It's important."

One or two would have anyone groggy and fatigued, but I'm worried that this is more severe. My medication is potent and could easily be deadly, especially in the hands of an addict who's used to doubling dosages.

Why in the world would I think it was okay to leave a pile of pills in a room with someone with an active addiction?

Lindsay's breaths are slowing as her body grows more limp in my arms.

Oh God, what have I done? What's happening to her?

"Lindsay, say something! Anything!"

259

Her mouth slightly parts, and her words come out in a low hum.

"I don't care if he hurts me anymore, but I can't live with him hurting you. I have to end this. All of it." She slurs as a small dribble of spit slides down her chin. She rolls her head around. "But isn't this everything he's always wanted? He rises while I fall."

I tie together her distorted words.

Was this an attempt to escape Dr. Beckham or her life? Or both?

I grab ahold of her neck, which has lost all strength to stay upright. Her skin is clammy and cold.

"I need to get Dr. Cassidy."

"No!" she screams, then begins incoherently spewing nonsensical sounds until she goes silent and her eyelids flutter closed. Her body begins to twitch.

"Lindsay? Are you okay?" I grab her chin, trying to regain her focus. "Lindsay, please answer me!"

Her frail body violently shakes in my arms, and foam runs from her mouth. I tightly wrap myself around her, trying to control her convulsing body, but I can't. A stream of tears bursts from my eyes.

"Someone help us!" I repeatedly scream at the top of my lungs from the porcelain-tiled floor until my burning throat gives out.

A ringing in my ears takes over, and everything slows down around me. Arms pull me away from her, and when she's released from my grip, her head droops to the side, and the color in her cheeks and lips has disappeared.

As I'm dragged out of the bathroom, two staff members I've never seen before rush in our room with a metal stretcher. "Code

Blue," one says into his radio. "We have an overdose at Awana Treatment Center. Twenty-two-year-old female, nonresponsive."

"Lindsay, please, you have to wake up! You can't leave me!" I cry out to her, trying to run back in, but Grace and a male nurse restrain me, shoving me face down onto my bed.

This can't be happening...

With my arms pinned behind my back, I lift my head to watch. When they strap her to the gurney, my thoughts torture me. I've been so worried about Gabriel's self-harm, I was oblivious to the fact that my best friend was capable of the same demise. But what ravages me the most is knowing that I supplied her with the weapon.

Her once-thrashing body is now stunned in place. I heave as the panic fully sets in. The nurses' faces and words are a blur as they try to calm me. My vision is tunneled around Lindsay as I helplessly watch her slip away right in front of me.

They roll her out with an oxygen mask covering her mouth. As they push out the door, my gasps and sobs turn into full-blown hysterics.

"Please, let me go with her! She needs me!" I wail, unable to control my hyperventilating shakes.

"You need to relax!" a nurse shouts in my ear, but I can't. Sorrow and fear have taken full control.

"No! Let me go! Please let me be with her. She needs me!"

My struggling arms break free. With all my force, I jab and scratch the limbs trying to ground me, desperately screaming out her name.

A needle breaks through my skin, and the living nightmare in front of me quickly melts like paint dripping down a canvas.

CHAPTER 19

Nine hours later, the sedative they injected in me has worn off, and I've spent the last hour in Lindsay's bed, praying for good news. My tears have stained the pillow that smells like her sweet scent. The horrifying images of her being taken away won't stop replaying behind my eyelids, and the what-ifs are running in my head on repeat.

How did I not see this coming? What if this is all my fault?

Things were far from great here for Lindsay, but I didn't think it was bad enough to lead her to this. How could I be so naive? She's been trapped and controlled by her vile abuser this whole time. Day after day, she was forced to engage with him in sessions, and during the nights, when I was too drugged to notice, he held her sexually hostage in our room like a cat stalking a mouse.

The worst what-if is the one that's crippling me, pinning me to this bed, making me ache from the inside out.

What if this secret kills my first and only best friend?

I should have spoken up the moment I suspected something was going on between them. Maybe then, none of this horror would have happened. But as much as I hate myself right now, I loathe Dr. Beckham more. It's his constant abuse that ate away at her soul and detrimentally caused her to do this.

My door creaks open and I jump up, hoping it's her. Dr. Cassidy walks in, and I analyze her expression for a clue to Lindsay's current state. She sits on the edge on Lindsay's mattress. Her normally comforting facial cues haven't appeared. Anxiety and fret are stomping harder on my chest every second she doesn't speak. She places a hand on my shaking knee.

"She's going to be just fine," she finally says, and it feels like the sun has broken through a disastrous storm. I squeeze my eyes shut and bite my lower lip, soaking in the immense relief.

I exhale as I reopen my eyelids. "When can I see her?"

"She's not coming back. Her parents are taking her back home. Awana isn't the right fit for her anymore."

As much as it stings to hear she won't be returning, I can't say I blame them. Their daughter overdosed on Awana's watch. I wonder how'd they react if they knew one of their doctors had been sexually assaulting her for months and basically blackmailed her into silence and submission.

"How is she?" I ask.

"She's doing well, considering she suffered a small seizure, but she's talking again and eating normally." Her tone grows more serious. "Natalia, she won't tell us where she got the pills from or why she took them. You're her closest friend. Is there any insight you can share with me?"

Lindsay has never ratted out for my strange morning behaviors or sneaking out. But the guilt gouges me. The pills were mine, and I know the reason she took them. She had been suffering, and it was the only way she knew how to cope.

It's time for me to be the friend Lindsay deserves. I kept my vow of silence about their relationship this long, but that may have been my worst mistake. Awana wasn't the right fit, but not because of her. I need to expose the doctor whose one job was to keep her safe, but instead he drove her to the brink.

"I know why she did it, and I know who's given her pills here before."

Dr. Cassidy narrows her eyes, tilting her head. "Go on."

I swallow a gulp that feels like a jagged rock.

"Dr. Beckham is a horrible, awful man." I tense, trying to fight back tears.

Dr. Cassidy moves next to me on my bed and rests her hand on mine. Her gesture brings me enough comfort to continue.

"I caught him and Lindsay together sexually when they both thought I was asleep during one of my studies. I confronted her the next day, and that's when she spilled that they had been hooking up frequently. She eventually wanted it to stop, but he wouldn't allow it. Not only that, but I saw him act violently toward her more than once. He was emotionally and physically abusing her constantly, and no one here ever noticed. He even gave her pills in secret so she'd be dependent on him, then used her own addiction against her when she'd threaten to expose what he was doing to her."

Dr. Cassidy's eyes widen with pure shock as she cups a hand over her mouth.

"Has he hurt you or anyone else that you know of?"

"Yes." I drop my head. "He strapped me to my bed in the middle of the night when he found out I knew what was going on. I think in a way it was to punish or try and silence me. I also don't want to speak for her, but I think he was sexually abusing Kookie too. Lindsay and I heard her talking about the relationship he had with her—a romantic one, she claimed. Lindsay and Kookie even got in a physical fight over him that he had to break apart."

She tucks in her lips and nods, trying to keep herself composed, but I can see fury forming in her eyes.

"I know I should have said something sooner. I'm sorry. Dr. Beckham told her that no one would believe her is she spoke up and that he would make her life a living hell if she dared to say anything, and she wholeheartedly believed it. She made me promise not to tell anyone because she was afraid of him."

Dr. Cassidy grabs my hand supportively, staying quiet while I rattle off the full story. I continue to explain to how I wanted Lindsay to come forward, but that she had convinced me that we as patients wouldn't be trusted against him, and we needed to bite our tongues.

Finally confessing this out loud feels like slow-killing venom has been sucked from my veins.

"I wanted to tell you the moment I found out. I *really* did. I was just too scared that I wouldn't be believed, or I'd get in trouble somehow."

Her brows lower as she rubs my hand.

"This is not your fault. You do not need to apologize or be afraid. You didn't do anything wrong. I understand how hard this type of thing can be to bring forward. I appreciate you being brave enough now to open up and tell me what he's been doing to all you girls. It's a serious crime, for which he will be punished. I will personally make sure of that."

It feels like I can finally breathe. Her supportive response is one I wasn't expecting but what I desperately needed to hear.

"So, you do believe me?" I ask, feeling my lip quiver.

"Of course I do. I'm sorry I didn't make you feel safe enough to come to me with this because you thought you would somehow be in trouble. Nothing could be further from the truth. Dr. Beckham is the only one to blame here and the only one who is trouble. I will be taking immediate action. I'm calling the police.

Effective immediately, he is suspended until the investigation is complete. He will need to leave campus and have no contact with any patients. You will not have to see him. He will not be able to approach you or speak to you. He can't hurt you. You're safe." She throws up her hands. "Hell, I would strangle him myself right now if I could. I won't let him get away with this. Trust me," she snarls.

I've never heard her speak this harshly about anyone. I can practically see the smoke coming from her ears. She's clearly shaken up and ready for vengeance. Dr. Cassidy is the fierce protector we've needed all along.

Her reassurance and the overwhelming release of this festering, dark secret clinging to my chest draws out tears. A crushing weight has been lifted. A hidden predator has finally been exposed.

"Thank you," I manage to say as I pull myself to my feet.

Dr. Cassidy also rises and stands facing me.

"I'm proud of you, Natalia. If there's one thing I've learned with men like him, it's that they won't stop what they're doing until they're caught. Because of you, he's never going to hurt anyone ever again."

I lean forward and latch on to her, letting the tears pour down my cheeks as she wraps her arms around me and holds me.

The destruction in Dr. Beckham's wake feels insurmountable. I even almost fell under his spell the first time I met him. I'm so thankful I didn't. When I imagine the look in Lindsay's eyes the night I saw him on top of her, I cringe. For a girl who lit up like a firework, he dimmed her completely. Despite his arrogance and manipulative ploys to suppress her, Lindsay is going to get the justice she deserves and will finally be set free from the ties Dr. Beckham bound her with.

***

A woman with a gun strapped to her waist and a gold badge resting on her hip just left my room after taking down my statement. Dr. Cassidy stayed right by my side the entire time for moral support. The words poured out faster than I could comprehend them all. I didn't hold back, telling her every detail. I even divulged my own strange experiences with him, like his lingering touches and the way he kept trying to bring the topic of sex into our therapy sessions. It sends a shiver down my spine, remembering all the times I thought he was a little off. But he really had a much more sinister intent behind what I know now were advances. He was testing me to see how I would respond.

A few moments after the officer leaves, I hear a commotion coming from outside my door. Dr. Cassidy had left with the officer and told me to stay in my room until Dr. Beckham was escorted out of the building, but I wasn't going to miss this. I rush out to see what's happening.

I need to see this asshole go down.

All the girls and the nursing staff stand in the living room with dropped jaws and arms crossed. Dr. Beckham is being handcuffed while yelling and struggling against his arrest.

"This is a huge mistake. That fucking bitch was lying! She's the one obsessed with me!" he shouts as two policemen force him out of the front door.

Everyone rushes to the window. I push past the crowd for a clear view of him being shoved into the back seat. For an instant, his eyes lock on mine menacingly through the glass. I return his scowl with wiggled fingers and a grin bursting with satisfaction.

"Bye, bye, Bennett," I mouth to him.

I wonder how he likes being restrained against his will.

Only one thing would make this sweeter: having Lindsay here to witness his fall from grace. The one person I wish could be here to see this moment in in the hospital because of this monster.

Don't worry, Lindsay. I got your revenge. He's done for.

***

The last twenty-four hours have turned Awana upside down. After my confession, the police raided Dr. Beckham's cabin. The pervert had a hidden drawer filled with love notes and nude Polaroids of past patients, some who were underage. He obviously had a sick fetish for those under his so-called care.

But justice is prevailing, not only because he'll lose his job and his medical license, but because after all the evidence the police found corroborating my story, I have no doubt that he'll be found guilty and will spend a good chunk of his life behind bars. I find it ironic, but also a very fitting punishment. I think Dr. Beckham got off on locking up his patients and grooming them to become reliant on him. Sadly, I saw it happen to my closest friend right in front of me.

I'm comforted now knowing he has lost all his authority and will be at the mercy of guards and other inmates. Maybe his good looks will attract the same types of crimes he enjoys inflicting on others.

My chest hurts thinking of Lindsay. Her parents don't want her to have any contact with anyone at Awana. I begged Dr. Cassidy to let me call her, but she legally can't allow it. She did inform me that Lindsay is safe at home now and has been cooperating with the police about her experiences. I can't begin to imagine what she's going through. I just wish I could be there for her.

All her stuff is gone. The pictures decorating her wall have been taken down, and her bed has been stripped bare. I've stayed in my room, unable to do anything else but hold my pillow and pray that she's doing okay.

My door opens, and it's the last face I was expecting to see. Standing there is Lindsay's biggest enemy—Kookie. I hope she's not coming here to talk shit since I'm the reason her secret lover was arrested.

She pops her head in but keeps it lowered, avoiding eye contact with me.

"Can I come in?" she asks quietly, and I nod in confusion. She settles down on Lindsay's mattress and taps her feet without saying anything.

I thought Kookie already left Awana and said her goodbyes.

Why on earth is she here?

"Why are you back?" I jump straight to it.

Kookie's normally tough expression softens. "The police came to my house. They told me everything. I get it now, why Lindsay was so angry that day when she overheard me talking about Bennett. I was hoping Lindsay would be here, because I owe her an apology. We were in the exact same situation. He was using both of us, and I was in denial the whole time."

A light bulb in my head brightens. Lindsay was right about Kookie and Dr. Beckham, but now with all his secrets unveiled, it's not all that shocking.

"I'm glad you've finally come to realize that. He really is a messed-up man."

Kookie releases a breath, then continues, "I know. I didn't even have the slightest clue that he was playing us both. He lied and told me Lindsay was the one constantly coming on to him. I

269

saw her as a threat, trying to get in between what we had, so I resented her for it. But then after our fight in the kitchen, I started to wonder. Her emotions were so raw and real. How could there not have been something going on between them? It wasn't until after I was discharged, and he decided to completely ignore me, that I began to really question him and his intentions. He lied to me, and I fell for it. I feel so stupid," she says, sniffling into her palms.

"He lied to everyone. He was scarily good it."

Kookie's pain is obvious. I'm seeing a softer side to her I never knew existed. I sit next to her and rub her back, and it causes her to spill more.

"And the shit they found in his cabin. I seriously thought he loved me... *only* me. Then I come to find out I'm just another girl in a photograph for his disturbing collection of conquests."

"He's disgusting," I assure her. "I can only imagine how much it hurts to find all this out."

There's a laundry list of fucked-up things he did to Lindsay, but it's not my place to share them with her, and who knows what he's done to Kookie that she's not mentioning.

"It's horrible. And I feel worse for how I acted toward Lindsay. Do you think she could ever forgive me?" Her tearful eyes peer up at me.

Though she had no right treating Lindsay the way she did, her remorse is clear.

"I do. I wish she was here so she could know that she never was alone."

"I wish I wasn't so blind to it all." She sighs and wipes her eyes.

"There's no way you could have known. Dr. Beckham was a mastermind at what he was doing. He knew pitting you two against each other would only benefit him."

She stands to straighten her blouse. "You're so right. Thank you for not holding all the shit I've said to you guys against me."

"Don't ever worry about it."

I'm shocked. I didn't think Kookie would ever admit to her wrongdoings or turn against Dr. Beckham, so I need to give her some serious credit.

Before she leaves, she stops in the doorway and turns back to me.

"I made a full statement to the police. I want to make sure the charges stick," Kookie says.

"Good. With all the statements against him, he's not going free."

We both wave goodbye, and though we might not ever see each other again, I see her in a different light. Yes, she said some truly cruel things, but she wasn't just a mean girl. She was also a vulnerable young woman who fell for a predator who knew how to pull her strings. He used her insecurities to his advantage and probably encouraged her to belittle Lindsay. All her bullying tactics were her way of defending her brainwashed version of love. She was just another one of his victims.

And now, she's free.

CHAPTER 20

Olga wants me home after she heard about the accusations against Dr. Beckham. Dr. Cassidy even offered to sign an early release if I wanted to go. I contemplated leaving, but I chose to stick out my last few days because amid the insane turmoil, there's one thing keeping me here, one person I'm still desperate to see before I leave. With Dr. Beckham gone and my last sleep study out of the way, I really have no reason to take my medication. I'm hoping tonight, Gabriel will be there waiting for me.

Waiting for Grace tonight is lonely. When she arrives, she hands me my pills, and after I pop them into my mouth, she doesn't leave after a quick inspection. Instead, she pulls out a tongue depressor and a light. I tense my tongue.

"New protocol."

I take a gulp and swallow the drugs, afraid she'll catch me. After she inspects every crevice of my mouth, she leaves, and my eyes water. I'm never going to see Gabriel before I have to leave. He's going to show up at my window, and I won't be there. When I saw him last, he was in a miserable state, and I just need to make sure he's okay. After almost losing Lindsay, it's impossible not to worry about him. But now I don't know how I'll make it.

Alone again, my heart feels bruised and battered. I never knew being heartbroken would physically hurt this much.

I pace my room, desperate to stay awake, but this medication is much stronger than my will. I slap my face and pinch my skin, hoping the pain will keep my mind alert, but the sedating substance makes my legs feel like heavy bricks and forces me to lie down. Within minutes, my mind is gone.

***

The sun blaring in my room is the reminder that I've spent one less night with Gabriel. I look out my window, hoping to find any trace of him, but all I see is the dried-up grass from the summer heat. The warmth from my window makes me ill, and the acid in my stomach crawls up my throat. I make it to the bathroom just in time and cling to the toilet. As I lean over the white porcelain bowl, an idea strikes me.

I think I've just found a way to stay awake so I can see Gabriel.

Once my stomach settles, I brush the acidic taste out of my mouth and hastily throw my shoes on to go downstairs. As I head down the hallway, a foul smell whiffs up my nose. There's vomit stuck between matted black strands of my hair. I take the scrunchie off my wrist and gather my hair back into a messy bun. At this point, I don't even care about my personal hygiene. I just need to get through this day so I can enact my plan later tonight.

Breakfast is quiet. There are no more crazy stories from Lindsay to keep me entertained, just the sounds of chewing and scraping forks. I'm sitting at a table with only Abby, who is quiet this morning, but I'll take her silence over any of her absurd comments. I can hardly eat, too anxious for breakfast and this whole day to end. Abby looks perplexed at her juice that's almost spilling out of the glass. I realize my shaking legs are causing the whole table to vibrate. I ditch her and my food. I'm too restless to be here any longer.

Arts and crafts is the same as breakfast—boring. With two girls gone, it's just Abby, me, Cheryl, and Kat, who now all keep to themselves. My stomach is still not right, and I struggle to do my poses in yoga, or maybe it's because of my complete lack of motivation to do anything other than see Gabriel.

When free time comes, I head straight for the willow tree. I figure I may as well use this time wisely. Maybe I'll find a hint that Gabriel was here last night. I inspect around the trunk and between the grass and leaves for a cigarette butt or his harmonica, but to my disappointment, there's nothing.

I peer toward the sliding door of the boys' house on the other side of the grass. The curtains are drawn with just a crack of space between.

If only I could get a closer look inside.

I glance around cautiously. No one is around except Dr. Cassidy, who's watering flowers in the garden to my left. She looks distracted enough.

Hell, what do I care if I get caught at the boys' house? I'm leaving soon anyways.

Now's my chance. I make a run for it.

The house is much farther than it looks, and with the blistering sun on my shoulders, I've broken out in a full-body sweat. I crouch down on a step leading to the doors and press my face against the glass where the parted drapes allow a view inside. A group of boys is having a good time playing a board game on a table, but not one of them is Gabriel.

A noise distracts me. It's the soft sound of music playing. I follow it, hoping it'll lead me to who I want to see. A window around the corner is open, but it's too high to know what's inside. I whisper his name, desperate for him to hear me, but nothing happens after my few attempts. I elevate my voice until I'm screaming.

"Gabriel!" I shout too loudly.

The music stops, and so does my racing heartbeat.

Somebody heard me.

I wait, silently praying that it's him. A hand lands on my shoulder, and my body shakes. I turn around to find a woman I don't know in a doctor's coat.

"You're not supposed to be over here." She looks at me quizzically. I glance back to the window, but it's now closed. "Do you need help? Are you lost? You look confused."

I don't answer any of her questions. I try to conjure a good lie quick, but one never comes.

"I-I'm… I'm just—" I stutter. But she doesn't let me finish.

"After everything that's happened recently, we're not taking any chances with boys and girls being near each other. We don't need any more scandals on our hands. I think it's time we bring you back to where you belong."

The older woman with a black bob wraps an arm around me and guides me to the girls' yard. Out of options, I follow her and slowly walk back toward my own dorm with a disappointed sigh. Dr. Cassidy spots us and meets us halfway.

"Is there a problem, Dr. Lee?"

"No, I don't think so. Just a wanderer. I found her in our yard, yelling something at our window."

"Natalia?" Dr. Cassidy looks at me sternly. "What were you doing over there?"

Screaming out the name of the boy I love so I can find him one last time before I leave this place and never see him again.

But I know I can't say that. I can't say anything about Gabriel without revealing weeks of lies and rule breaking. What if it would make them want to send me home right away? Any shot I would have at being reunited with him would be completely blown. So I just shrug, not giving her the real reason.

"This is Natalia," Dr. Cassidy says to the other woman. "She was Lindsay Cartwright's roommate. I think the incident has her feeling a little out of it today. Is that right?" she asks me, placing an arm tightly around my shoulders.

I nod, still not answering.

"Ah, yes. Understandable. Well, feel better, dear. Just be sure to stay over here. The boys are distracted enough, and a yelling girl had them all on their toes," Dr. Lee says with a wink, then heads off in the direction of the boys' house.

Dr. Cassidy leads me back with my head down. I feel defeated. My hope of seeing Gabriel is beginning to deteriorate.

What if I never see his face again?

***

Six weeks at Awana, yet the only thing I know about Grace is she's extremely punctual and likes to wear different printed socks each day of the week. I like to think that makes her personable, even if I've never seen the woman smile. She comes in not a minute late, and peeking from her canvas slip-on shoes tonight are small flamingos.

"Did you know flamingos like to dance?" I ask before she hands me my pill. She furrows her gray brows. "Yeah, it's actually a way to entice a mate. It's sort of their version of flirting."

A corner of Grace's mouth moves toward her cheek.

That was definitely a smirk. Maybe I've finally cracked her.

"They're my favorite animal."

"Great choice," I say before popping the pills into my mouth.

I thought some light conversation would distract her from her oral inspection, but she proceeds with her flashlight, so I'm forced to swallow them down.

As soon as Grace leaves, I resort to my original plan, the one I thought of this morning and am now dreading, but after all my failed attempts to see Gabriel, I know what I have to do. I kneel before the toilet and squeeze my eyes shut as I stick two fingers in my mouth. Saliva drips down my hand, but no gagging. My eyes water as I stick them in farther, to the point that I feel my own tonsils. My stomach retches and expels vomit into the water below.

Out of breath, I examine the half-digested pasta from dinner. When I spot the small yellow pills floating between basil chunks and spit, I sit up, knowing this sense of pride is a new level of dysfunctional for me.

Now it's time to wait. It's only a little after eight, so I have some time to kill.

I pace my room. I pick my split ends. I try on different outfits. I lie down. I do jumping jacks. I chew on my nails, then move on to the surrounding skin, then reprimand myself to stop.

The clock acts as my biggest enemy, dragging every minute out to an eternity. Finally, the moment arrives. At a little past two, I open my window, and a part of me withers away when all I see is darkness. No scent of a cigarette or sound of a harmonica.

But I won't lose hope, so I stay up. I hang upside down on my bed, feeling the blood rush to my head until I get dizzy. I attempt to braid my hair, but it ends up in knots. I pace and pace some more.

I am constantly checking out the window for his approach. Each hour that goes by leaves me more disappointed than the last.

Dawn is approaching. The haze of the morning rolls onto the wet grass. The sun is rising, but I want to scream at it to stop. It proves that Gabriel didn't come to see me last night.

Does he not even care enough to say goodbye?

I'm curled up in bed feeling utterly numb. My cracked, sleep-deprived eyes are unable to shed any tears.

I am broken.

CHAPTER 21

Two more days have passed, and Gabriel still hasn't appeared. Neither has my desire to sleep.

How could he do this to me? How could he care so little?

My last night at Awana is before me, and I've never felt more alone. Lindsay has disappeared from my life, and Gabriel doesn't want to see me. Olga will take me home tomorrow and will want me to go back to being isolated from the world and everything in it. But I'm a completely different person than the timid, obedient girl who first arrived at Awana. I've learned what true friendship is and how to stand up for myself and others who are being treated unjustly. I've shed the skin of who I once was, and it's toughened me into a young woman who won't tolerate my old desolate living conditions.

I'm sure my final meeting will go exactly as all the others have throughout the years.

Dr. Cassidy will instruct me to *"Take your medication and call us if your sleep patterns change."*

But I've hit the point where I don't care about my inability to sleep or if my horrific night terrors cause me physical harm.

Who cares about my fractured brain when it's my heart that hurts?

It's just after 5:00 p.m., and I drag my feet to my last meal at Awana. I'm in a fog as I go through the motions of putting food on my plate from the buffet. I've mentally checked out. My fingers are shaking as I push around my chicken and rice. My appetite must have decided to disappear too.

"You'll never see him again," I hear an ominous voice whisper.

Wait, was that in my head? Did I just think that, or did someone actually say that out loud?

Confused, I look around to see who's within earshot. As always, it's only me and Abby at the table. I squint my eyes at her, and she stares back.

"Did you say something?" I ask.

She ignores me and puts her head down.

My anger toward her has been growing hotter than lava, but it's her blatant disregard for me that causes me to fully erupt.

"Here we go again! Might as well finish our final dinner together with one last bizarre remark! Do you think this is some sort of joke? You say weird shit to mess with my head and then clam up when I call you out on it?" I bolt up from the table, slamming my fists hard against the top.

Abby recoils, quickly scooting back in her chair. She pulls her legs up and throws her arms around them, holding on to her knees in the fetal position. She's cowering as if I might strike her. But I won't fall for her scared, victim act.

I've had just about enough of this girl and her mind games.

"Say something, Abby! You're not a mute! You're lying to everyone. I know it. Say something!" I yell, feeling myself physically shaking.

She tucks her head into her legs and begins to cry loudly. Her sobs finally bring me out of the wave of rage that was ready to rip right through her.

What the hell am I doing? She's clearly terrified.

I lower my stance and voice. "I'm sorry. I didn't—"

Her cries grow louder, and before I can finish my apology, Dr. Cassidy runs in and rushes over to our table to comfort her.

"What is happening here? Natalia, you have no reason to be raising your voice," she says sternly while coddling Abby and stroking her shoulder.

I take a step back, unsure of what to do.

"I'm sorry. I really am, Abby."

"I know you've been through an ordeal, but that doesn't give you the right to shout at anyone. Abby does not deserve to be spoken to like that," Dr. Cassidy snaps. I've never been on the receiving end of her anger, and it doesn't feel good.

"You're right. I'm sorry," I say remorsefully, and I truly mean it.

Dr. Cassidy looks at me with disappointment in her eyes and nods her head. She helps a tearful and very shaken Abby up from her chair and walks her out of the kitchen.

What is happening to me? Why did I just completely lose my shit?

After I escort myself to my room, I sit on the floor with my back against my bed, trying to figure out the jigsaw of my emotions that are all over the place and uncontrollable at this point. I can't believe I lashed out at Abby like that.

My door opens, and I'm not surprised to see Dr. Cassidy. I knew my stunt at dinner would earn me a visit. I sit up and straighten the bottom of my dress over my knees. She pulls the desk chair close to me, a black notebook in her hands.

"I know this is your last night, and it does tend to bring heightened emotions, but is everything okay? You've never shown any sort of aggressive behavior before, so it does alarm me."

I was expecting some serious reprimanding for my actions, so I'm more than thankful for her empathetic concern.

"I'm fine," I say with a heavy sigh.

"It's okay if you're not. It's unrealistic to think you can never have bad days. Was today one of those days?"

"Sort of. I guess I just have some stuff on my mind."

That's a huge understatement.

"Well, I'm all ears."

The immense weight of it all feels unexplainable at this point, but I try.

"I just feel like everything is going to change when I go home. The relationships I've made here will disappear, and I'll be alone again."

Dr. Cassidy looks at Lindsay's bed.

"Do you know if she's doing okay?" I ask.

"I know you miss her. She's doing fine. They found a facility close to home. She has a lot of deep healing to do, and it's going to take time, but I think you stepping forward has allowed her to be in a safe place to do so. Here, I brought you this. A parting gift." She hands me the notebook. "I know it's a bit outdated, but the exercise still serves great purpose. Sometimes when we're forced to let people go, writing them letters can bring you a sense of closeness to them even when you're far away."

She pulls a pen from her pocket and sets it on my nightstand.

After she leaves, I open the notebook and find an envelope tucked into the first page. It's stamped and addressed to Lindsay Cartwright's home in Santa Barbara.

She's given me a lifeline to Lindsay. The perpetual frown I've been wearing finally lifts.

Lindsay's wild blue hair comes to mind. I run my fingers through mine and remember that the first time I ever felt beautiful was because of her. I miss her so much. I miss her loud music and silly dance moves. I miss her quick wit and her ability to always make me laugh even on the days I struggled the hardest. Though she was reckless and short-tempered at times, her heart was always in the right place. She cared for me deeply, and I couldn't ask for more in a first friend—my best friend. I'm left with a comforting hope that my friendship with Lindsay won't be left to die in the walls of this room.

After Grace comes and does her inspection, I stand with my back against the bathroom door. I'm torn. I'm running on only the couple of hours of sleep between dawn approaching and my blaring alarm. I'm exhausted, and the thought of shoving my fingers down my raw throat makes me shiver, but I twist the doorknob and do what I have to, throwing up everything in me until the little yellow pills appear. I know it seems insane, but I'm holding on to the tiniest speck of hope that on my last night, Gabriel will come to see me.

I lie in bed in my white nightgown, staring at the ceiling, trying to determine how long it's been. The strange thing about sleep deprivation is that time operates differently; minutes can feel like hours, and hours can feel like minutes. It's hard to keep track of the moments during the day. It's like I'm being pulled through a messy collage of memories that may or may not have already taken place.

Every evening I've spent with Gabriel is spinning through my head like a carousel, from the moment he rested his cigarette on my feeder to when I became his.

The clock strikes two, and the only thing worthy of noting outside is a crescent moon in the distance. My heart, which once felt woven into Gabriel's, now feels like it's being ripped at the seams as each second approaches closer to daylight. The hours I've spent waiting have been tortuous, and the sun will be making its arrival soon.

Though everything in me feels defeated, I grab the notebook and pen, and through my blurry vision, I scribble down one line. The last thing I'll never get to say to him.

Gabriel King, why would you come into my life only to disappear from it completely?

My falling tears smudge the blank ink. Every piece of me is shattering, but I pretend to be whole. My sorrow is turning into a jaded bitterness toward Gabriel. I don't leave him my address or number. He's the one who chose to sever us, so I'll respect his wishes.

I roll up the paper, and with my disintegrating strength, I pull myself out my window one last time to leave him the letter I hope one day he'll find after I'm gone. My feet land on the grass, but I immediately lose my balance, falling to my knees. I feel around the dirt to find a rock. A sharp one scrapes against my palm, and I place it over my letter to weigh it to the ground.

I'm shivering, but somehow, my skin is hot and sweaty, protecting me from the freezing winds around me. I crawl toward my window, too worn out to walk or climb back up. Instead, I rest my back against the wall to collect my disorganized thoughts. I close my eyes, trying to find some form of peace in the final moments of this weary night.

This truly is the end of Gabriel and me.

A cool breeze hits my sticky skin, sending chills through me. My eyes fly open and fixate on a blurry figure walking across the lawn, toward the trees in the distance. I dig my knuckles into my eyelids to make sure I'm not asleep. The sight becomes clear ahead of me.

It's him.

Gabriel is dressed up in a white button-up and tie, with his hair blowing in the wind. But he's not headed toward me.

Where is he going?

He doesn't see me, but I need to see him. I'm exhausted and weak, but this desperation to give our abandoned romance one last shot at closure forces me to my feet.

I'm not ready to give up on us yet.

I gather my strength and trample over the damp grass with my bare feet. Gabriel has already headed into the forest that lies at the property's edge. Sharp rocks pierce my skin, but I ignore the pain and push my legs to move faster, hurrying before I lose sight of him. I follow him into the darkness.

My panting creates clouds in the air, and when I make it close enough, I yell his name.

"Gabriel. Gabriel!" I call out to him, but he doesn't seem to hear me.

His back is to me, and the distance between us continues to grow. I try to keep my eyes on him, but it's difficult. I'm running fast, but I can't seem to catch up with him. The overgrown branches are casting shadows in every direction, and I have to keep looking down so that I don't trip. The moon is only half full, so there isn't much light in the night sky to guide me.

I catch a reflection from his bright shirt moving farther into the woods. I trail behind, afraid that if I don't reach him in time, this will be the last I ever see of him.

"Gabriel, stop! Please!" The sound of my voice bounces off the trees, and I can't imagine how he doesn't hear me.

Is he really choosing to ignore me right now?

I'm stepping over fallen leaves and leaping over broken logs that line the forest floor. We're reaching the area of the forest that clears, making way for the river. He heads down the embankment, staying close to the riverbank. The sound of the hissing water grows stronger, stopping me in my tracks, provoking the unexplainable harrowing feeling this river has always given me. Every hair on my body stands straight, and my flesh is covered in goose bumps.

Get a grip, Natalia. There's nothing to be afraid of.

Out of breath, I force myself to continue my chase. I've almost caught up to him. A gap in the branches above allows moonlight to shine through, offering a clear view of Gabriel making his way to the water's edge. Suddenly he stops, staring down into the choppy bank.

"Gabriel!" I call out in the loudest voice I can muster. The rushing water creates a white noise that is hard to hear over.

His shoulders twist, and I see his head turn back in my direction.

I think he finally heard me.

For an instance, his eyes lock with mine, and I freeze in place because of the startling sight before me. He doesn't look like the Gabriel I know and love. His eyes are dark, sunken in sorrow. All the warmth and charisma has vanished from his face.

What on earth is he doing?

As if he's read my thoughts, he shrugs apologetically and then jerks his body back around to face the open water. Gabriel spreads his arm out at his sides like a cross, and terror overtakes me.

"Gabriel, no! Don't!" I scream.

Only a few feet away, I lunge forward and reach out for him. But before I can wrap my arms around his chest, he escapes my grasp, dropping headfirst into the water. His limbs hit the surface with a cracking sound like a snapping branch.

"Gabriel!" I cry out, crouching down on the riverbank. "Swim to the edge!" I desperately reach my hand down for him, but my arm is too short.

Helpless and afraid, I watch the rapids thrash him around. His head floats above the waterline for a moment, and his shivering lips are violet blue. The hypothermia alone could kill him. As the waves continue to drag him under, I realize he's not struggling or attempting to swim. It's as if he wants the deadly waters to take him.

The harsh reality finally hits me.

He came here to take his own life. And he wants to drown.

I can't allow it. Not on my watch.

I look around for anything I can use to reach farther out to him, but there's nothing but mud and twigs. I run to the nearest tree and reach up toward a hanging branch. With all my body weight, I pull until the wood cracks and falls. Grabbing one end, I begin dragging it toward the river's edge. I cast it into the water inches away from him, holding on tight, praying he'll see and take ahold of it.

"Fuck! Gabriel, please grab on!" I yell.

But he never does. The catastrophic waters are winning the battle that I don't think Gabriel is willing to fight. His head plunges under, but this time he doesn't come back up.

I can't watch him die.

There's only one thing to do. He'll never survive the time it would take to go get help. Time is quickly running out. I have to act now.

I push away all my fear of the water, knowing there's only one way to rescue him. I have to go in and get him myself.

With a deep breath, I step off the bank and dive in after him, straight into the violent waves and crashing whitecaps. The icy water hits me like a thousand knives cutting my skin. The wind is instantly knocked out of me. I struggle to keep my head above the surface, gasping for air. I've underestimated the vigorous power of the current as it laps over my head, shoving me under.

All the chaos above slows down beneath the surface. All I can see is dark, murky blackness blanketing my vision. This is not a lucid dream or a night terror. The past intrusive nightmares that have haunted my unconscious mind have somehow manifested themselves into waking reality.

As I'm holding my breath, a peculiar sense of déjà vu washes over me like a premonition—or maybe more like a memory. This feels familiar, but different.

All this time, were my nightmares trying to warn me that this river would take both our lives?

My skin is numb, and it's becoming harder and harder to stay conscious as I lose more air.

I can't let us die here!

With the sliver of strength remaining, I fight for my life once more. I wave my arms up and down against the thick, heavy waters, slowly inching myself up. With one final push, I'm able to break the surface.

I scan for any sign of Gabriel. I open my mouth to scream for help, but as I yell, an unbearable amount of water funnels in, suffocating me. My muscles spasm. I've become too weak to swim any longer. My head drops back underwater, and as I sink farther into the depths of the river, I am brutally aware that Gabriel is gone, and so I am. The raging water inhales me, pulling me under, dragging me deeper.

Something hard and blunt smashes against my head. And in an instant, all my agonizing pain comes to an end.

***

"Pull her out!" a voice screams.

"Is she still breathing?" another asks.

"Give her CPR!" another commands.

As my back is dragged over rocks and dirt, my eyes open to a sky filled with hundreds of jeweled birds flying together. Their soft feathers swoop under me and lift me higher. Euphoria radiates down, enveloping me in warmth, and my teeth meet in a wide grin.

The beaming white light and tranquility vanish when pressure crushes my chest with repeated slams against my sternum. My throat burns as I gag. The choking ends when water spills out of my mouth and drips down my chin.

All my senses return to the sound of sirens and unknown faces strapping me to a cold gurney. A plastic mask is placed over my mouth, and with each breath, my vision slips from me.

CHAPTER 22

With a large gasp for air, I stretch my eyes open to find needles and wires stuck to the insides of my arms. The clouded haze over my mind is slowly clearing.

What's happening? Where am I?

Fully alert now, my heart pounds from the anxiety of the unknown. As my panic rises, a beeping noise quickens.

Lights above blind me, but when my eyes adjust, Olga's piercing ones appear before me.

"Natalia, it's okay! It's okay," she whispers and grabs my hand as I begin to move my head to look around. The warmth of her skin comforts me, and the details of her face become vivid. "You're in the hospital. You had a near-drowning accident and suffered a concussion, but you're safe now." The medical machines and dreary wallpaper stand out behind her. "Just a few more tests. Hang in there for me."

A throbbing sharp pain stands out at the back of my head.

What is she talking about? Why can't I remember anything?

I try to talk, but a tube in my mouth cuts my throat each time I attempt to make a sound. I'm physically forced to keep my questions inside.

"Just rest," Olga tells me, stroking my hair.

My eyelids feel like they're being tugged closed. I'm struggling to keep them open, trying to fight off the fatigue, but it's no use, so I do as she says, letting them close as my mind drifts.

***

As I become aware of my body again, my eyes flutter open to see the sterile white ceiling. I blink a few times to clear the blurriness from my eyes and find that I'm in a hospital room. There's a humming sound from the machines all around me. My heartbeat is pulsing on a monitor to my left. There's a table next to me with a pitcher of water and a cup. The tube has been removed, and the inside of my mouth feels dry and raw.

I lift myself up from the mattress, and all the blood rushes to my head. I pause for a moment to get my bearings, then grab the cup and swallow down a full glass of water. It helps to bring back my senses.

The door is closed, but I hear the movement of nurses bustling up and down the hallway. There's no one in my room. I peel off my thin blanket and pull the paper hospital gown up to reveal tan bandages wrapped around different parts of my body. Daylight shines in through the windows, shimmering on the greenery outside, but I have no clue what time it is.

How long have I been unconscious?

I throw my legs over the side of the bed, carefully navigating the needle and long clear tube inserted into the vein on the top of my hand. When I step down, every muscle in my body feels inflamed. My legs are sore, and it takes all my power to lift myself upright. I grip the handrail on the bed tightly so I don't tumble to the floor.

The door opens, and Olga appears with a handful of flowers.

"Natalia! Do not try to stand on your own!" she yells, rushing over. She reaches me before I can fully stand, holding her arms out to steady me. "Sit down, please. Don't hurt yourself. The drugs are still wearing off."

Her dainty arms maneuver me back into bed. After Olga places a blanket over my legs, the door opens again, and I'm puzzled when Dr. Cassidy walks in.

"You're awake! Wonderful!" she says, clapping her hands together with a bright smile. "You gave us quite a scare. How do you feel?"

What the hell is going on?

"I'm okay… I think," I mumble.

Olga drags a chair over for Dr. Cassidy and places it next to hers at the foot of my bed. They both take a seat, eagerly staring at me.

"What day is it?" I ask.

"Saturday. You've been in and out of consciousness for two days. From what I understand, your body desperately needed the sleep," Olga says, a hint of disappointment in her voice.

Two whole days?

I've never slept so much in my life.

"How did I get here? Why exactly am I in the hospital?"

Olga and Dr. Cassidy look at each other with worrisome eyes.

"You hit the back of your head. The concussion you suffered can make remembering things a little fuzzy," Olga states.

"Natalia, what's the last thing you remember before waking up today?" Dr. Cassidy asks.

Releasing a breath, I clench my eyes shut. Vivid visions begin to appear in my blank head: Darkness covering the sky. Tall trees encroaching all around me. Leafless branches scratching me as I run past them. Cold, wet mud and rocks that feel like razors against my bare feet. Swishing sounds and the piercing feelings of plunging into ice-cold water. The weight of the unforgiving river slowly choking and crushing me. A tormenting final image of losing him to a vicious, watery death trap.

"Gabriel!" I cry out in a panic. "He was in the river too! I jumped in trying to save him, but I couldn't! Please tell me he's okay. Please tell me he got out. Please!" My eyes overflow with tears as I plead.

Olga lunges toward me and places her hands over mine. The sympathetic and devasted look in her eyes is enough of an answer. My stomach caves, and the sudden wave of despair makes me nauseated enough to gag.

"No. No!" I scream.

"Natalia, I know this is going to be extremely hard to hear, and I need to brace you," Dr. Cassidy says.

"He's dead! Isn't he? Did he drown in the river?"

Dr. Cassidy and Olga exchange frowns.

"Just tell me!" I roar impatiently.

Olga squeezes my hands, but she remains silent.

"Tell me what happened!" I demand, now in hysterics.

A deep wrinkle forms between Dr. Cassidy's brows.

"There's no easy way to say this." She clears her throat. "Natalia, he isn't alive because he was never really there. He wasn't real. Gabriel was a delusion you created."

What? I just suffered a concussion. Why are they fucking with my head right now?

I shake my head fiercely in denial.

"He's a patient in the boys' house. You don't work over there, so you must have never met him," I assure her.

"Natalia, please let me explain more," Dr. Cassidy says.

"Please do!" I snap defensively.

Her voice amplifies in a chaotic swirl around me. "Yesterday, just before sunrise on your last day at Awana, Abby saw you from her room. She saw you on the lawn running into the woods. She said you were wearing only a nightgown and no shoes. Abby was worried, so she hopped out of her window and followed you. She said you looked manic. She heard you screaming the name Gabriel over and over. She realized something was very wrong, so she turned back and got help. By the time the night nurses and the techs got there, you were already in the water drowning. They were able to pull you out, but there was no boy with you. Gabriel was never in the river, Natalia, because he doesn't exist."

Her horrifying words suck me into a violent vortex, causing every one of my muscles to seize up.

No! I refuse to believe this. How dare they try to blame this on my sanity, or lack of it.

He's not alive, but not because he isn't real. It's because they didn't save him. My heart screams through my stunned body.

"He was there! But he was already at the bottom of the river. That's why no one saw him. And now he's dead. He's fucking dead!"

More tears burst from my eyes as I sob into my hands.

"Natalia, I need you to take a deep breath and listen to me. Lindsay told us all about Gabriel but said she had never met him. She told us about you skipping your meds most nights and how you weren't sleeping. Honey, those meds are extremely strong. When you go on and off them like that, you experience withdrawal symptoms. And some of the side effects are hallucinations. When paired with your sleep disorder and the fact that you were extremely sleep-deprived, your mind began to play tricks on you."

She stops to grab a file from her bag and shuffles through the papers.

"I read Dr. Beckham's notes from your sessions and looked through your records from previous hospitals. I don't think any doctor truly understood the gravity of your condition. I've spent the last two days doing research. Aside from night terrors while asleep, parasomnia can induce intense hallucinations while you're awake, creating delusions that feel so real, you can't tell that they're not. The imagined events can involve all five senses: touch, taste, sight, sound, and smell. You were awake. You were walking and talking and vividly feeling things, but the experience you created was not real, including Gabriel."

This is impossible. I didn't make him up. He was real. He is real!

My brain is struggling to comprehend her theory because my heart is refusing to accept it.

"This can't be true! I felt him when we touched, and the pain he shared with me couldn't be made up. Everything about Gabriel was real! You're wrong!"

Tears gather in Dr. Cassidy's eyes as she reaches forward, trying to wipe mine away. But they won't stop pouring, soaking my paper gown.

"I'm so sorry, sweetie, but it's true. I even checked the records to be sure, and there's no boy named Gabriel in the boys' dorm."

"Then he lied about his name," I insist, refusing to believe this cruel, fictitious story.

I don't know why Gabriel would lie about his real name, but it's easier to accept that than what they're telling me. I can forgive him for that untruth. I can't forgive him for not existing.

I can't forgive myself.

Olga runs to my side and buries my head into her chest. I've never needed her more. I weep as she rubs my back and rocks me back and forth. Olga is usually so stoic, but in this moment, it's like she's as broken as I am.

Dr. Cassidy gives us a moment, and after some pause, she continues, "Lindsay also told us that you only saw him at night. We have cameras in the yard, but we don't check them regularly unless there's a problem. We were able to go back and watch the videos of you sneaking out and interacting with... well, no one. You were talking to yourself. There was never anyone with you. I can show you," she says, pulling out a tablet.

Is everything they've been saying true? Did I make this all up in my head?

Maybe Lindsay was right all along about the black starling. She never saw it because it was never there. It only stalked me on the mornings I wasn't on medication.

A trail of memories cascades through my mind, and Gabriel disintegrates from each of them. Every time I climbed out of the window and our meaningful talks under the stars, all the way to when I leaped into the river. The disturbing truth goes off like a bomb inside my head. Gabriel was a mere side effect of withdrawal. The reality is, I was always alone. Our relationship was only ever me.

Their evidence is towering over any defense I have left. I have to accept it. I have to accept that I might actually just be fucking insane.

"Why would I ever want to watch that? Why would I want to see that psychotic version of myself?" I yell between tears. "Wait, Abby told on me. So she *does* talk!" I raise my voice louder, redirecting my anger at myself toward someone else.

"No, she doesn't talk. That was another delusion of yours. She wrote it all down for us. She wrote that you have accused her of talking a few times, which confused her. She was concerned about your behavior, so she kept an eye on you. She also saw you leave your room from your window the other night. She saw you do strange things, like talk or dance with yourself. She even saw you smoke cigarettes. You're lucky she saw you heading toward the river, and that they were able to save you when they did," Dr. Cassidy explains.

I feel utterly destroyed by my shame and sorrow.

"You should have let me drown." I clench my teeth. "You're telling me the one person I've ever been in love with is a fucking figment of my imagination. Why would anyone want to live after hearing that?"

I pry myself away from Olga, my body aching everywhere. I sob into my hands, praying this is all a nightmare and I'll wake up soon.

But I know better.

This is a horrifying reality.

Because you never actually feel pain in a dream, and right now, I've never felt anything more excruciating.

CHAPTER 23

I've been home three whole days now, but I'm still left with swollen eyes and a defeated soul. Physically, I'm getting better. The bandages are all off, and my energy is coming back, but I still refuse to leave my bed. My binoculars sit on my nightstand next to a vase Olga filled with the flowers she brought me in the hospital, hoping they might make me feel better. Today is the first day she's asked me to change out of my pajamas since Dr. Cassidy is coming over for a check-in visit. Though she'll be here any minute, I have no desire to get dressed for myself, let alone anyone else.

Olga has been a nervous wreck all day, cleaning every inch of our cabin compulsively. I know it's a been a while since we've had a visitor, but she's normally not this neurotic. I can't help but wonder if something else is on her mind.

As expected, my door opens, and Olga walks in first, glaring at my unkempt appearance.

"Natalia, Dr. Cassidy is here," she announces, and Dr. Cassidy comes in behind her.

"Here, please sit." Olga offers her a seat on my reading bench but doesn't sit herself. She's pacing around aimlessly, chewing on a nail, a habit of mine she hates. "I'm so sorry she isn't dressed. It's been a hard couple of days."

"There's no need to apologize. Natalia's attire is the least of my concerns. I just want to make sure she's doing okay. How are you doing today, Natalia?" She turns to me with a caring smile.

Does she want to know the truth?

I feel like someone sliced open my chest and drained all the blood and emotion out of me.

"I'm okay," I lie.

"I'm glad to hear you're feeling better. But I'm not just here to check in on you." She sighs. Confused, I tilt my head sideways. "Olga has divulged some serious things to me and asked if I would be here to help her share them with you."

"What sort of things?" I look at Olga, but she's pensively staring out the window.

"A big part of the equation into your psyche and why you have likely been suffering such a severe case of parasomnia all these years. She's explained something that happened to you in the first few years of your life, and I want to be here to walk you through it."

I thrust my torso up from my bed.

"Olga, I thought they were unknown. No one knows my past before the day at the train station. Right?" I ask nervously, curious.

Olga turns around and shakes her head deliberately.

"She can't know. We can't do this now. I'm so sorry I made you come all this way. You should just leave," she says to Dr. Cassidy.

I rip my quilt off and stand to my feet.

"I have spent my entire life feeling like a piece is missing from my brain. Months spent in institutions, hours upon hours of therapy, and no one has figured out anything about this hole inside my head. So, if you have even the slightest clue as to why I have traumatizing nightmares or delusions of people who convince me to do things like fall from a tree or jump into a river, then I think I have every right to know any information you've found."

Olga chokes on her words before murmuring, "You're right. You do deserve the truth."

Dr. Cassidy grabs a notebook and pen while Olga rushes to my side and helps me sit back down. Her hand trembles in mine and tears fall from her eyes. She's never been one to lose control of her emotions, but during these past few days, she can't seem to get ahold of them. I clutch onto her, and she buries her head in my hair, trying to hide her cries.

"Please don't hate me, Natalia. Please. I've only wanted to protect you."

"What is it? What could possibly be so terrible?" My chest tightens.

Olga lifts her head and continuously wipes her eyes and cheeks, trying to blot the tears. Dr. Cassidy reaches forward from her chair and squeezes her hand.

"You need to tell her. I can't do it," Olga says to her.

Dr. Cassidy sits back in her seat and gives Olga a confident nod.

"Natalia, Olga is your aunt." The words sound distorted coming out of her mouth.

My aunt? As in a blood relative?

This feels like a sick joke.

I turn to Olga.

"Is… is this true?" I stutter.

She keeps her chin low but moves her head up and down.

"How? Why would you keep that from me? My whole life, I thought I never had a family. I've spent all this time thinking I was someone's trash disposed on the side of the road."

Olga keeps nodding and biting her lower lip.

I stare into her sapphire eyes that I now realize resemble my own.

"Just give me a second to explain." She exhales deeply. "I haven't had to mention my brother—your father—since before we moved to America." She sighs again. "He was the wild one of the two of us. He was a harmonica player in a traveling band. He was outrageously gifted. That little instrument paid his bills, and after you were born, he said the melody helped you fall asleep. He tried so hard to be a good father, but he had demons in his head that ate away at him. Then one day, shortly after you were born, he took off with you and your mother, and I never saw him again." Olga's eyes tense, and she has to stop.

"My mother?" My voice weakens.

"Yes. She was beautiful and soft-spoken, just like you. You inherited her love for nature and the creatures that live in it. She loved putting you in pretty dresses. The first time I saw you after you were born, you looked like a little porcelain doll."

I've always dreamed of what my mother was like, and this whole time, Olga has kept her hidden her from me. Why would she do something so awful?

"Did she love me?" I cry.

Olga grabs my hand. "Of course she did, Natalia! She loved you so much. Your dad did too."

"Then why did they leave me? How could you leave someone you love at a train station? Or is that a lie too?"

I'm trying to sort this all out, but it's becoming way too mangled. I rip my hand from hers, and she frowns before speaking again.

"I'm afraid my history in Russia is much worse than I led on. Your grandmother, my single mother, died a year after you were born, and since I was only sixteen and my brother was still nowhere to be found, I went away to stay with the only living relative willing to take me. Little did I know, my uncle only wanted me for one thing—my body. Two years later, after living a life where I had to disconnect my soul from my physical being, he decided he wanted to sell me to someone else. That was my breaking point. I knew then that I'd rather die trying to escape than have that life be my chosen destiny. I was packed up and ready to flee, but then I received a call... There had been an accident."

She stops, her lip quivering. I can see it's physically torturing her to bring up the past.

What sort of accident?

I'm afraid to ask, but I need the answer.

I want to bombard her with questions, but my heart also hurts for her. No one should endure that kind of abuse. My instinct kicks in to comfort her, knowing she's in pain, but she pulls away as I reach for her.

"No, this isn't supposed to be a pity party for me. I just don't think I can say the rest. It's too painful."

Dr. Cassidy breaks the silence. "This is an intense process, Olga, and you did great." She then turns toward me. "Natalia, with your permission, I can help you remember your past on your own."

What could possibly be so bad that Olga is too distressed to share at this point? What could be worse than what I've already endured? If it's something *that* bad, do I even want to know?

As much as it scares me, it's something I need to find out.

I look up at Dr. Cassidy and muster the courage to say, "Please help me remember."

Dr. Cassidy sets up an arrangement of pillows for me to lie against. She dims the light and brings her chair right next to my bedside.

"Now, we're going to do a form of hypnotherapy," she explains. "I feel it's an appropriate technique to use since Olga has just revealed some parts of your past that were unknown to you. It's a good time to tap into an altered subconscious state to try to remember the rest. But first, I need to warn you that this type of exercise can cause physical sensations. Some are pleasant, others are not. Are you both okay with this?"

I'm unsure what to expect, but at this point, I can't keep going on like this. Whatever is suppressed in my memories is controlling the narrative of my life. I need to get to the truth before it ruins it completely.

Olga is positioned at the bottom of my bed. Her hand is pressed anxiously to her forehead, but she nods in approval.

"I'm ready," I tell Dr. Cassidy.

We start with my eyes closed and long, deep breaths. She then leads me through a series of instructions that seem silly at first. She has me extend my palms and pretend a ball is between them that I can't let drop.

"Focus on the ball in your head, and when I count to three, I want you to imagine it dropping from your hands." Slowly, she counts, "One... two... three."

On "three," a relaxed wave splashes over me. Dr. Cassidy is speaking, but her words become faint as my conscious mind fades. A combination of chills and sweat breaks out all over my body. Sharp flashes of light turn into a flutter of flashbacks behind my eyelids.

Dark waters are thrashing in chaos. Gabriel appears with his cherub features that were too good to be true. His face disappears, morphing into a young man with jet-black hair and brooding dark circles under his eyes. A woman appears behind him, wearing bright red lipstick and a slick bun with a white gardenia pinned to its side. Love and warmth radiate inside me when I look at her.

"Describe what you see and feel, Natalia." Dr. Cassidy's voice echoes around me.

Like a faulty video camera, I'm taken back to a time that flickers, shifting the scene in my mind, and I speak out loud.

"There's a gray sky behind raindrops tapping on glass. Buckles are strapped across my lace dress. I have a doll in my hands. I'm in the back seat of a car with a man and woman. I can only see the backs of their heads, but I know they're my parents because I have this distinct feeling that I belong to them."

"What are they doing?"

"They're screaming at each other. My father is behind the steering wheel, driving recklessly and very fast. We're swerving. I hear my own cries in the background," I say, trying to use the right words to paint the picture of the warped memory in my mind.

"And your mother?"

"My mother is speaking in Russian. I can't understand her, but when she turns to look at me, mascara is streaming down her face. It's as if she's pleading with him to stop. But he won't. He's too angry. I hear the engine being revved, and my mother lets out a final scream... so loud it causes my ears to ring. She desperately reaches back for me. Her beautiful features are now riddled with horror. But it's too late."

My body violently shakes, but I can't stop it or open my eyes.

"Keep going, Natalia. What are you seeing?" I faintly hear Dr. Cassidy call out.

"Glass shatters everywhere as my mother's head slams against the dashboard. My stomach drops, and the air is sucked from me until it suddenly feels like we're floating. A powerful wave rushes in, mixing with the deep rouge surrounding their bodies and my mother's tangled black hair. The cold water is rising every second, but I'm still strapped in my seat. I'm trapped. I'm struggling and crying. My dress is now soaked. My doll slips from my fingers and washes away. I'm fully submerged, suffocating slowly."

Drenched in sweat, I can't catch my breath. A flood of fear and grief pours over me. Every emotion on that day has come back to haunt me. My damaged lungs cough as if I'm still trying to fight for air.

My eyes open, and my vision slowly allows me back to see Olga's and Dr. Cassidy's red eyes staring at me.

The overwhelming release of everything buried inside my head causes me to fall into Olga's arms. Our sobs align as she rocks me, redundantly apologizing for everything.

***

The sunlight has faded, and Dr. Cassidy is still here. After she pulled me out of the hypnotic state, I cried for what felt like hours. No words have been spoken. There was just anguish and grief releasing with each heavy breath and tear.

The moon shines through the curtain cracks, casting a beam of light across my room. I'm sitting up in bed, staring at the floor, still not sure if I'm ready to process any more.

Olga brings in tea on a platter and hands me a mug. The soothing warmth hits my dry lips, and my shoulders ease toward my spine. Dr. Cassidy pulls back the drapes and opens a window. The evening breeze cuts through the thick tension in the air.

Olga sits on my reading bench and looks out at the trees. She doesn't turn around when she speaks for the first time in hours.

"It was familicide. I could never explain my brother's reasoning. He always struggled with his anger, but I never knew he would take it that far. I tell myself a demon must have possessed him. He drove off a small bridge, crashing full speed into the guardrail. Luckily, the lake beneath was shallow enough, and a group of passersby below saw everything. Your parents died on impact, but they were able to pull you out moments after the car went in. I received the call about what happened. The authorities said that if my uncle didn't take you, that you would be put in an orphanage. I wasn't going to let either of those things happen. I was only eighteen, but I couldn't let you be raised by the same man who tried to traffic me. So, I took you with me. We escaped. Once we made it to America, the home of fresh starts, my pain still had its claws in me, constantly tearing at me, making every day feel agonizing. I thought if I could bury the transgressions of your father in Russia, you'd be better off than me."

It feels like she just opened a mansion of family skeletons and dumped them all on me. How does she expect me to react after hearing so many horrid revelations and secrets she's kept from me?

"Why wouldn't you just tell me that my parents were dead and you're really my aunt?"

"Because it was too awful to explain to a child. You would ask questions that I just couldn't—wouldn't—answer. How could I tell you that your uncle was a pervert and a pedophile, or that your father murdered your mother and attempted to kill to you?" She gulps and goes silent.

My heart is divided, but anger outweighs my sorrow. "But at any time throughout all of this, did you think this hidden piece could have helped the doctors figure out what was wrong with me?"

"It crossed my mind, believe me. But I became terrified that your father's demons had been passed on to you after you sleepwalked into my room and tried to strangle me. You were only a little girl then. I figured there was still time to help you. I believed keeping you in institutions would be the only way to protect you from growing up and becoming him."

I squeeze my fingers into fists, and my nails cut into my palms.

"So, your only solution was to keep me locked away and let doctors come up with their make-believe assumptions on why I'm so fucked up? You had no right to do that or keep any of this from me!"

It's taking everything in me not to slap her across the face. It would be a small pain in comparison to how wretched her lies feel.

Her eyes water with remorse, but I don't know how to accept the apology that is almost twenty years too late.

"I'm so sorry. It's what I thought was right, and as the years went on, that vile secret hid further inside me, making it more impossible to dig it out. I couldn't tell you even if I wanted to. But after you almost killed yourself by jumping into that water... it was too eerily similar to what happened the day your parents died. Both times, you were so close to drowning. Except this time, I think it was my fault for trying to erase your history. I was ignorant to think you were too young to remember. The memory must have stuck with you and shaped you in more harmful ways than I'd ever imagined. I knew it was finally time to tell you, even if you hated me for it. I'm so sorry you have to face this now, but I think it's the only way you'll get better."

Hate isn't a strong enough word for what she did. Olga let me fester in mental hospitals and grow up thinking I was a terrible burden because of this poison in my mind. Meanwhile, she knew exactly where it came from. Her lies and secrets have robbed me of any sort of normal childhood. I can't help but wonder what my life could have looked like if I had known this sooner.

"All these years, you made me feel like I was broken. And you knew why. But you let me suffer and you said nothing!" I shout at her, my body flushing with heat.

Dr. Cassidy puts her hand on my shoulder. "Natalia, I know it's hard to understand Olga's reasonings, but you have to realize she was a victim herself, dealing with intense trauma. Dissociation is the most common response. It's a survival tactic. Withholding the truth and lying may have been wrong, but in her eyes, she was protecting you. She didn't want the truth to hurt you. It was her love for you that kept her silent."

Part of me knows Dr. Cassidy is right, but it's hard to recognize that as love when it's caused me so many years of tribulation.

Tears roll down Olga's cheeks, and she moves onto my bed, reaching out to hold me. I want to resist, but her comfort is all I've ever known. I rest my head against her, and she wraps her arms around my shoulders.

"I don't know if I'll be able to forgive you," I whisper in a low voice.

She kisses my head, then pulls back to look me in the eye.

"It's your life now. I can't tell you what to do. You don't have to ever speak to me again if that's what's going to help you get better."

Devoid of anything left to say, I move toward my window and focus into the night. Though the stars' lights are dimmed behind thick clouds, I still look to them for guidance.

I don't know how to go on with my life after everything that's happened in the last few days. Where would I even start?

How do I learn to live amid all these horrendous truths? My first love was an illusion, and I'll never see him again. My father is a murderer who committed the ultimate betrayal. A doctor who is supposed to heal broken minds left my best friend in the most injured mental state I'd ever seen her in. Now, I come to find my newfound aunt has been keeping secrets and detrimentally hid the most important parts of my identity.

I feel like a stranger in my own head. How do I trust myself when my own mind lied to

me with so many delusions? How can I trust anyone ever again after this much deceit?

Everything I've ever known has been a lie. No wonder I created Gabriel. I was already living in a life that wasn't real.

***

My torn leather bag that was never unpacked is rolled out to Dr. Cassidy's car. Olga leans against our cottage entryway. I stop, and we lock eyes before I close Dr. Cassidy's passenger door. With tears streaming down her cheeks, Olga waves one last goodbye.

CHAPTER 24

Today marks my final departure from Awana. It's nothing like it was when I first arrived: no Lindsay, no irresponsible doctors, and—a hard one for me to adjust to—no Gabriel King.

Six months after the drowning incident, a whole new group of girls lives in the house, and another patient is coming soon to take over my bed.

Awana isn't the only thing that's changed.

The first month back felt like torture. I never wanted to leave my dark room. My appetite was gone. My hair was starting to thin. I didn't want to socialize with anyone. I became a true recluse, not because I was forced to be, but because I was beginning to believe that what I'd gone through had left me wrecked beyond repair.

I already knew what resilience was. My life was spent in a constant state of it. This time, the battle was me against myself. I had to fight if I ever wanted to escape the depressive hell I was lost in.

So, I began fighting for the little things each day. I'd sit out in the sun, soaking in the rays and air around me. I'd listen to music, and on occasion, I'd get up and dance. I read endless books and admired the characters in them who showed strength in hardships. Though they were all small tasks, those tiny joys ended up being the biggest leaps I took toward my path to recovering.

After feeling a bit more like myself, I opened up to a few of the other girls—Cheryl, who was still there and whom I grew to like, and the girl I was afraid to face, Abby. I was so ashamed of what she'd witnessed, but then paintings began sliding under my door. She drew me birds and sunsets. For someone who doesn't speak, she showed me the greatest amount of compassion.

We began to hang out regularly. She told me about herself, not vocally but through her writing and artwork. I started studying her mannerisms and body language to figure out when she was frustrated or excited and all the emotions in between. I discovered we have a lot in common with our love for nature and art. It's not hard to communicate with someone who doesn't talk; you just need to take the time to understand them differently. I only wish I had done it sooner.

Abby's time at Awana finally came to an end. The day she left, I cried. She saved me from dying in the river. Even with all the chaos in my life, I'm still thankful to be alive.

With Dr. Cassidy's help, the sadness that seemed unending is numbing, and my anger toward Olga is dissolving. I've learned that it can be disastrous to allow painful emotions to harbor inside you for too long. After months spent piecing together the fragments of my life and pushing myself back up when everything inside me felt ruined, my mind is clear for the first time, free of terror and nightmares.

The therapy sessions in the beginning were the hardest. Dr. Cassidy brought up tough subjects and worked me through my wounds. At first, I thought they would never stop bleeding, but eventually the pain eased and scabs began to form. I know I will always have the scars, but they're the proof that I'm healing.

My perspective on therapy and medication has changed. They aren't the enemy, but not dealing with a dark past can be. I used to hate talking to therapists, but with time, I've seen how truly life-changing it can be. Even after I leave Awana, I'll continue to see one. I'm on a proper dosage of meds now that keep me from acting out in my sleep and seeing things that aren't there, all without sedating, sickening side effects.

My mental illness has been officially diagnosed as post-traumatic stress disorder that developed into severe parasomnia. My unresolved trauma had been eating away at my brain for so long that it seeped into my dreams and even began to control my waking life. The human mind is truly an enigma.

I wish Dr. Cassidy had been my doctor from the start. Her support and guidance these last few months are what I could have used all along. She determined that my PTSD didn't only stem from the tragic repressed memory of my parents. It was also from the years of terrible practices I endured in mental wards. Strapping me down was not only inhumane but an immediate trigger to the day I was stuck buckled in a car seat, waiting for a slow death.

I was surprised to learn the negligence from my very own "caretaker" exacerbated my symptoms. Olga's stern, cold temperament always made me feel like an outsider in my own home. Keeping me isolated from the world and kids my own age had an ill effect on my mental well-being. It made it impossible for me to learn how to make healthy connections and develop friendships. Maybe that's why it was so easy to create an imagined one.

Deep down, I know Olga has always loved me, but it's the ones who love us the most who can cause the most damage, even if they never meant to.

Dr. Cassidy has given me an emotional roadmap to lead a normal life without allowing my trauma to define me or deter me from moving forward. Not only that, but she also set me up with practical things too. She taught me how to drive and celebrated with me when I passed the driver's test. Then she helped me find a job a mile away from Awana at a local grocery store and took me to a bank to open an account so I could save my earnings.

After months of receiving paychecks, I was able to buy a '98 canary-yellow van. Though the interior is dingy and old, the radio works, and the engine is new. I've spent the last month tearing out the seats and laying down new carpet. It now has all the necessities to make it a functional place to live: a bed, a hot plate, a small refrigerator, and a battery-operated sink. I added a small bookcase, hung string lights for ambience, and decorated the walls with Abby's paintings.

During my treatment here, I haven't spoken to Olga. I've received small updates on her life from Dr. Cassidy, but I chose to separate myself from her completely. A massive part of my trauma was caused by her. I needed the distance to heal from it.

Lindsay and I have been exchanging handwritten letters throughout my time here since the strict "no phones" rule still applies. It has really proven her devotion to our friendship, because I know she would prefer technology any day for the obvious speed and convenience. Being able to write her letters and read hers has done more for me than she'll ever know. I've shared everything with her, and I think writing it all down has helped me during this process. She apologized for outing my delusional love affair with Gabriel, but I told her I didn't blame her. I had outed some of her secrets too. Sometimes, you have to speak up for your friends when you know they're in harm's way and won't do it for themselves. In a way, we both saved each other.

My last therapy session with Dr. Cassidy was yesterday. She asked me to do one final cathartic exercise. She wants me to send letters to two people with the hope that it'll bring me peace.

With my black notebook and pen in hand, I glance out my window that was once used as an escape from my reality. I open to a blank page and begin to write.

Dear Olga,

I know it's been a while since we've talked. Thank you for filing the court order to end our conservatorship. I realized our dependence on each other was doing us more harm than good. When you cling too hard to someone, you'll never know what it's like to stand on your own. I finally feel grounded.

With me being gone, I hope that's what you've learned to do. I hope you're not only able to look forward but also able to turn around and face your past. Like me, you were trapped in a world of your own demons. I hope you've set some of them free.

Although I will never agree with some of the choices you made, I wouldn't be who I am today if it wasn't for you. You chose to care for a child who wasn't your own. You saved me from the horrors that happened to you. Your intentions were good. You were trying to protect me, and for that, I'm eternally grateful.

Dr. Cassidy helped arrange something for us. I wrote a time and place on the back of this letter. I understand if it's not something you're ready to do. Either way, I'll be there.

Love,
Natalia

I rip the page from my notebook, folding it in half. I stare at the next blank page and take a deep breath to steady myself. This one will be harder than the last.

Dear Gabriel King,

Where do I begin?

It would be a lie to say that sometimes I didn't miss you, or that getting over us wasn't one of the toughest things I've had to do. I used you to try and fill the void in my head, but you started to leak out onto every part of my life.

The doctors have proven that you were just a mere figment of my imagination that my twisted head conjured up. I guess you could say that the years of abandonment and loneliness finally drove me mad. I created you as an internal savior to console me during a time when I was so broken I could no longer do it on my own.

But, Gabriel, you also came into my life to help reveal the darkest parts in me that were hidden and screaming to get out. In a way, you are me. Your pain and emotions were mine.

I dove into the river that night because maybe inside, I knew I had to. It would be the only way I'd learn about the tragic events that took place in my life.

Without you, I wouldn't have known my history or learned who I am.

I'm not mentally unstable or insane. I'm a survivor with a mind that is one of a kind.

Thank you, Gabriel King. You may no longer live in my head, but a small part of you will remain in my heart.

Under the same place and same stars, I'll always remember you.

Love,
Natalia

After the ink dries, I place the letters in stamped envelopes, then gather myself and walk to the main entrance. I step outside to stick one in the mailbox and nestle the other in my sweatshirt pocket. The sky is gloomy, and the wind chill bites, but I switch directions and trek through the dewy grass toward the woods that hold the river.

As I near the clearing, I hear rushing sounds, and I clench my eyes and fists, but then I reopen them, slowly reminding myself how far I've come since the last time I faced this water.

I'm not that same girl. I won't let this river dictate my emotions anymore.

When I arrive, I notice things I never saw before: Dandelions are sprinkled along the riverbank. There are apple trees down the way. A sliver of the sun breaks through the clouds, causing the water to shimmer.

The only thing the babbling noises of this river bring is a sense of calm—a feeling I didn't think I was capable of experiencing while standing in its presence.

I pull out the envelope with the name *Gabriel King* written across it. I place my lips to the seal, and with a gentle throw, I toss it in.

Goodbye, Gabriel. Loving you was worth losing you.

The letter trickles down the bank, giving me the closure to our relationship I never thought I'd receive.

CHAPTER 25

My van is packed, stocked with food, clothes, and everything I'll need for my next adventure.

Lindsay always wondered about my fascination with birds. At first, I thought it was their ability to love, but I've come to learn it's their freedom to fly anywhere at any time. And with my new home, I've finally found that.

Dr. Cassidy meets me in the driveway in a sundress covered in bright flowers. She no longer wears her doctor's coat, and I believe her new relaxed wardrobe suits her better, because she doesn't just medically treat here, she supports and loves each one of the patients under her care.

"You really fixed it up in here," she says, helping me place my bags inside.

"Thank you. I'm truly indebted to you for everything you've done to get me here."

"I've barely done anything. It was your strength that brought you to this point."

She removes one of her necklaces, a small one with an uncut purple gem, and places it around my neck.

"Amethyst, the stone known to provide protection. I want you to keep it." She smiles gently. "Please take care of yourself, dear. I know this is just the beginning of an incredible life ahead of you."

We stand outside the driver's door for a moment, and then I wrap my arms tight around her. She's the one person who has restored my faith in adults who are put in your life to protect you. The genuine care in her heart is grand enough to balance out some of the evil in this world.

After we let go, she says, "There's one more thing I think you'll want to take with you." I squint, puzzled. "Under the weeping willow. Go on. Go see for yourself."

I walk around my van for a better view.

The surprise waiting for me under my favorite tree sends tears sliding down my face and dripping into my smile. There, leaning against the trunk, is my best friend who, the last time I saw her, was fighting for her life in my arms. When she sees me, she grins, waving her right arm that is weighed down by a duffel bag dangling from it. Her hair is a new shade of pink, and she looks more radiant than ever.

She runs across the grass, straight to me, laughing and screaming my name while she bobs.

Her hug nearly knocks me over, but it's filled with the exuberant feeling when two separated hearts are united again.

"What are you doing here?" I ask with elation as I wipe the happy wetness off my cheeks.

"After you told me about your first destination in your new home, I knew it was something you shouldn't have to do alone. Plus, a six-hour trip up the coast sounds like a blast. Who doesn't love a good road trip? Now, where should I put my stuff?"

Katey Taylor

Lindsay hoists her luggage, which looks like it's filled with bricks, over her shoulder.

"Toss it next to mine. How much did you pack?" I laugh at her struggling before I lend a hand and help.

"Well, I know we have a lot of time to make up for, so if you don't mind, I thought I could stay with you for a while," she says, her lips stretched wide.

"Of course. There's no one else I'd want my copilot to be." I smile back.

I was ready to take on the world alone, but I'd much rather do it with my best friend.

I climb into the driver's seat with Lindsay by my side. We give our last wave to Dr. Cassidy and send a final salute to Awana's Treatment in the Trees.

We embark on our cruise along the Northern California coast into Oregon. The highway is covered in beach towns and sprawling seascapes. Lindsay has the music blaring while singing along even louder.

We make a pit stop at a taco shack near the shore and enjoy lunch with a view, allowing our legs to dangle out the van's open back doors.

As we both watch the glistening horizon, Lindsay swallows her last bite of food.

"I'm proud of you. You've really kicked some ass in the last six months," she tells me.

I admire her glowing skin and infectious grin. "Look at yourself! I'm so proud of *you!*"

Her smile fades as she lifts her legs and wraps her arms around her knees. "Thank you. I'm better now, but for months, it felt like I couldn't rub the scent of him off my skin. I kept seeing his face on strangers. To this day, he will still find a way into my thoughts, and I hate it. I hate him so much for what he did to me and all those other girls."

"He's the definition of evil, and evil can feel impossible to overcome. But you're doing it right now. You're surviving and taking care of yourself, and that is the biggest 'fuck you' you could give him."

Lindsay stretches herself back out.

"You're right. Even if it took a village of strong women to put someone as toxic as him in place, we did it, and now he's going to pay the price. Last I heard from the courts, he's being convicted for every girl in the photos they found. Underage or not, he abused his code of conduct, and I have a feeling he's going to be locked away for a long time."

We hug in triumph, and then she places her arm around me.

"Are you sure you're ready for this?"

I nod. I've already conquered so much, but I know there's still one last thing for me to face.

***

With Lindsay's hand laced in mine and my other gripped around a bouquet of white gardenias, we step through the arched wrought-iron entrance of a graveyard. The sun is setting, but the dark clouds hover over any color in the sky. I researched cemeteries for months, and when I stumbled across this place, I knew it was the one.

We march up a winding cement path between lush grass and rows of rosebushes. Once we make it to the top, the view is mesmerizing. Behind the array of tombstones is a vast dark lake with overgrown ivy crawling up the sides.

We walk farther through the graves until what's ahead steals my breath. Kneeled in front of a tombstone is a stunning woman in all black with distinct gray hair. Olga glances over her shoulder, and when our eyes meet, she stands to dust off her dress. Lindsay squeezes my hand, and we look at each other one last time before I meet Olga.

Once in her presence, everything stays quiet until she breaks the somber moment.

"It's absolutely perfect," she says with a light, loving expression that's a new look for her.

I bend down and place the white flowers in front of the grave. The etched name, Irina Sokolov, under the words *Beloved mother* stings my chest, but my pain is soothed with a comforting warmth knowing she has a beautiful place where she can be remembered. After her truth spent decades buried underwater, now we both can experience the peace we deserved all along.

"Thank you for coming. I know this wasn't an easy thing for you to do. I know you hate long drives," I say, turning to Olga.

Her solemnness eases.

"I would have driven across the country to see this—to see you. I've been working on myself since we last spoke. I get out more. I visit new places on the weekends. I'm doing all the things I should have done while you were growing up. I thought locking you away from the world would prevent you from seeing all the ugliness in it. But with time, I've learned there's so much good to see, and I deprived you of all of it. You're everything to me, Natalia, and I'm so sorry if that was poorly reflected. I know now that my means of care were done in vain and messed with you more than anything else. I don't know if I can ever forgive myself."

She places a trembling hand over her lips.

I reach for her, and when she clings to me, our tears pour out. In this moment, there is no anger. There is no resentment. There is only love.

"You did the best you could for someone who was surviving their own trauma," I whisper in her ear. "I forgive you, so please forgive yourself."

She moves back so she can look at me, sniffling as she runs her fingers along my hair.

"Thank you. I don't deserve your grace, but it's what will help allow me to heal."

Olga is the closest thing to a mother I ever had, and with deep open wounds on her back, she still carried me through life. She is my only living family I've ever known.

I signal for Lindsay to come over so the two most important people in my life can meet. After an exchange of greetings and hugs, a loud roar shakes the ground. Lightning streaks across the sky, releasing a downpour, soaking us all, but instead of running for shelter, we smile and laugh, embracing the cool raindrops hitting our skin.

Standing at the memorial where my mother's soul now rests, we reach for one another's hands. The strength we've each gained from overcoming our different life-shattering obstacles creates an electrifying power that radiates through our interlocked fingers. It's a blazing bright uniting force that will continue to outshine every dark day behind us.

THE END

ACKNOWLEDGMENTS

First and foremost, to my husband, Mike, thank you for your unwavering encouragement and inspiring me to reach for the stars. I am endlessly grateful for your love, belief in me, and constant presence in my corner.

To my family and friends, thank you for your unconditional support. Your enthusiasm and faith in my work means more to me than words can express.

To Kelly Thomas, this story would never be what it is today without your devotion and guidance. I cannot thank you enough for helping this book reach its full depth and potential.

To Kristin Scearce, thank you for your laser-sharp editing skills and incredible insight. Your talent is unmatched.

To my readers, thank you for welcoming my words into your minds and hearts. I appreciate each of you.

ABOUT THE AUTHOR

Katey Taylor is a San Francisco Bay Area-based author and published poet, with work featured in online magazines such as DarkWinter Lit, SWAAY, and Fauxmoir. She's recognized for her ability to address complex topics with sensitivity and depth.

To find out more about her previous and upcoming novels, visit www.kateytaylor.com

www.ingramcontent.com/pod-product-compliance
Lightning Source LLC
Chambersburg PA
CBHW030602180626
46816CB00005B/1638